PENGU

. THE END (

Vincent C. Sales has been a writer fc ʌɪ twenty-five years. He began his career as an advertising copywriter and spent a decade in the industry. As a journalist, he was editor-in-chief of a leading consumer electronics magazine. In recent years, he has been a content creator for several Asian online platforms.

During a five-year stint in his dream job as a stay-at-home dad, he wrote the novel *The End of All Skies*, the inception of which began at the turn of the millennium. He is the author of several other books, including a self-published anthology of short fiction, *Children in Exile*. He has also written a trilogy of best-selling genre novels. He has been published in the *Philippine Graphic* and is a fellow of the 34th University of the Philippines National Writer's Workshop.

He lives in Manila with his wife, three children, two hamsters, and a rabbit.

The End of All Skies

Vincent C. Sales

PENGUIN BOOKS

An imprint of Penguin Random House

PENGUIN BOOKS

USA | Canada | UK | Ireland | Australia
New Zealand | India | South Africa | China | Southeast Asia

Penguin Books is part of the Penguin Random House group of companies
whose addresses can be found at global.penguinrandomhouse.com

Published by Penguin Random House SEA Pte Ltd
9, Changi South Street 3, Level 08-01,
Singapore 486361

First published in Penguin Books by Penguin Random House SEA 2022

ISBN 9789815017823

Typeset in Garamond by MAP Systems, Bangalore, India

www.penguin.sg

Contents

For Frances

Part I: The Forgotten City

If you want to find the woman who sells dreams, go to the common market. Down a crowded alleyway without a name, you will find her selling dreams in glass bottles. She is a witch, she says, who remembers what no one else does. If you ask her about her past, she will tell you stories and lies. They are never the same stories twice.

She might begin her tale by saying, 'Sun Girna Ginar was a city on the greatest island of the Pacific, and it was founded by the gods.' Or, she might say, 'Only the sea remembers Sun Girna Ginar. The rest of us have forgotten it.' Sometimes, she will not use the name Sun Girna Ginar but Namayan, Nalandangan, or another name that will not stay in your memory.

She will tell you stories of the city's people: its soldiers, its beggars, its great Sultan. She will call the people by name as if they were known to her. At other times, she will forget their names, interchange them with others, or simply let them disappear from the story altogether.

Go down to the market, past the fruit vendors and the wholesale sellers of old clothes and when you reach the hawkers of trinkets and baubles, you will be close. You will find her there, dressed in rags, mouth void of teeth, selling bottles filled with dreams that she will say you can possess. And if you ask her, she will tell you of a city that no one else remembers but her—a city she swears existed hundreds of years ago, the city where she was born.

'The city lives on through song,' she might say. 'These songs tell of heroes, protected and guided by their ancestors. They tell of gods who toyed with the lives of men. These gods and heroes walked the streets of Sun Girna Ginar along with men, beasts, and ghosts. Some lived and some died. A few of them live forever.'

Often she will jump in with a fresh lie as if she had just thought of it:

'The storytellers sing of Sun Girna Ginar's general, Marandang, who was protected by powerful ancestors. He was famed for his victory against an army of giants he defeated with a host of creatures from Skyworld.

'They sing of the god of destruction, Kalaon, who was enslaved by the Sultan. Kalaon gave the Sultan the power to rule the heavens but when Kalaon was freed by the Sultan's enemies, he abandoned the Sultan.'

Or, softly, she might say, 'The singers whisper of the six-headed giant from the mountains of the north, who declared war upon Sun Girna Ginar. It was the oldest of its kind, born with the earth. And it will be there still when the earth dies.'

Even when she was lucid, nonsense spewed from her mouth.

They sing of the Sultan, son of Kabuniyan, ruler of the earth, the sea, and Skyworld, conqueror of the underworld, long may he reign. He ruled over all in a palace with eighty-eight towers. There, at the centre of Sun Girna Ginar, he surveyed the stars that told him of its destiny. He ruled over all the world, enslaving the nations whose people accepted him and destroying all others. He even climbed the heavens and conquered Skyworld, home to the gods.

In the Sultan's city, there was a woman born of a monster and a witch. When the woman was young, her beauty burned brightly in every eye. Men came from distant lands to love her, and in return, she devoured their souls one by one. When she was old, she sold dreams in the marketplace, the singers say. By luring the city into dreams, she destroyed Sun Girna Ginar, bringing it to its knees with hope.'

'This is the story I will tell you,' the old woman says, 'but it begins not with kings, or heroes, or in palaces or battlefields. It begins in the stink of the marketplace, with simple men born of unremarkable ancestors, best forgotten.'

1

Baningan

'How much?' Baningan asks, and the old woman replies, 'Five gold beads.'

In his hands, he holds a small vial in the shape of a woman's body. Inside is a liquid that looks like water with a thin tendril of blood that disappears as quickly as Baningan sees it.

'What is it?'

'A trinket,' the old woman replies. 'A trinket with the power to make your dreams come true.' Baningan sees through the years so cruelly etched on her face. He knows the woman was beautiful in her youth. He thinks she is beautiful still. The price is too much, but Baningan doesn't hesitate to buy it with the little money he has.

'A bargain for the power of dreams,' he says. Of course, he doesn't believe the old woman. He buys the vial because Tamisa loved glass things. He used to steal them for her just to see her smile.

As the old woman hands Baningan the vial, she says, 'Dreams come in through closed eyes. Drink this and perhaps you can open your dreaming eye.' She mimics drinking the liquid inside the bottle. 'Now tell me what your dream is, young man.'

He smiles and says without thinking, 'Just to see her again. Just once. Up close. Without her knowing.'

The old woman looks at him with pity and holds his hand in a tight grip. 'You are too good for her, you fool!'

Baningan laughs at the woman's words as he pockets the vial. 'You are the only one who thinks so,' he tells her, already walking away in the direction of the parade. 'I am an alipin, like you. Just a slave.'

* * *

The Sultan's wedding parade would go no nearer to the Slaves' Quarter than the bridge that led to the market. Baningan stands on top of the bridge now, waiting to see the parade. Underneath his feet, under the bridge, is his home, one among the dozens of others—a crude wooden platform hanging like a bird's nest to the pillars of the stone bridge. He lived there with Tamisa once, a lifetime ago.

For a free man, this was no place to live but a slave could hope for nothing better. What it lacked in comfort, it made up with its view. From Baningan's vantage on the bridge, he beholds the same view as that from his home—almost the entire city of Sun Girna Ginar.

The land slopes downwards from the city gates behind him to meet the sea. At the centre of the city is the Sultan's palace with its majestic towers. At the foot of the palace are the gardens of the Maharlika, glittering green and just beyond the domes of the Holy Quarter's one thousand temples. At the very edge of his vision, the city meets the sea. He sees the sails of boats and the flash of sunlight on the water. Closer to the bridge is the labyrinthine sprawl of the marketplace, spreading down from the ridge through the twisted, rotting maze where the slaves quarter where the alipin live. Below him is the river, once wide and mighty but now a pale memory of its old self, a brown stream choked with garbage.

Baningan chews betel nut and watches people while waiting for the parade. They are dressed in the manner of their tribes. The southern men are in loose pants, vests, and headscarves shaped like the horns of a demon, with kris knives hanging from the middle of their belts. The southern women wear long, narrow sarong skirts and woven shirts adorned with brass bells that ring like music when they move.

The women's heads are adorned in jewelled headpieces, also dressed up with the same brass bells. The mountain men of the north wear only loincloths, but their bodies are covered in tattoos. They always carry two weapons: a machete for traveling in the jungle and a head axe for fighting their enemies. Instead of loincloths, the mountain women wear short woven skirts that end below the knee; they too are heavily tattooed. On their arms are thick gold bracelets and around their necks are necklaces of coloured beads.

With little else to do, Baningan opens the glass vial. He looks around. The street is full of people, but no one is watching him. He swallows the liquid inside the bottle, hoping it is a drug that will make him forget his worries.

The liquid burns. Baningan closes his eyes in pain and falls to the ground. The fire burns his throat and the inside of his stomach, and then it radiates to every part of his body. He is burning, and there is nothing he can do.

A woman stops to see if he is alright, but he pushes her away, and the rest of the crowd gives him a wide berth. Just another crazy man, they mutter, another dirty alipin driven insane.

The fire gnaws at Baningan's spine, searing his flesh from the inside, reaching the tips of his fingers and his eyes. As he claws at his face to gouge out his eyes, a cracking sound erupts and the world splits open and the sky is torn apart. Many of the people in the crowd cower at the sound, or, like Baningan, fall to their knees. Others run for their lives.

It is the God Cannon, announcing the arrival of the Sultan. The cannon, a weapon General Marandang created to kill giants, is the length of three longhouses placed end to end. Storytellers say its cannonballs are iron boulders, and its sound is greater than thunder and more terrible than the end of all things.

As the panic in the crowd subsides, the burning in Baningan's body dies into embers, and he opens his eyes to wake as if in some kind of a dream. In his vision, everything is burning with holy light. The sky is red. The sun is white. The ground is burning coal.

Baningan looks up to see the parade coming down the road. He sees miracles.

Great burning banners are unfurled in the wind, carried by standard-bearers whose skin is the colour of red coral. In the vanguard of the parade are proud soldiers with burning swords and spears. Their armour is full of designs of fire. The captains are on great white fire mares, impatient in their slow march around the city.

Behind the soldiers are creatures from the kingdoms enslaved by the Sultan. There is a giant bird named Manaul whose wingspan shuts out the sky. The hunting dogs of Kabigat are large as horses. Bacunawa, the serpent who ate six of the seven moons, is a mile long. Following the serpent is a hairy kapre, ape-like, grey-skinned, and as large as a house, and last of all, the decapitated head of a giant dragged through the streets by fifty oxen. In Baningan's eyes, these creatures, like the soldiers, are aflame. Manaul's feathers are fire, the snake's eyes are burning embers, and the kapre is smoking a cigar—the brilliance of a sun is in its mouth. Smoke fills the sky.

Next, come the people enslaved by the Sultan. They pass in tight rows, almost like the soldiers, but they are all in chains, starved and branded, heads shaven, their eyes pointed at the ground. Their skin is covered in ash. There are thousands of them to represent every nation in the world.

Then, of course, there are the gods. In a golden cage, there is Galangkalulua in the shape of a winged head, who is responsible for creation. He is too bright to behold and it hurts Baningan's eyes to look at him. In another cage is Sinunggol, a powerful goddess whom the Sultan captured in the kingdom of death. She is chained in her cage but changes shape for all to see. One moment, she is a snake, the next a boar, and then an emerald dragonfly, but she can't escape from her chains no matter what form she takes. The other two cages hold the god of the harvest, Anianihan and the god who fathered thunder and lightning, Dumagid.

Rising high above the cages of the gods comes the Sultan and his bride. They sit on golden thrones placed on a massive wooden platform with one hundred steps. The platform is carried by five hundred slaves.

The Sultan's bride is radiant, aflame with beauty, for she is a diwata, the daughter of Taganlang. She wears a golden dress and a tall, golden crown on her beautiful head. And yet to Baningan's eyes, there is a sadness in her bearing. She looks no different from the enslaved gods in the Sultan's golden cages.

The Sultan looks over all—at the gods in chains at his feet, at the slaves carrying his throne, at the people cheering him on the streets, without any expression on his face.

Baningan curses the old woman, for everything he sees is full of fire. He runs after the Sultan as the others have, pushing each other aside and begging for his blessings.

Soon, the Sultan and his bride disappear, returning to the palace by way of the Holy Quarter.

Behind the Sultan comes his harem, each of the women upon a golden palanquin carried by more of the coral-coloured men. Each palanquin is heaped with silk. Hidden somewhere within, the beautiful concubines of the Sultan shelter themselves from the afternoon sun.

Palanquin after palanquin passes, each one anonymous until one stops in a spot right beside the bridge where he once lived with Tamisa.

A slender white hand reaches out and pulls aside one of the silk curtains. The woman inside moves forward ever so slightly to look outside, and sunlight falls upon her face.

She is beautiful, the crowd murmurs, but she pays no heed to them. Baningan's breath catches. It is Tamisa burning brightly in his vision.

She looks no older than Baningan remembers her, but her eyes betray the passage of the years. Still, she is beautiful, more so now than ever. Tamisa looks at the view of the city with her body partly outside the palanquin now. It is the same view she once shared with Baningan. She smiles as if she sees someone there, a ghost perhaps, then she looks away, with a hint of regret, and pulls the curtain back into its place in a slow, graceful movement.

In that instant, Baningan remembers. Memories return unheeded: his childhood years living on the streets, begging at the temples with the other children, stealing rice cakes for Tamisa whom he had loved from the start. Despite her tattered clothes, tangled hair, and the dirt that always clung to her like all street children, he saw her hidden beauty and made a promise to himself that they would never be apart.

Baningan remembers. Maybe he never stopped. She is with him always, weaving in and out of his days, like a waking dream.

He remembers whispered promises and unmade vows. He remembers the passing of those short years and the lingering moments that lasted forever, staring into Tamisa's eyes and Tamisa staring back, unafraid. He remembers Tamisa and all the reasons she gave for leaving.

A man had come to them and promised her a better life. She would never go hungry, he said. She would have everything she ever wanted. With her beauty, she could be the wife of a datu, or who knows? Maybe more. All she had to do was come with him and leave Baningan. The man would help her disguise herself as someone else, and start over anew.

Now, with Tamisa in front of him once again, Baningan almost calls out to her but he stops himself. She belongs to the Sultan now, and his shadow is everywhere.

Slowly, the parade passes in front of Baningan, and it is night when the last of the parade's wonders returns to the Sultan's palace. Baningan has seen many incredible things all day but remembers none. In his mind, there is only one memory that burns one silent name.

The fire in his sight fades as the moon rises high into the sky. Still, Baningan remembers. He remembers Tamisa as the fire goes out.

2

Aran

Aran sighs as she passes through the market. *Since the drought, there have been no flowers.* She remembers the flowers of Skyworld, the ones he used to give her when she was young. She recalls their otherworldly shapes, the intricate layers of gossamer petals, the colours she had no names for. *See*, she tells herself, *you are not too old to remember*.

Aran shakes her head to remove the memory of him from her mind. Again, she sighs. She has much to do. She has things to buy in the market, and precious little money to buy them with, but somehow, she will make it enough. The market will be crowded because of the Sultan's wedding. She must hurry. Aran looks up at the midday sun, and for a moment, she glimpses Skyworld.

She doesn't like thinking of him, especially these days, but her mind returns to her husband and Skyworld like it has a life of its own. Unlike the young these days, she is old enough to remember when Skyworld was just above the mountains. She would go there by climbing the gods' rainbow bridges.

Aran's grandmother told her of a time when Skyworld was lower still. 'The gods were angered,' she told her when Aran was just a child, 'when a woman kept hitting the floor of Skyworld with the tall pestle she used to husk rice.'

Aran looked at her grandmother with doubt.

'Nanay, that's too low!'

'Believe your grandmother, you shameless child! Since then,' she went on, 'Skyworld has been retreating from the world, going higher and higher into the heavens.'

Aran never believed her, but today she realized that she could barely catch a glimpse of the shores of Skyworld beyond the clouds.

Aran remembers what it was like to walk in Skyworld; few others did nowadays. The lowest level of Skyworld—Heaven Near the Earth, they called it—was little different from our world, but it always seemed to her that there, in the sky, she was farther from hunger, pain, and death. She couldn't explain it. It was just a feeling she had.

Of course, many other things in Skyworld were unlike on earth. For instance, some of the plants and animals looked strange to her. And when she looked up, she could see the six upper levels of Skyworld, traveling farther and farther from her with each moment. They were like distant shores on a sea of blue, full of unspoken promises. Right above Heaven Near the Earth, she could see The Embroidered Heaven and its gossamer mountain peaks. The other levels were often obscured by clouds, but she could almost always see the outline of The Circular Heaven close to the sun. And at the very edge of her vision, there was the seventh level of Skyworld, The End of All Skies.

At night, because Skyworld was closer to the bowl of the sky, the moon was larger, and more stars were visible. They were like iridescent gemstones that no one, not even the Sultan, could possess.

Twice in her travels to Skyworld, she met the gods. First, she met Manama, then Tungkung Langit, the king of the air. Both of them were tall, beautiful, and golden-skinned, with a light shining from their being. She could see their light from miles away. Once they were in sight, she would kneel and bow her head. The gods would pause in front of her and give their blessings. Then they would be gone.

Iraga, her husband, would also travel to Skyworld to trade with the creatures who lived on Heaven Near the Earth, the tikbalang, and the lesser gods, the diwata. He would always return to Aran with Skyworld's flowers.

Even after they were married, he would return with flowers in one arm. Iraga promised her wealth, undying love, and the moon, and she believed him. Since then, Aran has received only the moon.

It has been many years since her husband's death. One day, during the Sultan's war with the gods, he went to Skyworld as he always did, but this time he didn't return.

Aran still thinks of Iraga as her husband. Her friends told her to move on, to find another husband. She was still young enough, they said. But she couldn't, not after the horror of that day. To Aran, Iraga was her husband for always.

Aran longs for him. It is a physical ache she feels in her gut down to her sex. She longs to hold him and nuzzle the corner of his neck and shoulder, the place where he said she 'fits'. She wants to breathe him in, the smell of his skin, his hair, his sweat, and the musk odour where the beast dwells. She wants to feel his stubble in the palm of her hand, wants to rest in the warmth of his armpit. Eyes closed, imagining breathing his scent in, her fingertips travel over her skin, the back of her arms, her stomach.

The sound of the God Cannon pushes the memory aside. Its power pulses through the air, and Aran's eyes close involuntarily as she kneels on the ground and covers her head. Screaming erupts from the people around her. But she regains her composure before all the others because she knows it is just the God Cannon.

Aran gets to her feet and continues on her way as people around her run about in panic.

'It is just the general's cannon,' she says, but no one listens. She goes on her way, and after too long, things return to normal.

Aran walks through the market, past alms-barkers and meat vendors. They shout the price of their goods to her. She walks on.

The vegetable dealers have little to sell and their prices are outrageous. The crops have been poor, and what little they have come from far away, brought in by the great ships of the merchant kings. She walks on.

Aran passes the empty lane in the market where the flower vendors are meant to be. She remembers what the market used to look like during the festival of flowers. The place was transformed into a garden in full bloom. Now the lane is empty. She walks on.

She remembers Iraga of the flowers and his arrogant ways. He swore to her that they would be rich one day. She would have twenty servants for herself alone, he said, and sixty more to care for their house in the Maharlika Quarter. He promised that he would cover her body in gold from head to toe. She never believed him, but she liked to hear him talk that way. It made them both happy. These days, she is content to dream of having a little more rice than normal, or wish for something that has the semblance of steady work. Sometimes she dreams of even less.

She passes the place in the market where they sell all manner of things. They sell kitchenware, pottery, books, sitars, sundials, perfumes, oils, knives, and mirrors. An old woman calls out to her, 'Dreams.' Aran stops.

The old woman looks like a wilted flower: black, grey, and purple with a heart full of maggots.

'Dreams,' the old woman says, offering Aran an assortment of enchanted glass trinkets, 'dreams in bottles. For you, four gold beads.'

Aran frowns at the price, which is almost beyond her reach, but she is drawn to the woman's words. 'What kind of dreams?' Aran demands.

'Anything,' the old woman replies with a shrug. 'That's why they are dreams.'

A voice within Aran tells her that this is just a scam, but something deeper still silences that voice. Almost against her will, she hears herself speaking to the old woman, and is embarrassed by her own words.

'Flowers,' she says 'I would like flowers.' *Like the ones, he would give before.*

The old woman rummages in her stall and produces a simple glass vase, elegant and fragile.

'Fill it with water, and the next morning your dream will come true.'

Aran doesn't believe the old woman, but she takes the vase in two hands and forgets to haggle on the price. She goes home after her errands, fills the vase with water just like the old woman told her, and goes to bed early.

The next morning Aran wakes up before the sun, alone. She sighs. She goes about her morning tasks, prepares her breakfast, and as she passes by the table on which she had placed the vase the night before, she drops the earthenware plate she is holding. It shatters on the floor.

In front of her, she sees something there that should not be. There, in the thin vase she bought from the old woman, are the flowers of Skyworld.

She remembers Iraga from that final day. His broken body lay at the doorstep of their house, with a hastily painted sign tied around his neck. It proclaimed that Iraga was a criminal and a spy for the enemies of the Sultan. At first, she had trouble making the connection that this thing, this carcass with the swollen purple face and the gaping, red, stab wounds, was him, Iraga the boastful, her husband. He was many things, she knew this—sometimes a liar, often a man who drank too much. But a criminal? No. That was someone else. There had to have been some kind of mistake. Who had they thrown at her doorstep? Her husband was away in Skyworld. He would return one day with flowers. Yes, he would not forget. Despite all his shortcomings, he never forgot.

Her heart quivers. She holds her breath. She takes a step towards the flowers, feeling the pieces of the broken plate under her bare feet. They are so beautiful, she thinks. She touches the petals of one of the flowers still wet with morning dew. She bends over the flower and breathes in its fragrance. She remembers the past, of how love came and was taken away from her by the cruelty of beasts. Aran weeps because she is so happy.

3

Bagilat

In a faraway land that knows only rain, they worship him as a god. He is Bagilat, god of the rain and bringer of life, god of the flood and bringer of death. Here, they do not know him.

Bagilat walks the streets in the form of a cat. If he were to take his true form, people would recognize him as a god. And in this dry land, their need for him is greater than any other. So he passes in disguise, an alley cat with deep blue eyes like the sky.

The cat god walks the narrow alleys of the market with a stoic expression. He avoids the crush of passers-by and walks close to the stalls, underneath the legs of tables, over heavy crates full of fruits, through heaps of garbage already rotting. From below, he watches children running through the alleys, rough men carrying sacks of rice over their shoulders, and pickpockets lurking around corners.

'Greetings, my Lord Bagilat,' an old voice says from behind the cat.

Rising to its feet, the cat turns around gracefully and sees an old crone on her knees, head bowed, palms open on the ground in supplication.

'Oh, it's you,' the cat says, its face a mask that betrays no expression. 'This is a long way from hell.'

The old woman raises her head, careful not to look the god in the eye. 'It is not so far,' she says.

'Get up,' the cat commands. 'The mortals are starting to look.'

The old woman does as she is told, holding onto a nearby stall for support, her bony knees shaking with the effort it takes to rise.

The cat jumps up onto the old woman's stall, landing in an empty space among the glass bottles. Not a single bottle falls.

'What brings you to this land?' the cat asks. It sniffs a bottle and licks the glass. 'And what are these? Your stink is all over them.'

'They are dreams, my Lord,' the old woman replies. 'I sell them to the mortals.' She pauses as if thinking of what to say next. Finally, she says, 'I am here to destroy the city.'

The god looks at her and tilts its cat head to one side. The stoic cat mask lifts and rises at the corners. The god laughs.

'Sun Girna Ginar was created by the gods! It is protected by the Sultan and the power of the god of destruction, Kalaon, and guarded by the armies of General Marandang! You, you old crone, think you can destroy the greatest of all the cities of man?'

'No, my Lord,' the old woman says, eyes bowed, 'not I. Men will destroy the city. I promise you.'

Bagilat laughs from his belly. He rolls on the ground in his cat form and forgets where he is. After a moment, he composes himself and says, 'Men do not have this power. Surely you know this. Their lives are like the flickering of fireflies: the moon does not grow jealous of their light. Then, they are gone.'

The old woman doesn't take the god's mockery kindly. Her face hardens. She measures her words.

'Nevertheless' she says, 'that is what will come to pass. These men and women—' she gestures to the people around her haggling over the price of fish on one side and selling junk on the other, 'they are the instruments of my destruction.'

'These *people*?' Bagilat says the word with disdain.

'Yes,' the old woman replies in a patient tone, her emotions reined in. 'These very same ones.'

A chuckle escapes the god's mouth. He sniffs the air.

'You are joking.'

'I assure you, my Lord, I am not.'

'Perhaps you mean the datus or the vizier? Or that hero—what was his name? Amang?'

The old woman shakes her head.

'These people.'

Bagilat still refuses to believe. Once again the mockery escapes. 'Like that woman who asked you for flowers? Or that pathetic lovesick fool?'

The old woman shrugs.

'Not all seeds land on fertile ground,' she says, then seeing someone approaching from the corner of her eye, she smiles. 'You will see, my Lord,' she continues. 'My champions arrive.'

Bagilat looks to either side of him.

'I do not see them,' he says. 'All I see are ordinary men. I am growing quite sick of them.' He sniffs the air again. 'But yes, I smell a datu among them, though he is an old and broken one. A datu once perhaps, but no longer. The others are slaves mostly, or beggars. Are these the champions you speak of?'

'Yes,' the old woman replies. 'I am afraid there is little I can do to convince you. We will just have to wait. And watch.'

The cat sighs.

'That is so tiresome,' Bagilat says, growing pensive. 'I do little else these days. Men have forgotten their gods. They do not send sacrifices. There is no more slaughter of pigs or slaves. Now it is all about the Sultan and his great city! They do not pray to the gods; the Sultan is always listening, and he is jealous. They do not fear the gods; they fear the Sultan more.

'Believe me when I tell you that I too wish to see this city destroyed. But these dreams you peddle, they cannot help you. They will achieve nothing. This—' he searches for a word, '*pastime* of yours is beneath your great stature. Your place is in Skyworld, with your father.'

'Ah, but my father is not in Skyworld. He is here too, my Lord, as you know.'

Bagilat shrugs. 'He belongs in Skyworld too, on the highest of the seven levels, beside Magbabaya the creator.'

'He is where he deserves to be.'

Bagilat doesn't answer, only tilts his head in acknowledgement.

The old woman says nothing, and the cat gets up as if about to leave.

'A wager then?' the old woman says to the cat's tail. Bagilat stops, turns around, and looks at the old woman's face. A hint of a smile is playing on her lips.

'I say that men will destroy the city. You, my Lord, say that is beyond their power. I have chosen my champions. You will see them. They are the next three men who will stop at my stall. I have sold dreams to thousands of others, and I will sell dreams to thousands more, but these three men are more important than all the others combined.'

'Now I propose that you choose your own champions to defend the city of the gods. And we will see which one of us is right.

'Maybe the city will burn, or maybe it will be consumed by war. Or maybe the Sultan will finish conquering the world and cover it in peace.

'We will watch them fight and struggle, your champions and mine. They will kill and betray each other and some of them will die, all because of their compassion, their nobility, their base desires, and their thirst for revenge.'

Bagilat gives a wide smile.

'I like this game of yours,' the god says. 'Let us play.'

4

Magat

Magat awakens in the Pit to realize that all his fears have come true. *I am going to die here.* He looks to his right and sees the bloody, swollen stump where his hand once was. He then looks up and sees the soldiers guarding the mouth of the pit, the Sultan's prison.

Magat has heard rumours about the Pit before. The slaves believed that the Pit is located in a fort along the palace walls, and inside the fort is a hole that goes deep into the earth. This was the prison where the Sultan sent those who broke his laws. To be sent here was to be forgotten, never to return to memory. Some say it used to be a mine where the Sultan found his riches. Others claim it was a prison built for giants.

Magat finds himself lying on a mat on the ground near one of the four walls of the Pit. Hundreds of men lie around him. Most of them are asleep. They are sick, he realizes, or dying. Like he is dying.

Each of the men was punished according to the Sultan's laws. Their tongues were torn out for speaking against him. Their eyes were burnt in their sockets for laying eyes on the Sultan's wives. For raising a blade against the Maharlika, their arms were cut off.

As far as Magat's eye can estimate, the entire Pit is maybe five to six thousand talampakan long and just as wide. But there are so many men inside that there is hardly any empty room. The men huddle together in small groups, on their haunches, or they stand in what little shade they can find from the shadows of the walls. At night, Magat would soon discover, they are packed together, shoulder to shoulder, with another man at their feet.

An old, bearded man approaches Magat and kneels by his side. A bright red burn scar covers half his face. He examines Magat's arm and touches his forehead with rough and calloused hands. Magat flinches at the man's touch.

'You're an unlucky one,' he says. 'It looks like you will live. Right now, a demon has you in its grasp, but if the fever breaks, you might come to live with us in this paradise. Or who knows? You might walk out of this place one day. After all, you still have both of your legs.'

Magat laughs weakly.

'No one walks out of here,' he tells the old man, 'if what they say is true.'

'It is,' the old man says in a grave tone, 'but I will let you in on a secret. After all, we owe it all to you.'

Magat closes his eyes and lays his head down. He is tired and he doesn't want to hear the old man talk. He begins to shiver uncontrollably.

The old man gives Magat a drink of water from a flask. Magat takes the flask with one shaking hand.

'My name is Mapolumpun,' the old man says when Magat remains silent. 'And I have been here for a long time.'

Mapolumpun takes a deep breath that seems to be carrying all the regret in the world. 'When you have healed,' he says, 'you will learn that there is one way in and out of this place: a narrow stairway built into the western wall. It is always heavily guarded. Every morning, the guards bring in new prisoners. Every evening, they take away the dead. We have nothing here except our mats and our loincloths. I have my flask. I know a man who has a nose flute. We have no tools for digging, no weapons, no wood we can fashion into knives or tools. But when they threw you in here, they gave us the key out of this place—for they also threw in your hand.'

'We are saved then,' Magat says, wishing the old man would stop talking. 'We will slap the guards to death with my hand.'

Mapolumpun grins.

'Good!' he says. 'Good. You have some spirit left in you. You will need it here.'

Mapolumpun looks around him, as if to see if anyone is listening and then lies down beside Magat. In a low voice, the old man whispers into his ear. 'The answer to how to get out of here occurred to me while I was taking a piss. You see, we may be lower than slaves but we are not animals. We maintain some order here: we piss and shit in the southern corner of the Pit. So one day, I was there, with my cock in my hand. I saw all the thousands of men in the Pit and wondered, 'Where does all the piss go?' If each of us took a piss five times a day, we should all be drowning by nightfall. And if the earth swallowed it all, we should be standing in mud, but the ground under our feet is dry. Even when it rains, the water disappears in a matter of hours instead of turning this hole into a lake.'

'So where does it all go?' Magat asks, forcing the words out so Mapolumpun can finish.

'There are holes in the ground,' Mapolumpun whispers, 'in the southern corner, where the water goes. They are small holes, no bigger than your arm, but I believe they join together into a larger hole, not far from the surface. It has to because the amount of piss that travels out of here is great.'

'Where does it all go from there?'

Mapolumpun shrugs, but Magat doesn't see it from where he is lying.

'I don't know. To some kind of tunnel or sewer, then to the sea, I hope. But I really don't know. That is the truth.'

'And what does my hand have to do with this story of yours?'

'Your hand? It's useless to us. You can have it back if you want. But they cut it off with a good chunk of your forearm, and with that bone, we have something hard to pick at the stone with. The stone and mortar around the holes have grown soft because of the water. We've been at it for a day now, and it has been slow going, but it has been working so far. It may take weeks or months, but when the hole becomes big enough for a man to pass, we will tell you. We owe everything to you. There is hope. Don't die just yet.'

* * *

Magat's fever breaks on the seventh day. The swelling in his arm recedes, and soon he finds himself on his feet.

Mapolumpun finds him somehow in the sea of prisoners. Like all the other prisoners, Magat stands under the noon sun, unable to escape. Already, his ribs have begun to show, his chest has sunk, and there are black circles under his eyes.

'And they said you were going to die,' Mapolumpun greets him with a wide grin. 'I never believed them. "This one is important," I told them. "The gods have plans for him!"'

'They plan to kill me slowly in this hole,' Magat replies. 'Look! They've already placed us in our graves. They've just forgotten to shovel the dirt in.'

Mapolumpun scowls at Magat. 'Where are your good spirits now?' he asks. 'I liked you better when you were dying.'

Magat looks at Mapolumpun, then looks away, at the ground, an apology of sorts.

'I meant every word,' Mapolumpun says. 'I do believe you have a role to play in our struggle. I was a tanner once, a master of my craft—yes, I know, it is hard to believe underneath all of this.' Mapolumpun runs a hand through his thick beard, the longest among all the prisoners. 'In those days, I had many apprentices. And I always knew which of them would turn out to be special. You are one of the special ones, Magat. And it's not just because of your good looks.

'You mustn't give up hope. I know people always say that, but it's true. So we are already in our graves. So what? What has changed? Even when you were free, you were already dying.

'Tell me, my friend, why are you here? What did you do to make the Sultan hate you so much?'

Magat doesn't move or say a word. Mapolumpun waits for his answer. He doesn't have anything else to do.

'I am a thief,' Magat says, still without looking up. 'Or, rather, I was a thief. I am a prisoner now. I am sorry to disappoint you, Mapolumpun, but I am not like you or the others here. I cannot say that I was a Maharlika, or that I became too powerful so the Sultan destroyed my family. There is nothing special within me. Before I was a thief, I was the son of a blacksmith. But my father died before he could teach me the craft, so I became a beggar. Is that what you wanted to know?'

Mapolumpun ignores the question, hearing the hostility in Magat's voice, and asks another one instead.

'What did you steal?'

'Many things. Anything I could. I became a slave, an alipin in the palace of the Sultan. There were hundreds of us, all picked off the streets, just to clean the rooms in one of the wings of the palace. I had never seen wealth like that before. There were countless rooms but no one living in them. The walls were covered in gold. And I asked myself, 'How can one man have so much when so many of us had nothing?'

'So you stole from the Sultan.'

'Small things at first, some food, gold leaf. Then more, a small gemstone in inlay or a crystal figurine. I never regretted it. It felt like justice.'

'Then they caught you.'

'No, not for a while,' Magat shakes his head in disbelief. 'There was so much wealth in the palace that they didn't know anything had disappeared until weeks later. Still, they didn't know who was stealing these things. So when they found out, the soldiers gathered all of us alipin together and they said they would cut off everyone's right hand unless the thief confessed. And I—

Magat stops, not knowing how to go on. 'I . . . I said nothing.

'The soldiers grabbed one of us, a friend of mine, and cut off his hand, just like that. No warning. Everyone screamed. I never believed they would actually do that.

Again, Magat has difficulty saying more and pauses. When he finally continues, there is a hard edge to his voice.

'He never reached this place. He bled out right there.

'After that, I confessed. They cut off my hand. I wanted to die like my friend. But I lived.'

Mapolumpun nods his head.

'And now that you have seen the Sultan's cruelty, what would you do if you could escape from this place?'

'We are not getting out of this place.'

'It is just a matter of time,' Mapolumpun says, sure of himself. 'The hole is growing. Tell me. Please. What would you do?'

Magat remains silent, but eventually, he answers. The hard edge in his voice has become determination and an indomitable will.

'The only thing that is left to do.'

'And what is that?'

'The Sultan must be stopped.'

Now Mapolumpun looks at Magat with a wide smile on his face. 'See?' he says. 'You are a prisoner in the Sultan's Pit, thrown away and forgotten. You have one good hand and no real hope for escape. But you dare to talk to me about stopping the Sultan.

'I was right about you.'

Mapolumpun says nothing more.

* * *

Weeks pass, and Magat loses track of time. Then one day, just moments before word spreads around the Pit, Mapolumpun tells Magat that it is time to go. Together, they walk as fast as they can to the hole. It is mid-afternoon. There are no clouds, and the sun watches them with its burning eye.

Around the hole stands a wall of thirty men. They are there to protect the hole and the diggers from the eyes of the guards. When they see Mapolumpun, they move aside.

Behind the wall of men is the hole, and it is exactly that, just a hole in the stone floor. The place reeks of shit and piss. Rivulets of piss drain into the hole. It is no wider than a man's chest.

There is a short line of men in front of the hole, the diggers. Already, they have begun to escape. They pass through the hole one by one and disappear. To do this, they raise their hands over their head and slide into the darkness beyond.

Crude tools lie discarded on the ground—sharp rocks, a stick with human teeth on one end, Magat's arm bone, now worn down. From the darkness beyond the hole, Magat hears water, footsteps, and the voices of the men who have gone ahead.

'Come, Mapolumpun, Magat,' says the last man in the line. 'It is time to say goodbye to this place.' They get in line behind him.

Just beyond the wall of men, there is a crowd now, and they begin to push against the wall. They know about the hole.

A fight breaks out. The men from outside the wall break through and rush towards the hole. The thousands of prisoners in the Pit descend upon them.

High up at the mouth of the Pit, the guards see the rioting prisoners and begin firing volleys of arrows into the crowd. Some men get down to avoid getting shot, but most do not. Along the stairway, a company of soldiers armed with tall shields begins to descend.

Magat is close to the hole now. As the men in front of him drop into the hole one by one, the others behind him push against the sea of humanity that threatens to engulf them. Magat sees Mapolumpun go through the hole moments before someone knocks him off his feet. His ribs are crushed as dozens of men step over him to get to the hole. He thrashes about on the floor, desperately trying to find space to get up. He reaches out and grabs a leg. Someone falls close to him, and others tumble to the ground around him, blocking the oncoming crush of prisoners. On his stomach now, Magat sees the hole in front of him. He crawls through it head first, into darkness, towards freedom.

* * *

Mapolumpun is right. The hole leads to sewers large enough for a man to crawl through.

Magat can see nothing in the sewers. He follows the sounds of the men in front of him, and after a long hour of crawling, he hears the sea and smells salt in the air. He sees a blinding pinpoint of light in the distance—the end of the tunnel is near.

Soon, Magat is swimming towards the nearest beach. Most of the prisoners head for the city for fear of being caught again; only a few remain to see how many more will escape. After a couple of hundred men arrive at the beach, the flow of prisoners comes to a halt.

Magat looks for Mapolumpun but cannot find him, and knowing the Sultan's soldiers will be hunting them down, he gives up his search. He knows he must act swiftly.

Magat re-enters the city as a beggar once again. He sits at the Bone Gate with a borrowed beggar bowl. This gate is the only entrance to the city, a massive arch supposedly made from the ribcage of the stone-skinned dragon Isarog. All around him, slaves and freemen walk through the gate. There are traders' caravans with elephants laden with goods. Other traders stand at the head of lines of slaves carrying baskets upon their heads. There are beggars—leg-less, arm-less, and blind. Among them are mothers carrying borrowed babies, and barefoot children. Magat doesn't even need to pretend to be crippled to disappear among them. As a beggar, he is invisible to the Sultan's soldiers.

When night falls, Magat takes his earnings—a few small gold beads—and walks into the city. He heads straight to the market in search of food and a dry, quiet alley where he can sleep. Down one alley, he passes an old woman with an unusual scam. She claims to be selling dreams in bottles. She is so desperate that she even pesters beggars like him. Magat declines her offer as politely as he can. Dreams will have to wait.

5

Adlao

From a distance, the giant looks like a small mountain. It is sleeping on its side, and a forest grows where its shoulder rises, as well as down its massive, protruding belly. Adlao can make out the giant's legs further in the distance. They are two more mountain peaks etched against the sky, but sharper than the others. The giant's knees have fewer trees growing on them. Granite crags are exposed to the heavens.

On the opposite side of the mountain, Adlao can see one head of the giant, but the five others are hidden from view or slumber underground. From the shoulders of this six-headed giant grows a sinewy neck that stretches to the first head like a stone bridge. Adlao can see part of the second head, but most of it lies buried.

The witch is waiting for him. The young girl sits on a wooden chair heaped with pillows and Chinese silk fabric. Beside her, a male slave holds a parasol. Behind her, a retinue of forty maidens waits on her.

She is dressed in the manner of the mountain folk, in a narrow skirt woven with a repeated geometric pattern of black, red, yellow, and white. She is naked from the waist up, except for several stiff necklaces made of gold. Most of her torso is covered in tattoos—snake scales for protection and other symbols that Adlao is unfamiliar with. Her arms and shoulders are the most heavily tattooed, with tattoos reaching down to her fingertips.

Her face brightens when she sees him, but she does not smile.

'Shall we begin?' she calls out to Adlao. Her voice is low, but to Adlao, she sounds like a child who is asking him to play.

'How do we proceed?' Adlao asks when he is closer to the witch. He speaks in an even manner and rarely raises his voice.

'Amtalaw,' she says, gesturing to the slave holding her parasol, 'will light a fire and burn the forest on the giant's back.

'This will not wake him, not yet. This particular giant has been asleep for four hundred years, and it will not rouse easily. But the fire will be the start. Maybe it will stir. If it does, you can speak to it.

'Afterwards, we will make an offering. We will sacrifice your slaves. You will not need them for your voyage back to Sun Girna Ginar.'

Adlao frowns. 'Won't a pig or two do?'

'No.' The witch speaks with certainty. 'The giant of Gawi-Gawen hates mankind. It is good for us to remind him of the taste of blood.'

'Is it necessary?' Adlao asks.

When the witch says yes, Adlao pauses but doesn't protest.

'The giant may not wake otherwise,' she explains, and after another pause, Adlao nods. It is a small gesture that comes at a great price.

'How long will it take to wake up?'

'A week? A month? I cannot say for certain. After the sacrifice, return to your city. There will be nothing left to do but wait. I will leave Amtalaw to stand watch. He will send word as soon as the giant awakens.'

'How will we lead it to Sun Girna Ginar?'

'I already told you, Datu,' the witch says. 'I saw it in a vision. By chance, an envoy of Sun Girna Ginar will come across the wandering giant and challenge it to destroy the Sultan's great city. Once given this purpose, the giant will make haste to Sun Girna Ginar. You need not worry. It will come to pass.'

Adlao takes a deep breath. 'Very well then,' he says. 'Let us begin.'

The witch nods.

'Before we do,' she says, fixing him with her gaze, 'I need to know if you are sure of what you are about to do. Once awakened, the giant cannot be put back to sleep. It is the greatest of all its kind, and destruction follows in its wake. The giant is full of hate for mankind. It would kill us all if it could.'

Adlao looks at the mountain in front of him and replies, 'Yes. I need its power.'

The witch doesn't ask for an explanation. 'Then let us begin,' she says simply.

* * *

It takes a day and a night for the fire to die down. Even then, only a portion of the forest on the giant's back is burnt. The forest is still green.

Adlao and the witch watch the fire from afar—the black smoke that rises from the fire is strong and thick—but when the fire is spent, they approach the giant's head again. They do not speak to each other. It is dawn. The sky is lightening, but the sun is hidden behind the mountains.

Through the smoke that is still rising from the remnants of the fire, in the dim light of the sunrise, Adlao can barely see the face of the giant. He sees that its eyes are open but unseeing.

Something in Adlao, some primal instinct, compels him to turn around, run and keep running until the giant is far behind him. But at that moment, the witch speaks and the urge is silenced.

'Look!' she says, delight playing in her voice. 'It is awake already.' Unlike Adlao, she is unafraid, and she rushes closer to the giant's face.

'Come, Datu,' she calls out to him as he stands frozen in place. 'The giant will not rouse until weeks later. No harm will come to you.'

Adlao tries to move his legs but his body will not obey. When he still does not move, she coaxes him further, saying, 'Come, Datu! Tomorrow you will be far from this place, heading back to your beautiful city. Today, you are in the gaze of the oldest of the giants, whose eyes witnessed the creation of our earth. Speak, and it will hear you. Tell it what you want. You won't get another chance.'

Adlao remembers why he is there and steels himself for action. He moves forward with tentative steps. The witch watches Adlao struggle. Sweat begins to form on his back and his brow as he passes the young girl. He keeps walking until he is within earshot of the giant. He can feel its breath as it exhales through its mouth. Adlao falls to his knees.

He begins to speak without looking at the massive face in front of him. At first, the words seem trapped in his throat.

'My name is Datu Adlao,' he says. 'I come from Sun Girna Ginar, the city of the Sultan, ruler of the earth, conqueror of Skyworld and the underworld, son of Kabuniyan, the Immortal.'

Adlao looks up at the giant. Its face has not changed. It stares through him, into the morning mist, unblinking.

At that moment, Adlao finds his voice. He lets it carry to the mountain in front of him where it echoes among the ridges and cliffs. He stands up, rising to his full height, his head thrown back. He was a datu once, he remembers, a commander of men, and a king.

'It is I, Datu Adlao, who has awoken you from your sleep,' he says with an iron voice. 'I heard from the songs of your greatness, and I have come to ask you one thing.' Adlao pauses then releases the full power of his voice. 'Destroy the city of the Tyrant, ravager of nations, rapist of Skyworld, a traitor in league with the underworld, motherless son of demons, dead but undying. Destroy his city and end his reign. Only then will any of us be free.'

* * *

It all came to pass as the Witch Princess said it would, and after weeks of travel, Adlao returned to Sun Girna Ginar. Now, he stands before the Bone Gate, alone.

Maybe he will die here, he muses, even before his plans are executed. Adlao reminds himself that this is where he needs to be. There is much work to be done.

Amidst the chaos of passing merchants and the beggars stands Vizier Humadapnon, the Sultan's right hand. Behind him are three hundred soldiers armed with spears and shields. They are all waiting for Adlao.

Adlao approaches the vizier, unafraid. Compared to Humadapnon, Adlao looks like one of the beggars that line the road. The vizier—tall and overweight—is dressed like the Southerners, in trousers, vest, and headscarf though his are made of silk and woven in vibrant colours. Around his neck are gold necklaces. Golden armlets adorn his arms. Each of his fingers has a gold ring. Gold covers the faces of his teeth, too. At his side is a kris knife with a wooden kamagong handle and an ornate scabbard in gold and gemstones. He greets Adlao like an old friend.

'Big Brother!' Humadapnon calls out to Adlao. 'It has been too long. We have missed you. The palace has not been the same without you.'

Standing face to face with Adlao, the vizier does not extend his arm in greeting, and neither does Adlao.

'Vizier,' Adlao says with a deep bow.

'Come now, Big Brother, we do not need such formalities. Have we not travelled the years by each other's side? I cannot recall a time when I did not know you. A lifetime has passed since last we spoke, but I like to think I know you still.'

Adlao says nothing. The smile on Humadapnon's face flickers, but he maintains it.

'Do not worry, Big Brother. The Sultan loves you still. Has he not kept his promise that no harm would come to you so long as you remained in exile?'

Forced to reply, Adlao says, 'He has.'

'And today is an auspicious day. The Sultan is to be wed—'

'Again? What country does he seek to enslave now?'

The vizier ignores Adlao's words. 'The Sultan's wife-to-be is a goddess from the Embroidered Heaven, the daughter of Taganlang,' he says. 'It will be a blessed, prosperous union. Peace will flourish in both our lands. So today is a day of celebration. We have much to be grateful for . . .

'And now our brother has returned. We do not know if you bear us hatred in your heart, but so long as you obey the Sultan's laws, you are safe here.

'That is how our Sultan loves those who served him well, even those who betrayed him.' A pained expression crosses Humadapnon's face. 'And your betrayal was a heavy one. But he loved you most of all.'

Humadapnon pauses. Sweat pours down his brow. He decides to deliver the message he was sent to give Adlao.

'I bear a message from the Sultan. He bids you welcome and good fortune. He gives me the power to allow you to enter the Sultan's city. He assures me no harm shall come to you as long as you obey his laws. In memory of the times you have shared, you are free to go about your business, but you shall attempt no acts of treason or rebellion. You will be free to travel in the city, but may not set foot in the palace or the Maharlika Quarter.'

'I understand,' Adlao says.

'Do you understand?' Humadapnon asks. The smile is gone now. 'You know the Sultan is always watching. What do you hope to achieve here?'

Now it is Adlao's turn to put on a smiling mask.

'Little Brother,' he says, 'I only wish to visit my home one more time before I grow old. Now please let me pass.'

The vizier's frown deepens, but he steps aside. The soldiers step aside as well, forming two ranks on either side of Adlao.

'Welcome home,' the vizier says, his voice heavy with mockery as Adlao steps through the Bone Gate into the city of Sun Girna Ginar.

* * *

The city has changed little since Adlao's exile. He finds most things as he remembers them. The ribs of the dragon still line the road from the Bone Gate. The minarets are in their place in the sky, rising from the Holy Quarter. The stink spreading from the market is there as well, just as he recalls.

Without thinking, Adlao turns to enter the market. Here, people press in on him from all sides, pushing and shoving. Their smells assault him, their hot sweat and stale breath, and the dry smell of the sun on their skin. He lets himself be carried along by the crowd. He hardly notices the things being sold around him—the steel knives and scissors, or the poisons and traps. He is led deeper and deeper by the crowd into the market, along unmarked alleys, through covered walkways beside festering canals.

When the God Cannon goes off, the people in the crowd disappear faster than Adlao thought was possible. The sound sends them tumbling to the ground, but before the sound of the cannon shot is gone, they have scrambled to their feet and run away.

With the alipin and freemen gone, Adlao is the only one who remains standing in the alley, but after a moment, he realizes he is not alone. An old woman behind a stall littered with glass vials is also standing on her feet, motioning to him to come nearer.

Adlao walks towards her. The old woman stares at him.

'You are Datu Adlao,' she says when he stands in front of her. 'I know you. You are a great man, a good man.'

'How—'

The old woman brushes Adlao's question aside. 'You will not remember me,' she says. 'I am no one.' There is something familiar about the old woman, but Adlao decides that she is probably right.

'Would you buy a dream from me, Datu?'

'Is that what these are?' he asks, picking up one of the bottles in front of him. Inside the bottle is a dead spider.

'Yes, Datu. One of them can be yours.'

Adlao returns the bottle to its place.

'At my age,' he says, 'one puts little faith in dreams. A man's actions are more trustworthy. They are like seeds. When planted in the past, they bear fruit in the future. I have little use for dreamy notions.' Adlao thinks of the giant of Gawi-Gawen, of the revolution to come, and the death of the Tyrant. 'You should know this! You are older than I am.'

The old woman looks offended. 'I am not a great lord, but maybe I know something you don't, eh? After all, as you said, I am older than you. Everyone dreams of something. You are not so different. Surely there is something you wish for?'

'I wish for the people to be free,' Adlao says right away.

The old woman looks triumphant.

'I have done all I can to make them free,' Adlao continues. 'I have set plans into motion. I have laboured for years. Now, I have wagered my life for the people. They are worth dying for.'

The triumph on the woman's face fades.

'I've never heard of anything so stupid,' she says. 'These people don't know you. They don't remember you. You don't owe them anything. They'll take it anyway, mind you. But why rush towards death? It will come soon enough, as it does for us all.'

'No, of course not,' Adlao says, shaking his head. 'I don't want to die. There is simply no other way. And I am willing to pay the price.'

An expression of begrudging respect crosses the old woman's face, but she replaces it quickly with a blank smile. She turns around and takes a bottle from a box behind her. She presents it to Adlao with a flourish and a bow.

'This is for you,' she says. 'It is three gold beads if you want it.'

Adlao bows in return. 'It is worth more, if only for the pleasure of your conversation,' he says, without really meaning it. 'What does it do?'

The old woman shrugs. 'It makes your dream come true,' she says, 'but you said you have no use for such things.'

Adlao is curious now. 'How does it work?' he asks. The glass thing in his hands is a common bottle used for holding coconut wine. There is water inside, but it is dark and muddy. The larger pieces of rock and dirt have settled to the bottom.

'It is always different,' she says. 'For you, you must find any spot of earth, then pour the contents of the bottle on the ground. Mix the water with the dirt and you are done. It will save your life.' She pauses for effect. 'Maybe it will make you live forever.'

Adlao reaches for three gold beads from a pouch on his belt. He doesn't believe a word the old woman says, but he is fascinated by how she has just sold him a bottle of muddy water, and how he is grateful for it.

6

Sakandal

Sakandal runs when he sees smoke rising from his village. He knows right away that something is wrong and leaves the deer on his back by the side of the hunting trail.

As the hunter gets closer to the village, he can see the smoke is made of many small columns. The largest one comes from the main village, but there is fire everywhere, even on the outskirts, where his house is located.

Sakandal knows what he will find when he gets to his house, but nothing could prepare him for what he sees.

The burning house has fallen from where it once stood, but Sakandal can still recognize the house's stilts, as well as remnants of the ladder he had once used to climb inside. Everything else has turned to black ash.

Sakandal crawls over the scorched earth, searching. Beside the doorway is what's left of a table and a chair. The wooden beams of the roof lie on top of them. Further on is the space where his family once slept. On the ground is his son's wooden top. Hanging from a burnt post, a blackened metal hook marks where the baby's hammock used to hang from. And in the corner of the house, there are three blackened shapes that look like bodies, burnt beyond recognition.

One is the size of a woman, and two are the size of children clinging to the woman's body, almost like suckling pigs. They are all curled up in a foetal position, and in the arms of the woman is a white skull peeking out from the woman's breast, the body of an infant.

Sakandal hears a low sound, one he recognizes as a human voice. It is a low moan that carries over the burnt houses of the village, rising from the pit of a man's stomach to find release in his tired, choked throat. He hears the voice fall and rise, and fall again. It is a familiar sound, one he has heard before, at funerals. The bereaved made that sound when they hung the dead in their coffins in the caves that led to the afterlife, and it carried all the grief that could not be contained inside any man's body. Today, it is Sakandal's voice.

Memory passes from that moment. Sakandal remembers trying to lift the bodies of his family, to go somewhere else, somewhere where they couldn't be hurt anymore, but they had become brittle, blackened meat attached to bone. Their sides had fused to the remains of the wooden floor, so Sakandal is forced to leave them where they lay. He doesn't want to break their bodies.

Not knowing what else to do, Sakandal stays beside his family, sitting down with his legs folded beneath him, one hand on his beloved's hand. Over the hours, his face, arms, and legs become covered in soot, but he isn't aware of how this happened.

His eyes look straight ahead, unseeing. His mind is motionless and empty. Time passes, but he remains unmoving.

As the sun hangs low in the sky, he begins to see. He sees the houses of his neighbours, burnt like his own. A fire in one house would never have spread to the next, Sakandal thinks absently. People would never have been caught inside unless they were kept there, or slaughtered first. He sees other bodies on the road between the houses. They too were burnt, but in their hands are spears, bucklers, or head axes.

Sakandal realizes that a war party had come, but he does not know from where. They had no enemies. And yet these men came with steel and fire and took everything from him.

It is sunset when the Sultan's soldiers find Sakandal. There are five of them, dressed for war in steel breastplates. Four of them carry a spear and shield, and on their belts hang long knives. The fifth, their commander, has a sword on his belt.

Sakandal reaches for the head axe at his side. He has lost his bow and arrows and his machete, but his axe is still there. The hardwood handle feels good in his palm.

'I told you there is no one here,' one of the men says. He is older than the others. His skin is lined and tough like leather and his cropped hair has white in it. 'We should get back to the others.'

'I heard something, I swear,' the one with the sword replies. 'And you know what the captain said. We can't let anyone escape. Or the vizier will kill us himself.'

'I'd like to see that pig try,' the older one snorts.

Sakandal wraps two hands around the handle of the head axe, and rises to a crouch. These men killed my family, he tells himself.

Sakandal watches the soldiers walk past the remains of his house. Covered in ash and obscured by a burnt wall in the failing light of the day, he is hidden from their sight. When they turn away from him, Sakandal crouches and leaps over the crumbling wall, closing the distance between them. The soldier with the sword and the older one are arguing, but Sakandal no longer hears them. There is only his heartbeat thundering in his chest, and his breath, traveling slow and even through his nose, as he raises the axe above his head, and takes aim at the last soldier. He strikes at the man's neck with all his strength.

The soldier's head falls to the ground, followed by the crash of his armoured body. The other soldiers turn around and raise their spears, but Sakandal has already raised his axe again. He lets it fall on the next soldier's neck.

Sakandal misses but hits the man's shoulder instead, where the blow breaks through steel and flesh, and the bone beneath. Blood gushes out of the soldier's mouth as he dies.

The two remaining spearmen advance on Sakandal with their shields raised. Their commander backs away and draws his sword. Sakandal struggles to remove his axe from where it is lodged in the second soldier. He manages to free it just as the third soldier jabs at him with his spear. Sakandal loses balance as he dislodges the axe but he swings wildly at the nearest soldier and strikes him in the knee. The man falls to the ground with a shout.

The old soldier, less foolhardy than the others, waits. He sees an opening. Sakandal is fully extended, his axe still in the soldier's leg. The old soldier rushes forward with his shield. He knocks Sakandal to the ground, and the hunter loses his grip on his axe.

The commander is at the old soldier's side in an instant, sword pointed at Sakandal's throat.

'What are you waiting for?' the old soldier says. 'Kill him.'

Sakandal doesn't move. He lies as still as he can, breathing heavily. He is ready to die.

'The captain said we might find someone,' he says. 'He told me not to kill him.'

'Why? He's nobody. It would almost be a kindness.' The old soldier puts his guard down, lowering his shield. 'We probably killed his family. I bet that's why he fought like a demon.'

The commander says nothing to the old soldier at first, but just before he pulls his arm back to strike Sakandal on the head with the hilt of his sword, he says something that Sakandal struggles to comprehend.

'The vizier himself wants him,' he says. The commander strikes. Sakandal reels from the blow. Blood pours over his eyes. Everything goes black.

* * *

Sakandal awakes in a prison cell. His mouth is parched. Dried blood cakes the right side of his face. One eye is swollen shut. His entire body is in pain.

Gradually, he remembers how he got here. After weeks of travel on foot, the soldiers brought him here, to a small fort in the wall of Sun Girna Ginar. They beat him and threw him into a small room with an iron door and bars on the windows.

It is night. Around him are over a dozen shapes, men, prisoners like him. Outside, the crescent moon casts little light.

The man beside Sakandal coughs. He has been sick long before Sakandal arrived in the cell. Seized by a fit, the man wakes up, raises himself on his elbows, and lets out a series of coughs that shake his whole body. He gasps for air, opening and closing his mouth like a fish, then his eyes roll back into his head as convulsions wrack his body.

Sakandal kneels beside the man, grabs his shoulders, and pushes him to the ground so that he won't hurt himself. As he does, the man's legs begin kicking into the air. Sakandal pushes the man's legs down with one arm and presses his body, shoulder first, into the man's chest. He stays that way until the man's convulsions stop. Some of the other prisoners are roused by the commotion, but they go back to sleep when they figure out what is going on.

The sick man passes out after his convulsions, but he wakes again after a few minutes. He coughs weakly.

'Thank you,' the man says, his voice dry, barely a whisper.

Sakandal says nothing in reply.

'Can I ask one more thing of you?' the man asks.

Sakandal looks at the man's face. In the darkness, he can see only the whites of his eyes. They are begging Sakandal.

'When I passed out,' the man says in his whisper of a voice, 'I thought I had died. I saw my ancestors, my father, my grandfather, and his father in a golden land that must have been Skyworld. And they told me that the man who just helped me was a great man, a warrior, and a king. They spoke of you. "He will help you end your life," they said.'

Sakandal wants to tell the man that his ancestors were wrong. He is none of those things.

'This is all I can give you,' the man says, placing something in Sakandal's hand. It is a rough, wooden carving, a statuette of the man's ancestors.

'He will help you to find justice for your family,' the man says, his voice growing weaker. 'My life has gone on for too long. I am tired. And a demon has me in its claws. It will not release me, but you can. You can free me from this prison. Then you can live. You can fly from this place. My ancestors will help you.'

'What is your name?' Sakandal asks, hoping the man would stop talking nonsense. He has no wish to kill this man.

'My name is not important. I am only the last in the line of my ancestors, and the least among them. Call me by the name of the first. Call me Asuang, who stole fire from Gugurang, the god of Mount Mayon. Or call me by the name of Asuang's creator, Ogassi of the underworld, of darkness and shadow. It doesn't matter.'

Sakandal closes his eyes. He thinks of his family. He thinks of all of the men who had wronged them, the soldiers, the captain of the war party, the vizier, the Sultan.

Sakandal's hands form into fists. His grief flows into the sorrow of this man's life. Intermingled, the emotions turn into anger and erupt without conscious thought into action.

When he opens his eyes again, he finds his hands wrapped around the man's throat. The man was weak and didn't struggle for long.

The man's death wakes a few of the prisoners, but none of them move when they see Sakandal hovering over the dead body.

Sakandal doesn't know why, but something about the way the man spoke to him makes him go to his cell's door. It is unlocked.

At the end of a short hallway, Sakandal finds two guards sleeping. He kills them with their own knives. He climbs out a window and finds himself free in the city of Sun Girna Ginar.

* * *

Sakandal is holding a bottle full of ash in his hands. He forces himself back to the present, away from the past. 'What is this?' Sakandal asks the old woman behind the market stall, curious about the thing that took him back to the past in such vivid detail. But she doesn't hear him. His voice is soft, and she is busy tending to another customer.

Sakandal waits and inspects the other bottles. In one, he sees the skull of a bird. In another, a baby's shrivelled and dried umbilical cord.

Sakandal asks the question again, louder this time. As the other customer walks away, the old woman turns to face him. He sees cataracts in her eyes, but her movements, swift and sure, tell him she is not as old as she looks.

'These bottles,' she says, her voice that of a crone, 'have the power to make dreams come true.'

'Can they raise the dead?' Sakandal asks.

She shakes her head.

'That is for the gods, not for witches.'

'Then what use are they?'

The old woman lifts her hands into the air, an indifferent gesture.

'Perhaps,' she says, peering into Sakandal's face, 'you seek the opposite of life. Perhaps you want your enemies dead. Dreams can do that, yes. They can do a great number of terrible things.'

Sakandal thinks of the blood he has spilled and the blood he still seeks: the vizier and the Sultan. He wants to ask the old woman how she knows about his hunt. Instead, he says, 'If this is all your bottles can do, then I do not need them.'

'Ah!' the old woman says, grinning. 'They can do more. They can do much more.'

Sakandal's interest is captured again. 'Tell me.'

'Ask,' the old woman replies, rising to the challenge. 'All you have to do is ask.'

'Can I become rich and powerful? Like Vizier Humadapnon?'

The old woman looks unimpressed. She says, 'Many have already asked. Humadapnon's wealth has been eclipsed. You can do better. Ask for more.'

'Can I be as powerful as the Sultan?'

The old woman locks eyes with Sakandal, and for a moment, it seems to him that the cataracts are gone. Her eyes are clear, her hair long and black, no longer white, her skin unlined. For a flickering moment, she looks like a young girl.

'More,' she says.

'Can I be the Sultan?' Sakandal asks.

The girl looks away and becomes the old woman again. Her back is stooped; her limbs are weak. Her hands are nothing but bone wrapped in skin. They shake as she points to the bottle in Sakandal's hands.

'You already hold that dream in your hands,' she says. Sakandal closes his fist around it.

'When your revenge is complete,' the old woman continues, 'open the bottle and let the wind have the ash inside. Then you will be the Sultan, my Lord.'

The old woman steps outside her narrow stall, gets down on her knees, and bows at Sakandal's feet until her forehead touches the ground.

'Long may you reign,' she says.

7

Bagilat

Bagilat, the god of lightning and rain, watches Sakandal walk away with an amused expression on his cat face. He looks at the old woman as if he wants to say something, but he holds his tongue. When there are no other people nearby, the god says, 'That was clever of you. Does he know what you gave him?'

The old woman looks around the alley and puts a handful of gold beads in a small bag she keeps hidden underneath her clothes.

'Of course, he knows,' the old woman says, 'but he does not believe just yet. When the day comes, I hope he will remember.'

Bagilat considers her answer. 'Is that how it works then?' he asks. 'Do you just give away your power?'

'My Lord knows nothing is that simple. But yes. They ask. I give. Are you any different, my Lord?'

Bagilat pauses then shakes his head.

The old woman says nothing more as if she has suddenly grown weary. But Bagilat is curious now. He wants to know more.

'Are those your champions then?' Bagilat asks the old woman. 'I can see how the hunter is a formidable man, and how your power can help him become more. But what about the other two? The broken datu woke the giant on his own. Maybe he does not need your help.'

'Nevertheless, he has it now.'

'The Sultan will kill him, you know.'

'Maybe, like the Sultan, Datu Adlao will live forever.'

'And the thief with one hand?'

'His name is Magat.'

'You gave him nothing!'

'He asked for nothing. He will find me again when he is ready. Then, he will know what he wants.'

Bagilat looks at the old woman with doubt. 'If I didn't know better, I would think that you don't want to win this wager. And yet, there is no doubt in your heart. Why are you so sure of yourself?'

The old woman shrugs. She says, 'I have lived with the people of this city for many years. I know what they are capable of. That is what you, my Lord, are unaware of in your seat in Skyworld. That is the heart of our wager.'

Bagilat contemplates her words.

'Perhaps you are right,' he says. 'But now it is my turn, yes?'

The old woman nods.

'And I can choose anyone in the city to give my power to—to "make their dreams real," as you say.'

Again, the old woman nods. 'Yes. They will come to me and I will give them your blessings.'

'Then I have won already!' Bagilat crows. 'I will choose great warriors who will protect the city from destruction. Your small men do not stand a chance. But don't worry. The first of them, like your champions, is nothing, a man without powerful ancestors. I wish I could say the same about the other two to make you feel better, but they are practically gods themselves. You may have heard of their stories before. Their stories will live forever.'

The old woman remains silent, letting the rain god claim victory for now. She knows there is nothing that can stop the flood and the fire to come.

8

Tagkan

On the day of the Sultan's wedding, Tagkan, who will one day be Sun
Girna Ginar's greatest hero, can think only of leaving the city.

Everyone is out on the streets to see the parade, as is Tagkan,
packed shoulder to shoulder with them, facing the road.

There are no clouds in the sky, and the afternoon sun beats down
on their shoulders without mercy. To Tagkan, the sun is like a weight
on his back. He feels it pushing down on him, crushing him. He can
hardly breathe.

Tagkan sees an old woman selling what she claims are dreams
in bottles, and goes to her to get away from the press of the crowd.
To his eyes, she looks like the rest of the city: dry and tired. She has
wilted under the sun, seemingly without the energy to call passers-by
to her stall.

He doesn't believe the old witch's scam, but he asks, 'Nanay, do
you have any bottles with rain?'

'Rain,' she mutters to herself, rummaging among her bottles,
'another dream for rain . . . must have another one of those
somewhere . . . '

After a few moments, she pulls out a large glass flask full of a dark
blue liquid. Tagkan takes the flask in his hands, and perhaps it is a trick

of the light or a reflection in the glass, but he imagines he sees rain clouds inside. And he remembers his home, the grey clouds of his childhood, and all the different kinds of rain. His favourite was the rain that was like a light spray, almost a mist, but he also favoured the hard, painful rain that stung the skin. There were warm showers that co-existed with sunshine and the typhoon that uprooted trees. Each year, the monsoon came and did not stop for weeks, until storm season came and flooded the lowlands. Tagkan thinks he can see them all inside the flask.

He takes the bottle in two hands and buys it without a second thought. He doesn't stay for the parade. By the time the God Cannon announces the marriage of the Sultan to the daughter of Taganlang, Tagkan is long gone.

* * *

The next day is even hotter. The heat possesses Tagkan's body, and he is unable to do anything. He cannot even think. His entire body feels like it has been reduced to ashes.

Tagkan sits on a stool outside, behind the single-room apartment he shares with five others. In the narrow space between their house and the next, scarcely wider than his shoulders, two windowless walls face each other. Tagkan goes there on hot days because, in that space, the wind often blows. But today there isn't even a breeze.

Tagkan holds the glass flask he brought from the old woman in his hands. It is cool to the touch, and he presses his face against it and runs it over his neck, chest, and belly. It is the only relief he has received all day. He looks deep inside the flask and again sees rain clouds in the dark fluid.

A smile touches the edge of his lips, and perhaps still possessed by the heat, he stands up. Without thinking, he uncaps the flask, and in one fluid motion, throws the water inside upon an empty wall.

Tagkan is surrounded by the smell of the rain.

The dark fluid from the flask pours down the wall. It becomes lighter as it falls, and pools on the floor. There, it becomes clear, merely water.

Tagkan looks at the pool of water on the ground and sees the wall reflected in it, but where the reflection is supposed to be that of a blank wall, there is, to his surprise, a wall with a window.

Tagkan's gaze shoots up to the wall. He blinks and stares. There is a window there. He knows there can't be a window there. On the other side of the wall is another mud shanty, but the window doesn't lead to that place. Tagkan cannot believe it, but there is no denying it either: the window is there.

He walks up to the window and a cool breeze blows in his face. Tagkan sees his homeland through the window. Green trees cover the horizon, competing for the sky. It is raining. He can smell the wet earth from the ground beneath the window.

Tagkan stretches a hand out the window and looks up at the grey skies. When he pulls his hand back, it is wet. He licks the rainwater from his hands and laughs. With the laughter still strong in his lungs, he leans as far as he can out the window. The rain soaks his hair and runs over his body. He lets out a shout and it carries far in the valley before him.

Tagkan pulls his body back and looks up. He sees only cloudless skies and the burning white eye of the sun.

* * *

Many days pass and Tagkan is content. He guards his secret jealously, barricading himself within his narrow alley.

He spends every day at his window of rain. He sits on a stool facing the window and looks at the rain until the sun sets. At night, he chews betel nut by the window. Sometimes he falls asleep to the sound of the rain.

It doesn't take long for Tagkan's contentment to evaporate in the heat of the sun. One day, he discovers, to his disappointment, that the window of rain is no longer enough. He stands in front of the window throughout the night. He listens to the voice of the rain speaking to him in his mother tongue and calling him by his childhood name.

Morning comes and Tagkan still remains in front of the window. As it becomes light, the rhythmic music of the agong from the distance breaks the early morning silence, bearing news from distant lands. It will soon be time to leave his window of rain. But when the hour comes, he climbs upon the window sill instead. Then without hesitation, he steps through the window and makes a short jump to the earth below.

Heralded by rain, his journey begins. He doesn't look back.

9

Lam-Ang

Seven days after Lam-Ang set out to find the head-hunters, he returned to Nalbuan with the head of his father.

The village knows of Lam-Ang's triumph, for the river ran red with blood and they knew it was a sign of victory.

Three days after that sign, Lam-Ang's sisters find him on the outskirts of the village. He is weary with travel and covered in the blood of his enemies. His spear arm hangs low, but his eyes are bright when he sees them.

'It is done,' he says.

* * *

Lam-Ang spends the first day of his return bathing in the river. The blood of the head-hunters is so thick on his skin that it turns the river red again, and the oracle who lives downstream augurs the end of the world and the destruction of Sun Girna Ginar. Lam-Ang's sisters wash his hair with soap made from burnt straw, and they need so much of it that the smoke from the fire causes the neighbouring town to think that war is coming their way. They gather all the people working in the fields and hide in the town, building barricades on their roads when they see the black smoke rising in the sky.

Lam-Ang is oblivious to all this. He sleeps the whole day as his sisters tend to him, his campilan lying idle in the grass. He travelled far, he fought a mighty battle, and he won. But today is not the day to speak of it. When night falls, one sister returns to the village to fetch their household's alipin, and together, they carry him home in a palanquin as he sleeps. Lam-Ang's mother, Namungan, weeps when she sees her son even though her daughter already told her of his return. The sight of him fills her heart with joy.

Preparations for the feast begin at daybreak. A calf is killed as well as a dozen pigs. Jars of tuba are sent for. And the musicians are paid in advance.

Just before noon, Lam-Ang wakes up, and his alipin dresses him in the finest clothes, a vest threaded with gold, and a gold and silver headpiece that shines like the sun. Then they bring him to the centre of the town for the feast. Lam-Ang's mother sits by his right side, at the place of honour, and she beams in the light of her only son.

'I always knew you would do great things,' she tells him, her hand over his. 'When I was pregnant with you, I prayed to the gods that you would bring us honour and slay our enemies. And in a dream, Aponibolinayen came from Skyworld and told me, "Namungan, go to Sun Girna Ginar and seek the witch who sells dreams. Buy one from her, and you will have a son who will be like the gods, beautiful and strong, but also knowledgeable and wise."

'I made the journey while I was heavy with child, but we made it—thanks to your father. It took us three days to find the witch in the bazaar, but all the hardships we endured were worth it. Two months later, I gave birth to you, my son. You were born before your time, but it was just as Aponibolinayen told me. While you were still a baby, you spoke as if you were fully grown. You knew the names of things and the ways of our people. You grew with the blessings of the gods. Before you were a man, you were taller than any in the village. You could beat them all in wrestling matches. Your spear travelled farthest in matches of strength. And too soon, you set aside your childhood when the Igorot took your father. I thought I had lost you both that day.'

Namungan turns away from her son then to hide the tears in her eyes.

'Enough,' she says. 'Enough of this old woman. Before you arrived, we had already heard of your great deeds. But now you are here, we would hear it from your mouth so that the singers may spread the story of your victory to Sun Girna Ginar and all its nations.'

Lam-Ang speaks then before the elders and the whole village. He speaks in clear, simple words. He speaks in facts and actions, and his story is soon over. This is not that story. This is Lam-Ang's story as the singers tell it.

* * *

On the day after Lam-Ang's father was meant to return to Nalbuan from a trading expedition, Lam-Ang had a dream. He was wrestling a giant crocodile in the river. He fought the beast for days, and in the end, he was victorious. Then the body of the crocodile turned into his father.

'Father, is it really you?' Lam-Ang asked. 'Or am I just dreaming? Why haven't you returned?'

His father's face changed then, becoming serious, more like the mask he always wore.

'You are dreaming, my son. I was slain by the Igorot as we crossed their lands. I will not be returning home.'

Lam-Ang shivered at the mention of the Igorot. They were head-hunters who lived in the mountains in the North. Warlike and proud, they were capable warriors and friends of the giants. They believed the heads of their enemies gave them strength and the favour of their gods.

'You will return,' Lam-Ang promised. 'I will travel to the lands of the Igorot. I will kill them all to avenge your death. I will bring your body home where we will bury you in the ways of our ancestors.'

In Lam-Ang's dream, his father said nothing, only touched the head of his son in blessing.

Lam-Ang awoke in the hour before dawn. It was silent except for the sound of weeping. He went in search of the source of the sound and found his mother sitting on the floor in tears.

'Your father is dead,' she said when she saw Lam-Ang.

'I know,' he said and wrapped her in his arms.

* * *

Hours later, Lam-Ang prepared to leave for the mountains of the Igorot. He brought his spear and his tall shield, which they called a kalasag. On his back, he bore the great sword, the campilan of his father. It was a cruel sword, made for war, broadening as it reached its double-pronged tip. This made the campilan almost an axe with a heavy head. Its weight and momentum in battle were unstoppable. It broke shields, snapped lesser blades in two, and tore through armour. If in the right hands, it could be used to split a man from head to groin.

The campilan shone in the light of the sun, its golden hilt reflecting the heavens. Its scarlet bombol, made from the hair of his widowed grandmother, hung from the hilt like the flash of blood on the battlefield. Lam-Ang's kalasag too shone in the sun. Its grip was made of pure gold, and the shield's face was inlaid with pearl by his sisters.

Around his neck, Lam-Ang wore two amulets. The first was a wild carabao's amulet, fashioned from its horns. The second was the Amulet of the Centipede, which blessed the traveller with good fortune.

Before he left, he knelt before his mother to ask for her blessing. She was still overcome by grief, but she called Lam-Ang by his name and raised her hand in blessing, the back of her aged hand grazing his forehead ever so slightly.

Lam-Ang left the village with purpose in his step. He headed towards the mountains, where his enemies waited for him, to war.

10

Aponi-tolau

Aponi-tolau, son of Lang-An of Kadalayapan, goddess of the wind and rain, has never seen anything like the sea. He stands by the shore for more than an hour, just staring at the water. *Its vastness is like the sky*, he muses, *but it is never still.* Also, unlike the sky, there is danger in the sea. He hears thunder in the waves, and unspoken threats from the deep.

I want to see more, Aponi-tolau says aloud to no one. In moments, the young god creates a raft out of rattan and crafts a paddle from some flotsam. He takes the hook that was given to him by an old woman in Sun Girna Ginar and places it on his belt. The hook is shaped just like the ones used by fishermen to catch fish, and is attached to a length of rope. It is almost the size of Aponi-tolau's hand, and its edges are jagged and serrated, giving it a cruel appearance.

Aponi-tolau sets out to sea without hesitation. He travels for days under the burning gaze of the sun. Over shallows, past still coves, beyond the sight of land, over mountainous swells, he paddles until he reaches the place where the sea and the sky meet.

There, a jagged rock as large as a mountain rises out of the sea. Before the mountain is a wall of smaller rocks that surrounds the mountain like a wall. In front of him, the wall is interrupted by a massive stone arch.

'What is this place?' Aponi-tolau calls out. 'Is anyone there?'

At first, there is no reply. Then he hears voices.

'It is a man,' a girl's voice says in a whisper, but her voice carries over the water.

'No, Sister,' another voice says, also in a whisper. 'He is a mountain god. I recognize his kind.'

'He is ugly. Are they all ugly like him?'

'Yes. Their creator was careless when he made them.'

Aponi-tolau announces himself. 'My name is Aponi-tolau, son of Lang-An of Kadalayapan. I mean you no harm. Please show yourself. I have travelled far to learn more about your world.'

The voices—there are more than two of them now—erupt into laughter. It is a beautiful sound, like falling water.

'Do you think he can swim?' a new voice asks.

'I bet you he can't.'

From the corner of his eye, Aponi-tolau can see something glitter, but before he can find its source, he is falling. His raft has flipped over, and he is in the water.

But Aponi-tolau is a god so he does not drown. Neither does he struggle; he just lets himself sink into the sea. Sound abandons him. He opens his eyes.

Now that he is underwater, he realizes that he was wrong about everything he saw on the surface. He cannot see the sea floor, but rising out of the darkness below is a palace. It is a massive structure of stone and gold, and the jagged mountain that rises above the water is merely its crown.

'Who is the master of this place?' Aponi-tolau asks. He chokes a little as the water enters his lungs, but he quickly grows accustomed to it. His voice carries far in the water.

'And he is ignorant too,' says one of the voices. The voices are louder now, clearer.

More voices join in.

'Ugly *and* ignorant. Are you sure he is a god?'

'Maybe he is just a man.'

'Then he would drown.'

'Maybe he is a trickster or a demon.'

'Maybe he is both.'

'Let's kill him then.'

'No, Sister. You are too rash. Let us speak to him first.'

Aponi-tolau searches for the source of the voices. He finds them swimming near the surface of the water, close to the wall and the arch. He counts nine of them. They are diwata—goddesses. Each of them is beautiful—more beautiful than any woman or goddess he has ever known—glowing with white light as if they are aflame. Their hair is green, with silver and gold reflected from the sun above, and in their hands, they carry spears.

The closest diwata swims in front of him and speaks.

'This is the home of Tau-mari-u, lord of the sea,' she says, 'and we are his daughters. What brings you to this holy place? What do you seek?'

She brandishes her spear in Aponi-tolau's face.

'I only came here,' Aponi-tolau replies, 'to see this world and witness its wonders. I thought your father's kingdom was the greatest of all the things I have seen, but I was wrong. It is you, his daughters. There is nothing more beautiful on earth or all the seven levels of Skyworld.'

'Begone!' hisses one of the sisters, growing suspicious.

The others join in. 'Begone!' They raise their spears.

'We have heard your words before, from other men,' the diwata in front of Aponi-tolau says, 'They tried to enslave us. As you would.'

'Begone!' the sisters say again.

The youngest of the diwata, Humitau, swims around behind Aponi-tolau and jabs at him with her spear. She cuts him on his upper arm.

Aponi-tolau turns around to see who attacked him. A tendril of red blood swims in the water between him and Humitau. It is then that Aponi-tolau sees that Humitau is the most beautiful of the sisters, and at that moment, he decides that he has to have her as his wife.

Aponi-tolau reaches for the hook the old woman gave him. Its metal is cold to the touch. Humitau swims away when she sees him reach for a weapon, but she is not fast enough to escape. He throws the hook in a deadly arc. Its point buries itself in Humitau's side. She screams.

When they hear the cry from Humitau, half of her sisters hide. They swim back to the wall or the palace. The other half swims towards Humitau, to save her, but it is too late. Aponi-tolau swims swiftly to the raft and pulls her to the surface as if she were a fish. Humitau tries to fight him, but the hook has made her weak. Once she is on the raft with Aponi-tolau, he paddles in the direction of Sun Girna Ginar with his prize, fast as an arrow on the wind.

Humitau struggles to fight the poison in her blood, but Aponi-tolau calms her with a hand on her cheek. He knows they have far to travel until they reach the safety of land.

* * *

Tau-mari-u's anger is terrible to behold. When he learns that his daughter has been stolen by Aponi-tolau, he summons the waves to chase the mountain god. The skies darken. The seas rise. White-capped waves like mountains appear behind Aponi-tolau. The seas move in every direction, and the young god is lost.

Despite Aponi-tolau's inexperience on the sea, he still has the strength of a god. He paddles harder than ever and speeds over the water until he is exhausted. But refusing to give up his prize, he continues to head towards land.

Tau-mari-u calls on all the creatures of the sea to find his daughter and bring her back to him. Fastest among them, the tuna, form a giant school and pursue Aponi-tolau. He sees their dark shapes beneath the surface of the water, each larger than his raft. When they are close, they jump into the air to knock Aponi-tolau off the boat, but he lies flat on the raft, beside Humitau, to avoid their attacks.

With Tau-mari-u's kingdom chasing him, Aponi-tolau grows afraid and prays to his mother to deliver him from the sea.

'Mother!' Aponi-tolau calls out. 'Mother, it is your son Aponi-tolau. Hear my prayer!

'My strength is spent. The lord of the sea seeks to drown me. I have claimed a great prize that will bring glory to your name. For ages to come, the singers will tell of how Aponi-tolau, son of Lang-an, beat Tau-mari-u himself.

'Yet, I am powerless here. Mother, I beg you, take me to land.'

For a long moment, the heavens are silent, and Aponi-tolau almost despairs. But Lang-an hears him from Skyworld and commands a wave to carry her son to shore.

Aponi-tolau and Humitau travel the remaining distance to land as if a hand has lifted their raft and carried them there. They come to shore in a fishing village not far from Sun Girna Ginar.

The fishermen are preparing for the storm, bringing in their nets and their belongings, when they see Aponi-tolau and Humitau descend from the sky. At first, they are afraid but seeing the sick girl, the fishermen let them into one of their homes and give them food to eat. Aponi-tolau eats to regain his strength, but Humitau refuses the food, throwing up all that they give her. Thinking that food will make her better, they force-feed her until she swallows some rice mixed with water.

The sea continues to rise. Tau-mari-u swears to invade the land until his daughter is returned to him, so he sends a flood to the village. All night long, the water rises until the flood surpasses the height of the stilts the houses are built on. Then the flood creeps into the houses in search of Humitau.

The water wakes Aponi-tolau. Though he is still too weak to go any further, he picks up Humitau and prepares to swim to higher ground, to Sun Girna Ginar, or the mountains. The fishermen's boats have all been lost, smashed upon the rocks by Tau-mari-u's waves.

Aponi-tolau enters the water and begins swimming. Though he is slowed down because of Humitau whom he carries, Aponi-tolau is strong and determined. He sets off as fast as he can.

Aponi-tolau knows that Humitau can breathe underwater, so he does not worry about her. But he is forced to stop when he hears her fighting for air. Humitau is thrashing in his grasp, trying to reach the surface. She is drowning.

Aponi-tolau treads water and helps Humitau float on her back, an arm supporting her neck to raise her head above water. He knows he can no longer make it to the mountains or even the city this way.

There is no other way to save Humitau, so Aponi-tolau does the only thing he can.

'Tau-mari-u!' Aponi-tolau calls out, letting his voice travel over the surface of the sea. 'Tau-mari-u! Lord of the sea! Your daughter is dying!'

The wind dies down. The storm is silenced. A stillness lies over the water as Tau-mari-u listens.

'Send back your flood!' Aponi-tolau commands. 'Your daughter is yours no longer. She does not belong to the sea. She has eaten the food of man. She belongs to me now. She will be my wife.'

The sea surges in anger. Currents reach out to pull Aponi-tolau into the deep.

'If you do not send back your flood, she will drown, killed by your own hand. Take your flood back, and she will live. Let there be peace between us.'

Tau-mari-u hears Aponi-tolau. For long moments, the sea is still, then just as Aponi-tolau loses hope, the flood begins to recede.

* * *

The singers tell this tale to celebrate how Aponi-tolau saved Sun Girna Ginar from the flood, for all time. It is through Tau-mari-u's great love for his daughter and Aponi-tolau's trickery that the god of the sea has promised never again to send his flood.

Humitau goes to the mountains to live with Aponi-tolau, and she becomes his wife. But she often travels to Sun Girna Ginar to look at the sea.

Despite his promise of peace, Tau-mari-u's hatred of Aponi-tolau and mankind grows each day. That is why the lord of the sea tries to destroy all the ships that come into his kingdom and attempts to drown any man who dares to venture into the sea. After all these centuries, men have forgotten the tale of how Aponi-tolau saved the Sultan's city from the flood. It is Tau-mari-u alone who has never forgotten.

Part II: Men of Insignificant Ancestors

Some call the city by another name. They call it Nalandangan after the ancient fortress in the heart of the city. It has other names as well: Yendang, Libalan, Newili-an. But like Nalandangan, all these names are forgotten now, like the city itself.

Nalandangan was founded by chosen people beloved by the highest god of Skyworld. They came from a distant land called Aruman, also forgotten, and travelled across the sea on a huge ship that became the great hall of the fortress city.

On the fortress eaves was a frieze of red warriors in battle, and on top of the building were golden statues—each as tall as ten men—of Nalandangan warriors made of solid gold. Facing the sunset was a statue of a maiden washing herself in a stream. Towards the sunrise, a monkey-eating eagle with its wings spread wide. The courtyard of the palace was made entirely of silver and was blinding to look at in the sun.

In front of the walls stood the iron and steel fort of the hero Agyu, who saved Nalandangan from the jealous Datu Padsilung. Possessed by hatred, the datu transformed himself into a giant snake and swallowed the city. Agyu was poisoned by the datu's daughter, Sawalan, but he travelled through death to resurrect Nalandangan's inhabitants and rally the people to defeat the datu and his allies. It is said that after Nalandangan was rebuilt, no invaders ever made it past the fort of Agyu.

Beyond the fort of Agyu, lay a mountain of broken shields and spear shafts. They remained there from previous battles to remind invaders of the strength and power of Nalandangan. They lie there still, buried in the earth. If you look closely, you can find the place. It is now in the shape of an ordinary hill, forgotten by Agyu's descendants.

1

Aya, Magat, and Adlao

Once outside the palace, Aya walks with her face covered so as not to be identified by the Sultan's spies. From the palace walls, she passes the mansions of the Maharlika, the Holy Quarter, and the market; she walks down a dirty street, turns at an alley, and stops at a locked door. She looks both ways to check if she is being followed. When she is satisfied, she knocks on the door.

As always, Magat opens the door and Aya rushes in breathlessly. She kisses him on the lips, her hands already removing his clothes. She thinks Magat loves her.

Many months have passed since Magat escaped from the Sultan's prison. Since then, he has regained his health, and now, in the service of a new master, his strength.

'How long do you have?' Magat asks Aya.

'An hour,' she says.

Magat steadies himself against the wall with the hand that the Sultan did not take from him, then he reaches for the courtesan. Somewhere in the tangle of arms and clothes, something tears. Aya's clothes fall to the ground and she emerges, naked, perfect, hungry. Magat takes her against the door.

* * *

An hour later, they are lying entwined on the floor. Aya rolls on her back and reaches for her clothes.

'Don't go,' Magat says and climbs on top of her, pinning her to the ground. It is difficult with one arm, but Magat manages somehow. She doesn't fight him.

'If that is what you wish,' she says and nuzzles his neck. 'I will do whatever you want. For you are my god.' She grabs his hardening cock, and he lets out a grunt. He kisses her hard on the lips and enters her.

'But a few moments from now, the palace guards will look for me. They need to prepare for the visit of the—'

'Shhh . . . Don't say his name.'

Aya laughs.

'What have you to be jealous about? He is my Sultan. You are my god. Now hurry. We still have a few minutes.' She begins to thrust against him.

'Next week,' Magat says.

'Yes,' Aya replies, 'I will be here again.'

'No,' he says, suddenly serious. 'You promised me you would talk to my master. You can help us. All of us. You can help the whole sultanate.'

'I haven't forgotten,' Aya says, growing serious as well.

'It may be dangerous,' Magat says. 'But I will make sure that you will be safe.'

'I wish you could be there.'

'As do I. But there is much work to be done.'

'Then finish what you started,' Aya says, mischief returning to her eye. 'I can be late by a few minutes. Hurry.'

* * *

A week has passed. Aya travels through the secret passage in the Sultan's palace to the exit along the walls as she does every week. Covered in a veil, she passes the mansions of the Maharlika, the Holy Quarter, and the market, to walk down a dirty street, but today it is a different street. She knocks on the door, but when there is no answer she almost walks away. Aya remembers her promise to Magat and decides to linger a little longer. After a moment, she hears footsteps.

The door opens and Aya steps inside. The man who opens the door—some kind of soldier judging by the stoic look on his face, and the cropped hair—says nothing. She finds Magat's master sitting at a table in the middle of the room. On the table are a lamp, a bag, a glass bottle, and a long knife. He stands up when he sees Aya and offers her a chair.

'Please,' he says, 'sit.'

This is not his house. Aya knows right away. It is obvious to her that Magat's master is familiar with power like the Sultan, but the home they are in belongs to a man without powerful ancestors—a cart driver perhaps or a man who works at the docks. There is a woven mat in one corner, a wood stove in another corner, and a table with four chairs. No one lives here now, that much is clear. There are no clothes or shoes or carved gods anywhere. Just a lamp, a bag, a glass bottle, and a long knife.

The door opens and another man enters, exchanging looks with Magat's master as he does so. It is obvious to Aya that he too is a soldier, a man who does what he is told without hesitation.

'She was not followed,' the man says. Magat's master nods almost imperceptibly.

'Please,' he says again, 'sit.'

Aya sits across from Magat's master. The man who just came in does not sit at the table. He stands by the shuttered windows with the first soldier and peers out into the street.

Aya removes her veil, revealing to anyone with eyes to see that she is beautiful in a way that other beautiful women are not. It is not that her beauty is uncommon—Aya was gifted to the Sultan in Antar A Langit, a kingdom renowned for the beauty of its women. Her kind of beauty is the kind that men would pay any price to possess.

But Magat's master is not the kind of man who is moved by beauty. He meets her unveiled gaze.

'Do you know who I am?'

Aya nods. 'Magat says you are Datu Adlao. The exile.'

Adlao acknowledges this with a grunt, then says, 'I am told that you can get something for us, from the Tyrant. It would go a long way in helping our cause.'

'The Sultan—'

Adlao raises a hand to silence Aya.

'We do not say his name. Or call him by his titles. His witches are always listening. And when you say his name, they hear you speak. Say the wrong words, and his assassins will come to your door.

'I'm sure you've heard it said before—names have power. That is because names belong to the person named. Speaking a name acknowledges this truth. When you speak their titles, you accept their power over you, you accept who they claim to be. You say lord and he is your lord. Call him a god, and it is so.

'So we name him instead. We call him Tyrant. We call him Lord of Lies, False Prophet, Murderer. By naming him, we gain power over him. He accepts our authority without his knowledge. He becomes who we say he is. He is reduced to who we know him to be. And the witches are unable to hear our voices.

'Call him the Tyrant.'

Adlao withdraws his hand from the hilt of the long knife. Aya never noticed that his hand was there, but having seen it now, she remains unafraid. Instead, she is filled with defiance at the threat.

'In the palace,' Aya says, 'a sculpture portrays the Tyrant as Malakas, the first man, springing forth from a bamboo plant split in two. Opposite him, on the other half of the split bamboo, is Maganda, the first woman. I know this is a lie, like the lies of the Tyrant's godhood.

'The Tyrant is no god. He fucks like a man. He comes to my chambers at night, for he is lonely and finds no solace with his wives. He drinks himself to oblivion. On other nights, he prefers opium, and we slip into the warm darkness together. But mostly, he comes to me to fuck. He likes how I do it, he says. He fucks with abandon, and he takes enjoyment in his pain. His wives will not harm the man-god. But to me, he is like a little child who comes to my bed to play a game.

He cannot bear what his life has become, or the things he must do to go on. He speaks little of his troubles, but a woman knows. A lover knows these things.'

Adlao listens with keen interest, but his face betrays no other emotion. Aya recognizes what she sees in Adlao: it is an obsession.

'So the answer is yes. I can get what you need for your cause if the Tyrant keeps it on his body. He adorns himself with little. The crowns and headpieces are only for ceremony. He removes them as soon as he can. Other baubles come and go. Sometimes a wife or an ally will gift him with a bracelet or a ring, and he will wear it for a while to show his gratitude. They are soon lost or forgotten.

'Only one thing remains constant: the amulet he wears around his neck, a piece of glass on a string.'

'I want you to bring the amulet here,' Adlao says.

Aya looks into Adlao's eyes, straight into the fire of his obsession, and for the first time that day, she is afraid.

2

Tagkan

Tagkan steps through the window of rain and walks into a familiar place. Without looking back, he heads straight to the mountains in the distance.

He knows where he is. This is his home. The mountain on the horizon is old man Mugao. At the foot of the mountain where the river broadens is the town where he was born, Buwayang Bato. It is not far, he can tell, perhaps half a day's walk.

Tagkan revels in the falling rain, the strong and steady downpour of the monsoon, and heads in the direction of home. But as the sun sets, Tagkan admits to himself that he is lost. He can't explain how this happened. He took the right path, he is sure of that, but the road kept rising towards the mountains instead of heading down to the river.

Maybe I am cursed, he thinks to himself. Isn't that what his mother always told him because he was constantly getting lost? She believed a tikbalang had cursed him. Tagkan has never seen a tikbalang and has no idea when he was cursed or why.

It is already starting to get dark, and cold. So, Tagkan makes a small shelter under the shade of a large tree. The tree's canopy is so thick that the ground underneath is dry, and with some branches, he makes a small fire. He tends to the fire until it grows into a bright blaze.

The earth shifts underneath Tagkan's feet. The mountain moves.

At first, he thinks it is an earthquake, but soon he realizes it is more than that. One moment he is standing on firm ground. The next, the ground is the side of a cliff and he is falling. He flails wildly with his arms and legs and lands on what was a ridge a few moments ago. Earth and sky are moving all around him.

From the sky, he sees a giant hand descend on where he stood moments before. The hand darkens the sky, and it smothers the fire in an instant. It looks as if the hand is made of stone, or carved from the earth itself. The knuckles are massive boulders. Sheets of granite form the nails on the hand.

A voice fills the air: 'Little man. Tell me why I should let you live.'

The voice seems to be coming from everywhere, from the sky itself. He has never heard anything so powerful, or so old.

Slowly, Tagkan comes to realize why he is lost. What he thought was a hill was not a hill at all but a sleeping giant and Tagkan lit a fire upon its body. When the path should have descended into the valley, it climbed instead, for he was steadily climbing the giant itself.

'Who are you?' he shouts at the top of his voice. 'Show yourself.'

The earth shakes, and Tagkan is falling again. This time, the fall is a short one; he lands in one of the giant's hands. He gets to his feet and discovers that the giant has raised its hand to its face. Tagkan looks into eyes that are as old as the earth.

'Behold the oldest of the giants, little man. I am your death.'

Before him is the giant's head, but to either side of the head that spoke to him are two more, sprouting from the same massive neck. As the giant's hand continues to move, he sees three more heads. The head that speaks to him has a proud and noble visage, but the other heads are ugly and deformed—each head more misshapen than the last.

Tagkan has heard of the six-headed giant of Gawi-Gawen before, in stories and songs, but he never expected to see it himself.

'Little man, tell me why I should let you live,' the giant says again.

Not knowing what to say, Tagkan decides to lie. Speaking as loudly as he can, he tells the giant, 'I am at your mercy, my Lord.' He gets on his knees and raises his arms in supplication. His mind races.

'But you should know before you kill me that I am . . . an emissary of Sun Girna Ginar.'

Tagkan holds onto the lie, his voice shaking. The rest of the lie tumbles out in fragments. 'My word is the Sultan's . . . My life is the Sultan's . . . and his alone. By ending my life, you declare war on the greatest of the cities of man.'

The earth shakes again. He realizes that this time it is laughter.

'There are no cities of man that are worthy of being called great. I have destroyed every city I have encountered like a volcano ravages the land at its feet. It does not give it a second thought.'

Tagkan has nothing to lose, so he decides to lie some more. In the back of his mind, he wonders if the giant has destroyed his town too. But he doesn't let his fears distract him. As Tagkan's confidence grows, the lies come easily.

'Then you have never seen Sun Girna Ginar,' Tagkan says at the top of his voice so the giant can hear him. 'You are mighty, but surely, if you saw this city, even you would be humbled. The walls of Sun Girna Ginar dwarf your magnificence. They are as strong as mountains. The city's towers surpass your height. They graze the dome of the sky.'

'Walls are merely bricks and mortar. My skin is stone. The earth is my blood.'

Once more, Tagkan decides to lie. 'The city is blessed with the children of powerful ancestors,' he continues. 'Kabuniyan, father of the gods, sired its Sultan. And the city is protected by General Marandang. You are powerful, I will admit. I have never seen the likes of you before. But you are no match for General Marandang's army. You are one. His army is like the stars in the sky, armed with steel and fire. He has killed hundreds of giants before. Those he didn't kill, he enslaved. He keeps them in the dungeons underneath the city. They are bound by dark magic, tortured, and enslaved, for the general hates all of your kind.'

At the mention of the murder of giants, the earth shakes. The six-headed giant rises to its full height and a low, menacing rumble escapes from its mouth.

'Tell your General Marandang I am coming,' the giant tells Tagkan.

Tagkan continues to lie, but this time, he knows the giant believes him. And he knows he is going to live.

3

Aya and Magat

Aya is lost. She doesn't know what to do, or what to say. When Magat asks Aya to do what Adlao asked of her, she is certain of the truth. She knows that Magat does not love her.

'Will you do it for us?' he asks her.

It has been a week since Aya spoke to Adlao, and now she is in the same dusty apartment as before, with Magat. It is the same time of day as always when she is here—the height of the afternoon just before the call to prayer wafts over the city. When it begins to get dark, she will know that it is time to go. She has always hated that hour. She would remove it from the day if she could so that she could remain here with Magat. But not today. Today, she wanted to leave as soon as the question erupted from Magat's mouth. She wanted to put on her clothes and storm out the door. But instead, she lies perfectly still. Her back is to him. He can't see her face.

'Is that what you want?' she asks him.

'What I want,' he says, kissing the back of her neck, 'is for us to get away, away from this city. I want us to go somewhere beautiful, where it actually rains sometimes. And you'll have to leave the city anyway if you help us. It won't be safe here anymore.'

'I know it won't be safe,' she says, 'but I will do it if that is what you want.'

'Aya,' Magat says, sensing the edges of her anger, 'what have I done?'

'Nothing.'

'Aya, listen to me. I only want us to be together. I know it is dangerous, but there is no other way. How will a man like me get rid of a man like the Tyrant?'

There it is, Aya thinks to herself, *he has admitted it. He has said his name aloud and revealed where his allegiances lie. To lesser men, he would still be 'the Sultan.' To a man who was his equal, he would be 'my rival.' To a jealous man, he would be 'your keeper.' To Magat, he is 'The Tyrant.'*

What was it that Adlao said? 'We name him instead. We call him Tyrant. We call him Lord of Lies, False Prophet, Murderer.'

No, he doesn't love me. He only needs me for the Sultan's amulet.

'Do you know what they will do to me if they catch me?' Aya asks Magat.

'I have some idea. Adlao told me what goes on in the Tyrant's prison.' Magat risks the lie. It is a small one. She cannot know how deep his hatred for the Tyrant goes.

'The Sultan himself will not care what happens to me. He will say nothing and give me to his guards. If he says something, then there may be some chance that I will be saved or granted a quick death. Silence means that the law will decide my fate, and to the law, I am nothing, worse than a whore. Concubines are not allowed to live outside the Sultan's grace, but the law is silent about how concubines are to die. It is a cruel death prepared for us.'

Fury flashes in Aya's eyes as she continues. 'I know this because the guards relish in telling us what will happen when the Sultan gets tired of us. First, the vizier will see to it that I am locked in a cell in his tower, and fed enough only not to die. The vizier will return when his whim suits him, and by then, I will be his plaything.'

The rest of Aya's words are released in an angry torrent. 'He will tear out my tongue so I will tell no secrets about the Sultan. Or, maybe, he will do that later if he has other plans for my mouth. He will break my spirit first, make me cry out in pain, beg him to stop, teach me there is no hope, that I am nothing, I am his—I am whatever he wants me to be. Once I am broken, the spirit will be gone, and it will be time to consume my body, one morsel at a time, or limbless given to the guards to play with like a man would give a bone to a dog.'

Aya pauses, breathless, spent. Then she turns to face Magat, and he sees there are tears in her eyes. Magat returns Aya's gaze evenly.

'This is what I risk for you every time I come here,' Aya says. 'So if you tell me that you want me to steal that thing from the Sultan, I will do it. But don't tell me that we will run away together and live in the mountains when we both know that's a lie.'

Magat says nothing at first, but when he finally speaks, Aya remembers why she loves him.

'I wish there were another way, but this is the only way the people will be free. If I could do what you can to save the people of our sultanate, I would do it. But I can't. I am counting on you instead.'

Aya watches Magat's face change when he talks about the people. His face almost takes on a light as if he were talking about his children or a woman he loves. And for a moment, Aya is jealous.

'We are ready to fight the Tyrant's armies,' Magat continues, 'but we are no match for the Tyrant himself. The amulet gives him control of Kalaon, who gives him the power of a god.'

'And what then? What if I steal the amulet? What would you do to him? Kill him?'

'If we kill him, another man will take his place. We want more than that. We want to take apart the entire sultanate, and to do that, first, we must destroy the Tyrant's city.'

Aya laughs, a beautiful sound that enslaves men.

'Destroy the city!' she says, incredulous. 'I knew you were ambitious, but now you are just mad. Sun Girna Ginar was created by the gods.'

'And men like me will destroy it with the help of the gods!' Magat rises to Aya's challenge. 'Adlao has awoken the six-headed giant. It marches southward as we speak.'

Aya's mind recoils in horror, at the thought of the giant, at what Magat and Adlao are capable of.

'The Tyrant might be able to stop the giant with Kalaon,' Magat continues, 'but without him, the city will fall.'

'The general will save the city.'

'We have infiltrated his armies. His men will not follow him. The giant will come, and the city will fall. The people of the sultanate will be free.'

Aya looks at Magat, the man who has only pretended to love her. She wonders if she ever truly knew him. *Did he know who she was from the start? Did he set out to seduce her with his humour and his easy smile? How did he really lose his hand?* She almost doesn't want to know the answers to her questions. She knows why she loves him still, and why she will do anything he asks.

'And now you know our plan,' Magat says. 'Now you can tell the Tyrant everything and have us arrested. Our insurrection will be crushed, and the giant will be defeated by Kalaon and Marandang's armies. Our lives are in your hands. My life is in your hands, Aya.'

'Tell me what you want.'

'We need you to steal the Tyrant's amulet.'

'No,' Aya raises a hand to his lips. 'Tell me what *you* want.'

Behind Aya's hand, Magat smiles. He knows he has won.

'I want you,' Magat says slowly, 'to steal the Tyrant's amulet. Give it to Adlao, throw it away, or destroy it. It makes no difference to me. Just take it away from the Tyrant. Then come back to me, and we will leave this doomed city and travel somewhere beautiful, someplace where it still rains.'

4

Tagkan

The town is gone.

Buwayang Bato used to sit between a deep harbour in the river and the mountains. Tagkan is sure that this is that harbour. Now there is nothing here.

Tagkan wishes he could see the multi-coloured sails of the karakoas and the praos again, but it is clear now that he never will. There are still a few boats on the river, but they are capsized and broken by the river's edge. It looks like the mountainside collapsed onto the town. A mudslide has swallowed Buwayang Bato, the destruction in the wake of the giant of Gawi-Gawen.

All that remains of the town are parts of the harbour and some small houses by the riverside. Tagkan walks to the edge of the mudslide and climbs to where the town's main road once was. At the end of the road was the temple where the Baliana, the priestesses, would bless the new boats and make sacrifices to the rain. As if to mark the place where the temple stood, a boulder the size of a horse rises out of the mud.

Tagkan continues to walk over the buried town. He finds the palace of the datu. One of the sarimanok carvings that adorned the roof rises from the mud. Its tail feathers are as long as Tagkan's arm, and the earth has a hold of them, making it look like the mud is giving birth to this creature of fire and magic. The sarimanok is now no different from any common rooster, unable to fly, its talons bound to the earth.

Tagkan walks on. At the datu's palace, he turns right and keeps on walking. He looks around him as if he is getting his bearing, and then he walks in a straight line for over a thousand steps. He stops where his ancestral home once stood, the home of his father and seven generations before him. Once, it was a compound of six other houses where his brothers lived, built around the central home. Now there is no trace of it.

Tagkan gets on his knees and digs his fingers into the wet mud, not really knowing what he's going to do. But soon he finds himself moving clumps of earth aside. He keeps on digging, not knowing why he is doing it. After an hour, his fingers are raw and bleeding.

He digs for days with an improvised shovel made from planks of wood. He does not rest. He eats only once a day and sleeps for short periods. He stops digging only to fish in the river, then he returns to his digging soon after. During those days, it rains constantly.

After seven days of digging, Tagkan finds the body of his father and mother, and two of his brothers. He is unable to find his other brothers, their wives, and their children. The rain keeps most of the flies away, but the smell of rot is everywhere.

On the eighth day, the rain stops, and Tagkan builds a pyre. He kneels a short distance from the pyre without moving, nor does he speak or cry. He just sits there as the fire rages. Shortly after the fire dies out, the rain begins again. He does not move from his place.

* * *

When night falls, something steps out of the shadows and takes pity on Tagkan. It is a tikbalang.

He might have been horrified by the creature's appearance—it has the head of a horse on top of a man's body—but instead, Tagkan looks up at the tikbalang without fear or surprise and stands up to greet him.

'What is your name?' the tikbalang asks. Its voice is deeper than any human voice could be.

'Tagkan.'

'I am Saragnayan,' the beast says. 'I know you.'

The man studies the tikbalang's bestial features and realizes that Saragnayan is telling the truth. The beast's breathing is calm, its manner gentle, and there is no lie in its equine eyes.

A part of Tagkan recognizes that he should be afraid to meet a creature that roams both Skyworld and underworld. But after the events of the past few days, he is beyond fear. He finds that he is only curious.

'I know you too,' Tagkan says. 'How is this possible?'

The tikbalang replies, 'I have known you since you first stepped foot outside your town when your bare feet touched the wet stones of the road for the first time, and you walked to your uncle's house down the river. I walked with you when you explored Buwayang Bato's backroads when you were older, and it was I who tricked you when you got lost. How I laughed at you then. So scared, pretending to be brave, you took off all your clothes and put them on backwards to turn back my magic. But you got lost again anyway, all on your own, and you didn't find your way back home until midnight, but only because I took pity on you and showed you the way. Your mother was so angry.

'I walked with you when you left your home and headed south to the great city of the gods. I was with you on the dry road when you first walked beneath the Bone Gate, and you wondered if you would ever see your home again.

'I know all this because I am a tikbalang. The gods gave us this knowledge and this responsibility. We guide the lost. We waylay the wicked. We lead those who are willing to pay the price.'

Tagkan takes in all that Saragnayan says and knows that the creature speaks the truth. 'Truly, the gods have sent you,' Tagkan says, 'for there is only one wish in my heart right now, and that is to stop the giant of Gawi-Gawen. I must warn Sun Girna Ginar that it is coming. But I do not know the way. Can you guide me?'

'As with all things,' Saragnayan says, 'there is a price that must be paid. Are you willing to pay that price?'

'I am willing to pay any price, but I am afraid that I have lost everything.'

Saragnayan shakes its head. 'I do not seek payment in gold.'

'Then name your price.'

The tikbalang nods. It has been waiting a long time for this.

'I shall tell you what I know of your road, Tagkan,' Saragnayan says, 'and why I have followed you all these years.

'Down one path, you become a great man, the saviour of Sun Girna Ginar; down another, you are led to a long, quiet life spent not far from here, beside a noisy river in a blessed place. All other paths lead to violent deaths. That is all I can tell you.'

Tagkan is surprised, but he accepts what Saragnayan says without saying a word.

'I will help you find the path you wish to take—the same path that the giant walks. And one day, if we are successful, when the entire sultanate knows your name, I will ask for payment.'

Tagkan considers the tikbalang's words and frowns.

'I cannot promise you what I don't have.'

Saragnayan nods.

'I can only promise you that our trade will be fair.'

Tagkan is not convinced.

'We cannot move forward,' he says. 'I have given you nothing. I have received nothing in return. Nothing binds us.'

Saragnayan is silent for a moment. They are at an impasse.

'Then let our blood be our contract,' the tikbalang says.

'You would do that?' Tagkan asks Saragnayan. 'Once the blood compact is made, it cannot be broken. The gods will destroy us.'

Saragnayan says nothing in reply, but draws the knife at its side.

The tikbalang takes the knife in its left hand and cuts itself on its right forearm. Dark blood flows from the wound. Saragnayan passes the knife to Tagkan.

He takes the knife, saying 'Then let the gods bear witness.'

He hesitates for just a moment, then cuts his own forearm, gritting his teeth in pain.

With fisted hands, the man and the tikbalang raise their bloody forearms and press their wounds against each other until their blood mingles.

'It is done,' Tagkan says. 'Show me the way, Saragnayan. We have a long way to travel.'

* * *

In the morning, Tagkan scans the horizon and finds no sign of the six-headed giant. At nightfall yesterday, the giant's back looked like a small mountain set against the mountain range. Today, that mountain is gone.

He turns around and calls to Saragnayan. The beast is always thirty paces or so behind him. Saragnayan said that other people can't see it unless it wants them to, but it also said that it would hide if they came across anyone on the road.

'We will not catch up with the giant on this road,' the tikbalang says.

'What road should we take then?'

'Nor any other road.'

'No,' Tagkan says, growing impatient. 'There must be some way. If we travel by sea, we can overtake the giant.'

Saragnayan is silent. Tagkan thinks the tikbalang is considering it, but he cannot read the beast's face.

'I have seen all roads,' the tikbalang says, 'and there is no path we can take to reach Sun Girna Ginar before the giant. Yes, it slows when it crosses the sea, but it is still not enough.'

'No,' Tagkan says again, refusing to accept Saragnayan's answer. 'There must be a way. Perhaps you are mistaken. There is always a way.'

Saragnayan stares at Tagkan, and again Tagkan is unsure what emotion, if any, is being conveyed.

'My days are spent walking down different roads. In my mind's eye, I have travelled them all,' the tikbalang says. 'There is no road that will let you overtake the giant of Gawi-Gawen, except for the one where you seek the magic of the witch.'

Tagkan considers the tikbalang's words.

'Then take me to the road that leads to the witch,' he says.

'The witch will ask you for something in return,' Saragnayan warns him.

'I know,' Tagkan says. 'There is always a price.'

5

Adlao

Adlao knows the time has come to die. The giant of Gawi-Gawen is coming. And while the Tyrant's fate is uncertain, all he can do is trust in Magat and the concubine, Aya. There is only one thing left for him to do: leave the shadows and stand against the Tyrant. Adlao does not doubt that doing so will lead to his death.

Other doubts persist too. He wonders if the people will remember him. He has been in exile for far too long. He is also unsure if the Maharlika will stand with him. He has spoken in secret to his allies in the palace, and they swore to support him. But Adlao knows they are afraid. Adlao is afraid as well, but he reminds himself who he is. *You are a datu,* he tells himself, *a king.*

His work is done. Today, he will walk the streets of Sun Girna Ginar under the light of the sun, and he will tell the people that the Tyrant's rule is over. He will ask them to join him, to stand against the Tyrant and fight, for they are many, and the Tyrant is just one man.

The time for silence is over. He will shout and rage. He will walk into the Maharlika Quarter with the people at his side. He will march with them into the Tyrant's palace and challenge the self-proclaimed god who has enslaved them: Surrender your power, step down from the throne!

Or maybe the Tyrant will kill you, Adlao tells himself and laughs. *The old woman was right, after all,* he thinks. *I don't want to die.*

Adlao prepares to leave the room he has been hiding in for the past weeks. He looks at his belongings on the table—a lamp, a pouch of gold beads, a knife, the bottle he bought from the old woman—and decides that he won't need any of them.

He takes the bottle, opens it, and pours the muddy water onto the dry floor, just as the old woman told him to. With his hands, he mixes the water with the dirt until the hard-packed ground becomes loose. Then he empties the flask and continues mixing the dirt and the water with his fingers until the mixture becomes brown clay.

The clay begins to grow, becoming a mound that rises from the earth. Adlao steps back, thinking he has been betrayed and the Tyrant has found him. He thinks of his knife, but the clay thing is between him and the table.

Before Adlao's eyes, the clay begins to take shape. Arms and legs form, and finally, a head. *It is a man,* Adlao realizes in disbelief. *No,* he corrects himself, *it is a golem.*

The golem turns and faces Adlao, and as it does, its surface begins to dry and takes on the hue of skin. Silver hair grows on its head. And its face assumes a familiar shape, his own.

Without saying a word, the golem dresses itself in Adlao's clothes. Adlao remains where he is standing, unsure what to do. The golem ignores him, its face expressionless. Once dressed, it opens the door and walks into the market streets.

After a few moments, Adlao follows the golem from a distance and covers his head with a headscarf. He watches it from behind a market stall, and wonders where it is going.

Soon, a woman stops the golem, and says in a loud voice, 'You are Datu Adlao!'

'Yes,' the golem says in Adlao's voice.

'The Sultan sent you into exile,' she says.

'Yes,' the golem says again. 'I have returned.'

A ripple passes through the crowd. Adlao hears the people talking among themselves.

'Who is Datu Adlao?'

'He was a great man. The right hand of the Sultan. Before the vizier.'

'He's a dead man. The Sultan will kill him if he finds out he's here.'

'Why have you returned, Datu?'

'Didn't you promise to set the city free?'

'Are you going to fight the Sultan?'

The golem doesn't answer. It keeps walking. Adlao follows. He is not the only one.

Soon, word spreads that Datu Adlao has returned from exile. Those who remember Adlao take to the streets and follow the golem, thinking that the datu has returned to lead them. Free men and slaves follow the golem, mixing with Adlao's allies. The streets swell with their numbers.

By the time the golem reaches the Holy Quarter, a large crowd is following it. They swarm around it, looking upon the image of Adlao with hope that they can't contain. They chant his name. There is even singing.

Adlao looks at the face of the golem and sees a benign expression there. He looks behind him and sees that the crowd has grown large. It snakes along the streets as far as the eye can see.

'Datu Adlao has returned!' they call out ahead of him.

'Save us!' they implore the golem.

'Give us food! We are hungry.'

The golem says nothing.

'Death to the Sultan!'

The golem continues walking. It reaches a crossroad, and there, three crowds converge. There is cheering when they see the golem. It only smiles and walks on, in the direction of the Maharlika Quarter, to the Sultan's palace.

6

Aya

Hours after leaving Magat, Aya sits in her room in the palace, waiting for the Sultan to arrive. She has been bathed, made-up, and dressed by her handmaidens in a pale blue dress that she chose, one that reminds her of the sea, of home.

Aya is alone for now. After her handmaidens leave, she waits a few minutes and takes out the glass figurine that she bought from an old woman in the market. It glints in the lamplight, like a fish in the sun.

'Pray to him,' the old woman told her. 'Place him on your altar, beside your anito. He will give you the strength to do what you need to do.'

Aya decides not to hide the figurine. She places the little god on her altar in the corner of her room, alongside the wooden carvings of her ancestors. She closes her eyes and prays but can think only of Magat.

She thinks of him sometimes as a god, powerful, relentless, and tempestuous as the sea. To her, he is the king of the silent depths, Tau-mari-u, Lord of Storms. His voice commands the waves, and his whispers carry all the promises of the tides. His kiss is the caress of the surf. His taste is salt. His memory surrounds her, like water on her skin, enfolding her in the wonders of the thousand kingdoms of the sea, carrying her down in his embrace, down below the storm, down to where it is silent and warm, and there is only him.

The door opens and the Sultan enters with his entourage. Aya greets the Sultan by getting on her knees and bowing at his feet, her forehead touching the ground in front of him. His guards stand by the door. His servants remove his robes and his slippers, bow, and leave the room with their heads held low, never looking at the Sultan or Aya.

The Sultan gestures for Aya to sit, and she does so on the edge of a nearby divan, attentive and ready. The guards step outside with the servants. The door closes, and she is alone with the living god.

Before her is a man. There is no mistaking what he is. A wealthy man, a powerful man, yes. But there is no mistaking him for a god. They say he is hundreds of years old, but he looks like a middle-aged man—hair greying prematurely, hairline receding, brow lined with worry. His body has begun its decline. His gut is soft and grows every month while his arms and legs are shrinking, becoming thinner, and losing their strength. Clad in a loincloth, the Sultan's penis stands proud like a god, but these days it follows its own bidding more and more, grows distracted, retreats into its own concerns.

Without saying a word, he signals towards the bed, and Aya stands up. She knows what he wants.

* * *

Asleep in her arms, the Sultan looks to Aya like a little boy, hardly a man. A part of her wants to protect him, but she needs only to think of Magat and the conviction of his vision to steel herself for what she must do. She needs only to think of the sea, of its ebbs and flows, its cycles and seasons, to acknowledge that the Sultan's time, his reign of daily cruelties over her, is over.

Once she moves, there is no turning back, she knows. She watches his breathing for an hour and when he moves onto his back and begins to snore lightly, she knows his sleep is at its deepest. She lifts an arm to see if he will wake. She pokes and prods him, but he does not stir.

To remove the amulet, first she reaches underneath the bed for a small knife she has hidden. With one hand, she picks up the amulet by the string that suspends it around the Sultan's neck so that it hardly touches his skin. Then swift as a snake, she severs the string with the knife and pulls. The string tugs at the skin of the Sultan's neck as the amulet comes loose. He begins to wake.

Aya moves quickly. She hides the amulet in one hand, then she rolls towards the Sultan, pressing her weight on his side and arm. He wakes briefly to find Aya's face close to his. 'Go back to sleep,' she says and kisses him roughly on the lips.

When he is asleep again, she places another identical amulet around the Sultan's neck. Adlao had them made so the Sultan would not know his amulet had been stolen from him. Through a small space between the Sultan's neck and the bed, she threads one end of the string around his neck and ties a simple knot.

Aya stands up and walks to the adjoining room of her suite. There, behind a lounge chair is an engraving of an eight-pointed star upon the wall. She crouches down and breathes on it, and a hidden door opens with an audible click. She steps inside, naked, and closes the door. On the other side, there is a change of clothes and a pair of sandals.

She leaves everything behind, all her belongings, the dresses, the jewellery, the figurines of her ancestors, and the glass figurine of her god. There is no turning back now. If they catch her, they will kill her. So she walks forward in the darkness of the secret tunnel, her footsteps sure, with her fingertips tracing the side of one wall and her other hand in front of her because she doesn't dare to light a lamp.

She leaves behind her imprisoned life as the Sultan's favourite concubine without regret. Through this secret passageway, she found her freedom. When she first discovered it, she spent the afternoons roaming the city and the market. Then she met Magat and learnt that love freely given is still greater than love taken—even when it is not given in return.

It does not matter to Aya. All is behind her. She reaches a spiral staircase cut from stone, and descends. From the bottom of the stairs, it is half an hour's walk to the other side of the passage, where there is another secret door on the palace wall.

The door opens and the city lights greet her with a multitude of colours. For a brief moment, she thinks she is watching the city burn. She imagines a firestorm raging through the mansions of the Maharlika and a magical blue fire consuming the walls as giants walk into the city to cleanse it of the wicked. But she is mistaken. There is only the light from the street lamps and a bonfire somewhere in the Artists' Quarter.

Aya keeps walking until she reaches the Holy Quarter, making sure that she is not followed. There, in a small temple to the gods of Antar A Langit, she takes out the Sultan's amulet, places it on the ground, and picks up a rock. Quick as a snake, she smashes the amulet. The glass shatters and there is a flash of lightning, but no sound of thunder.

That same night, Aya leaves Sun Girna Ginar and all its sorrows. The moon is high when she steps outside the city gates. The air is brisk. She is free.

7

Tagkan

The witch is expecting them. When Tagkan and Saragnayan arrive at her estate—a plantation not far from Buwayang Bato—they find the witch's alipin waiting for them. She told the alipin that they would be coming on this day, so he took his umbrella and his betel nut chew to wait for them. She is not mistaken about their arrival. She never is, the alipin says.

It is the alipin's first time seeing a tikbalang. He bows deeply to the beast and welcomes him formally, but the effect is comic. Afterwards, he stares rudely but Saragnayan makes no sign that it is bothered by the alipin.

'How is it that you can see my companion?' Tagkan asks.

'My master knows a great many things,' the alipin replies in a boastful tone. 'She said to me, "A great man and a tikbalang will visit us. Prepare a feast. Slaughter a young pig. Tomorrow, come and greet them at the turn in the road. They will have no trouble finding their way, but we must show such esteemed guests that we are honoured that they come to us for counsel."'

'Refreshments? The house is still a few hours away.'

At that point, the alipin produces a tray of rice cakes wrapped in banana leaves, earthenware cups, and a pitcher of water from beside the

woven banig mat that he was sitting on just moments before Tagkan
and the tikbalang arrived.

Tagkan shrugs, takes a cup, but does not touch the food. He is
more tired than hungry.

'You still haven't answered the question,' he reminds the alipin.

'Ah yes! So my master says to me, "Amtalaw," for that is me, that
is my name—' Amtalaw smiles widely to reveal that half his teeth are
missing. '"Amtalaw," she says, "you cannot see a tikbalang with your
own eyes if it does not want to be seen. You must borrow spirit eyes
from a beast. To do this, find a sleeping dog and gather the dust that
dries around its eyes and place that same dust into your eyes. With the
dog's spirit eyes, you will be able to see the tikbalang until you take a
bath or wash your face." So that is how I can see your companion.'
Amtalaw bows to the tikbalang again.

Without a word, Saragnayan walks away, towards the witch's house.
Amtalaw rolls up his banig in a hurry, drinks what's left of the water in
large gulps, and stuffs the rice cakes into a little bag—all while Tagkan
watches him. Finally, Amtalaw grabs his parasol and rushes after the
tikbalang. Tagkan follows in no particular hurry.

'Tell me more about your master,' Tagkan says.

Tagkan has heard of the witch before. News of the Witch
Princess—that is what they called her—had reached Sun Girna Ginar.
Tagkan took interest because they were also tidings of home. She was
said to have declared war on all the witches in the north at the age of
sixteen. After years of bitter conflict in this world and the spirit world,
she emerged triumphant, and now she rules over all the northern
witches who remain.

'I could not ask for a better master,' Amtalaw says, again displaying
his missing teeth. 'She is kind and fair and wise.' Tagkan could see that
Amtalaw meant it too.

'And quite beautiful, I've heard.'

Amtalaw smiles conspiratorially and scratches his head. 'Yes, that
never hurts,' Amtalaw says, 'but she's really not my type. Too skinny.
Too . . . pointed. I like my women simple.'

'You are not married?'

'Bathala has chosen not to bless me with a wife. I leave that to him. I serve my master.'

'And your master is not a simple woman?'

'She is braver and more cunning than any man I have ever met,' Amtalaw says. 'And she is a witch, you know. That changes everything.'

Tagkan is impressed by the loyalty the Witch Princess inspires.

'In the south, we call her the Witch Princess.'

'I have heard the name.'

'Saragnayan calls her "The Witch". As if she were the only one.'

Amtalaw shrugs and says nothing, but something on his face gives away that he agrees.

'How am I to address her? I do not want to give offence.'

'Call my master by her name.' Amtalaw says.

'And what would that be?'

'Gaygayuma.'

'That is a very old name.'

'She is not as young as she looks.'

* * *

Three hours later, Tagkan and Saragnayan await the arrival of the Witch Princess in her receiving room. The room is large enough to fit several houses inside but is almost empty. Tagkan and Saragnayan are sitting on oversized cushions while a dozen of the witch's alipin—all women—face the two travellers. They kneel on the floor with their feet tucked underneath.

Amtalaw leaves Tagkan and the tikbalang at the steps leading up to the massive stone building which is the witch's home. Like all houses in the North, this one too is raised from the ground. Around it, there are smaller houses made of wood and bamboo. They house enough alipin to constitute a small army, and it is obvious that some of the alipin wandering the grounds are warriors. Many of the men carry silver axes as well as the kalasag, the tall shield of the region.

Beyond the Witch Princess' house are rice paddies cut out of the hills like the rice terraces of the Ifugao mountain folk. From where he is sitting, Tagkan can see the fields glittering in the sun like an iridescent green beetle.

A set of double doors open on the far side of the hall. Four more alipin walk through the door before the Witch Princess enters herself. Everyone in the room stands up.

Tagkan knows it is her right away. The girl must be twenty years old now by Tagkan's count, but she is small and thin, which makes her look sixteen. Rumours of her beauty are also true. Her features are fine and delicate that heighten the illusion that she is little more than a child. But it is her eyes that disarm Tagkan. A fierce intelligence burns behind them as well as something else. *Playfulness? Mischief?* She commands her alipin with a glance. She sizes up Tagkan with another. She takes in the presence of the immense tikbalang without blinking.

'You are welcome here,' the Witch Princess says when she reaches her place in the centre of the room.

What follows are a series of formalities. Tagkan and the tikbalang bow to their host who bows back. They bow lower. Gaygayuma greets Saragnayan in his language. He expresses his appreciation and gratitude for her. She then greets Tagkan, and Tagkan in turn thanks her for her hospitality and generosity.

With the formalities over, silence falls between them. It is the Witch Princess who speaks first. Her voice is deep and controlled.

'Sun Girna Ginar's doom marches towards it, and you seek to stop it. What makes you think you can? You are just a man, a man without powerful ancestors.'

'Lady Gaygayuma, if I may ask, how do you know these things?'

She only smiles. Again, there is mischief in her eyes. 'That does not matter. What matters is that they are true. Why even try to stop the giant of Gawi-Gawen? You might as well try to stop a landslide.'

'I have seen the giant,' Tagkan says, 'and I know its power. You speak the truth when you say I cannot stop it. But others can. I seek only to warn Sun Girna Ginar of the giant's coming before it reaches the city walls. General Marandang can stop the giant. He has killed giants before. He can do so again.'

The Witch Princess looks thoughtful.

'The question remains: why, Tagkan, son of no one?'

'The giant took everything from me,' Tagkan says. 'It destroyed my home town, killed my family, and everyone I once knew.'

'Revenge, then,' the Witch Princess says. 'I can understand revenge.'

Tagkan pauses, remembering how Amtalaw said the witch believed he was a great man. For a moment, he is afraid that revenge was not enough. A great man would have better reasons. So he decides to lie.

'No,' Tagkan says. 'It is love for the city.' The young witch looks at him with veiled disbelief.

'All I have is the city that took me in, years ago. It has become part of me. Sun Girna Ginar is all that I have left.

'My family is dead. Revenge is meaningless. There is nothing more I can do for them, except seek honour in this life.'

The Witch Princess' eyes narrow slightly, then she nods her head and says, 'You are a noble man, Tagkan, son of no one. But there is another question we must answer: Why should I help you?'

Tagkan has thought about this and tells the witch the only answer he has found.

'It is true,' Tagkan says, 'that I am only the son of a merchant. I am not a Maharlika, nor am I a renowned warrior. But my companion, Saragnayan, has revealed something of my fate. On one road, he says, I am the saviour of Sun Girna Ginar. So while my ancestors may be nothing, I am something. Or, will be. And if you help me succeed, you can name your price later on, as long as the trade is fair.'

The Witch Princess looks into Tagkan's eyes, then she fixes the tikbalang with the same look.

'And you, Saragnayan, why do you help this man?'

'We have a contract,' Saragnayan replies without emotion.

The witch weighs its words and stares at the tikbalang as if searching for meaning in the beast's eyes. Her eyes grow wide and her head turns to one side, but Saragnayan only stares into space.

The Witch Princess closes her eyes and bows her head. 'Very well,' she says. 'I will help you, Tagkan, son of no one. You have shown nobility of spirit. I have much to gain if you succeed and nothing to lose if you fail. And all you require is counsel.

'You seek to outrun the giant of Gawi-Gawen and warn Sun Girna Ginar of its coming.' Tagkan nods his head.

'You are already too late,' the Witch Princess says. 'The giant is approaching the city gates as we speak. A revolt has begun in the streets. The army will abandon the general. He will not be able to defend the city.'

Tagkan feels as if he has been struck in the face. Blood rushes to his head. He looks down at his hands. *I have failed.*

But the Witch Princess is not finished. 'Do not lose heart. There is still a way for you to reach Sun Girna Ginar.'

Tagkan catches his breath. He looks up at the Witch Princess.

'Have you heard of the sigbin?' she asks.

Tagkan shakes his head while Saragnayan does not answer.

'It is a beast from Skyworld. You can still find some herds here if you know where and how to look. Sigbin are able to travel very fast if you can catch and ride one. And when confronted by danger, they can blink from one place to another by jumping on lightning.

'At the centre of time, there is a storm. So, by jumping on lightning, not only can they travel great distances but they can also travel to a time that has passed, to yesterday or last week if you know how to make it do so.

'With one of these beasts, you can arrive at Sun Girna Ginar days before the giant of Gawi-Gawen.'

Tagkan releases a breath he did not realize he was holding.

'There is a trick in making the sigbin do your bidding. My alipin, Amtalaw, will show you how. For now, you should rest. If this is the road you wish to take, there is no hurry.'

'Thank you, Lady Gaygayuma,' Tagkan says, bowing in his seat. 'I was praying you would bless us with your counsel. My prayers have been answered.'

'There is more, Tagkan, son of no one,' the Witch Princess says. To Tagkan's surprise, her lips do not move when she says this. He soon realizes he is hearing her speaking to his spirit. And only he can hear her.

'Do not trust the tikbalang,' she says to Tagkan. 'His kind is full of malice and deceit. This one is no exception. He seeks to lead you astray. He wants you to travel a road of his choice.'

Tagkan rejects the witch's words at first, but at the same time, he knows she speaks the truth.

'How do you know this?' Tagkan asks through his spirit. Somehow Gaygayuma hears.

'That is not important,' she replies. 'Just beware. Be on your guard. Be watchful of turns in the road.'

'How can I trust you? I have just met you while I have known Saragnayan all my life. The tikbalang warned me about you. He told me to heed your counsel but not to trust you. He said you cannot trust a witch.'

The Witch Princess smiles.

'Then you have a choice to make, Tagkan, son of no one.'

Tagkan thinks the Witch Princess looks beautiful when she smiles that way, her head turning to one side. She looks like a naughty child playing a game. He knows she is capable of lying, but what would she gain? He looks to his side, at his companion. Its equine eyes look gentle and tranquil. But Tagkan knows it is not of this world. For the first time, he realizes that the tikbalang only looks like it has the head of a horse. It is not a horse's head at all. Its teeth are all wrong. And some of them are sharp, like a boar's tusks.

'Perhaps one of us is lying,' the Witch Princess says to him, still silent. 'Or both of us. Or perhaps we are both telling the truth, and neither of us can be trusted. It doesn't matter. The question you need to answer is not which one of us is lying, but why do either of us care what happens to you, Tagkan, son of no one?'

'Stay the night,' the Witch Princess says, aloud this time. The sound of her voice shocks Tagkan back to this time, this place. 'You have travelled far, and you have farther still to travel. The sigbin will carry you through time and distance, past the giant. Tonight, you need warm food and sleep. Put away your concerns. You are safe here.'

8

Sakandal

Vizier Humadapnon doesn't see Sakandal until the hunter's knife is at his throat. He lets out a shout before Sakandal pushes him against the wall, but there is no one to hear him. Sakandal has made sure of that. All of the guards in the vizier's tower are dead.

To silence the vizier, Sakandal adds a small amount of pressure on the knife until a scarlet line of blood appears under the blade. Humadapnon winces and stops shouting. He begins quivering. His breathing comes in rapid gasps.

'I have gold,' Humadapnon says. 'Take what you want.'

Sakandal barely glances at the gold or the jewels in the vizier's quarters. He cares little for the rare and precious things the vizier has amassed.

'I came here for two things,' Sakandal says, his voice just above a whisper, 'to ask you a question, and to take your life. I have no need of anything else.'

Humadapnon's quivering turns into shaking, almost as if he is suffering convulsions. Sweat breaks out on his face.

'Who are you?' the vizier asks.

For a moment, Sakandal doesn't know what to say. His name was Sakandal once, but they don't call him that anymore. He is someone else now.

He remembers the days after his escape, living on the streets of Sun Girna Ginar as a beggar. He lived like this for a year, to atone for his sins.

One day as he begged for alms at one of the temples in the Holy Quarter, a babaylan stopped in front of him. The priest knelt beside him on the dusty ground as if he too would beg for alms.

'A man with such powerful ancestors should not be here begging. Come with me. Please,' he said, his made-up face smiling. Sakandal followed him.

The babaylan brought Sakandal into the temple where alipin bathed and fed him. When he was clean, they brought him to a room full of statues of anitos. Unlike Sakandal's hand-carved anito, these statues were as large as men. They carried head axes and shields in their stone hands. He found the babaylan praying in a corner.

'What is your name?' the babaylan asked.

'Sakandal,' he replied.

'I know your anito, Sakandal,' the babaylan said without looking at him. The babaylan's long hair reached past his waist.

Sakandal struggled to understand what the babaylan was telling him. He kept the anito in a bag around his waist with what few possessions he had. He didn't think of it much.

'He was a gifted killer, your anito, perhaps the most gifted the world has ever known. If he wished your death, it was said, you would be dead by the time the cocks were crowing. He also possessed a thirst for blood that could not be quenched.'

'How do you know this?' Sakandal asked.

'I am a babaylan of Bathala,' he said simply, as if that answered everything, 'the one god who is the union of woman, babae, and man, lalaki, fused together as the divine spirit. I possess the duality of Bathala, both man and woman, both spirit and flesh.

'As a babaylan, I speak to the living and the dead. I help the living make peace with the dead. I help the dead aid the living. They long to see their descendants become great.'

Sakandal considered what the babaylan was saying. His hand grasped the anito through the bag around his waist.

'What do the dead tell you about me?' Sakandal asked.

The babaylan turned around then and smiled at Sakandal, leaning his head forward as he did so. He looked beautiful in that pose.

'They say you have your anito's thirst for blood.'

The babaylan looked down at the floor, almost with regret, then raised his eyes to stare into Sakandal's.

'They say you can be Asuang.'

Sakandal's training began soon after. The babaylan communed with the anito and taught Sakandal the ways of Ogassi, Asuang, and his children. He led Sakandal into the dream world where the hunter received instruction from his anito, learning the way of the knife and how to become one with darkness. And after years of training, he mastered all the arts and shed the name Sakandal. He was now Asuang, and his hunt began anew.

Yes, he remembers now. He tells Vizier Humadapnon, 'My name is Asuang.'

'Years ago, Vizier, you sent a war party to my village. Your soldiers killed everyone they found there. They killed my wife and children and burned their bodies. But they spared me. They brought me to the city to be executed. The soldiers said you wanted to see me die yourself. You and the Sultan. Why?'

There is panic in Humadapnon's eyes. Asuang sees it. *He doesn't remember.*

Asuang suppresses the urge to slit the vizier's throat.

'Think,' he whispers to Humadapnon. 'Or I will make your death long and painful.'

Still, there is no answer from Humadapnon. Asuang plunges the tip of his knife into the vizier's liver. Humadapnon gasps, then a flash of recognition enters his eyes.

'I remember!' the vizier says desperately. 'I remember. The witches. One of them had a vision. She said a hunter from your village would kill the Sultan one day. If we burnt the village down, she said, we would find you. The Sultan wanted to see his would-be killer, to see you die with his own eyes. I did it to save him. I only did it for the Sultan.'

Asuang pulls out the knife and raises it to the vizier's face. He sees that Humadapnon's blood is thin. He licks the knife. The blood tastes sweet.

'Please,' Humadapnon says, his shaking more violent now. 'Please believe me. I beg you. We weren't going to kill you. The Sultan only wanted to talk. Everything can be solved. I have riches you cannot imagine. They are yours. I can show you.'

Asuang knows Humadapnon is lying. He laughs. In one swift motion, he makes a deep cut across the vizier's throat. Humadapnon's neck splits open, exposing thick layers of fat. His thin blood floods down his neck and stains his silks in a rich, scarlet hue.

9

Tagkan

'They are quite delicious,' Amtalaw says, 'when you grill them. Many hunters eat them like that in the wild. But I like them deep-fried. The skin turns crisp, that's the best part if you ask me. The rest of them is full of small bones, which makes them tricky to eat. But if you're not picky, just chop them up, lightly season and serve with soy sauce and calamansi. They're a real treat.'

Tagkan and Amtalaw look upon the herd of sigbin from behind some low branches. The beasts are in a clearing on a mountainside, gathered around the carcass of a pig that Amtalaw used to lure them together. In the moonless night, Tagkan can barely see the shapes of the sigbin, but their red eyes are clear in the darkness.

The sigbin are about the length of a small pony with great hind legs, small front legs, narrow bodies, and long tails. The animals often stand on their hind legs, looking almost like men when they do. Their faces are feral, with long snouts, and ears that look like the wings of a bat.

Tagkan doubts these sigbin can carry the weight of a man, and he has trouble believing Amtalaw's explanation.

'Tell me the plan again,' Tagkan asks Amtalaw.

'The two of us will hide here on one side of the clearing. Our mighty tikbalang will come from the other side and scare the sigbin towards us. We will have to be fast. These sigbin can run.'

'And then what do we do?' Tagkan wants to hear it all again just to make sure.

'Once we have one sigbin for you and one for the mighty tikbalang, we inflate them so they can carry you.'

'How do we do this again?'

Amtalaw stops his explanation. 'You don't believe me,' he says, catching on. 'Why don't you believe me?' Now he acts hurt.

'I don't mean to offend you,' Tagkan tells Amtalaw. 'But it is somewhat difficult to believe. You have to see it from my side.'

Amtalaw considers this for a moment and decides not to be offended. He breaks out his tooth-deprived smile. 'You will see. I am telling you the truth. You just have to grab the sigbin, push aside its tail and blow air into its ass.'

'And this will work . . . ?'

'You have to do it a few times and then the sigbin inflates on its own until it's the size of a pony . . . well, a pony with a very large stomach.'

Amtalaw senses that Tagkan still doesn't believe him.

'Look, do you want to get to Sun Girna Ginar or not?'

'Of course!'

'Then, that is what you have to do,' Amtalaw says, exasperated. 'You'll see. You'll see.'

'I believe you,' Tagkan tells Amtalaw, hoping the lie does not show in his voice.

'Good!' Amtalaw looks pleased. 'Then let us do this. The sooner I get back, the better. I am hungry.' He raises his hands to his mouth and makes a sound with his lips, a bird call, their signal to the tikbalang. The shape of Amtalaw's hands propels the bird call forward.

From across the clearing, Saragnayan springs into action. It lets out a roar that is unlike any sound Tagkan has heard before, and the night is filled with terror.

The cries of the panicked sigbin follow. It is not the sound that Tagkan expects, almost like the crying of children. Before Tagkan can react, the sigbin come bearing down upon him, tearing through the jungle, red-eyed and afraid.

'Quick!' Amtalaw says, and Tagkan leaps towards the nearest sigbin, pinning it to the ground. It doesn't stop struggling and continues to scream until Amtalaw tells Tagkan to hold the sigbin by the neck. When he does, it goes limp, but it continues to watch him from its position on the ground.

Not far from where Tagkan lies on the ground, Amtalaw stands up, holding two sigbin by their necks. He is grinning widely.

'I caught another one!' Amtalaw says with pride. 'Maybe I will go with you, after all. Or maybe I will just make a stew.'

* * *

Tagkan wakes to a strange sky. He doesn't recognize the stars. He moves to get up, but pain shoots through his leg and up his side. Saragnayan's horse head appears between him and the sky.

'You were in an accident,' the tikbalang says. 'Can you move?'

'Yes,' Tagkan replies. It occurs to him that he is supposed to remember something, but his mind is cloudy. There is also a pain radiating from his chest. There is more pain, distant but greater in magnitude, in his leg. It occurs to Tagkan that he should raise his head and look down at his body to survey the damage. Maybe something is broken. Instead, Tagkan pursues neither remembering nor finding the source of the pain. He is too busy looking at the stars.

The stars Tagkan sees are not the stars he knows. Instead of tiny white points in the sky, each star tonight is a sphere of light. There are other stars like the ones Tagkan is familiar with, but there are a million more of them, scattered behind the constellations.

'You are in Skyworld,' Saragnayan says at the same time Tagkan realizes that the stars of the constellations are suns, only farther away. He is adrift in a sea of suns.

'Rest,' the tikbalang says. 'The road ahead is long. But we have come far. You should rest for now.'

Tagkan struggles to remember. As he falls back to sleep, a dream rises to greet him. Tagkan recognizes it as the same dream he had upon waking. In his dream, they were riding the sigbin. Saragnayan was to his left and Amtalaw was to his right. The witch's alipin had decided to come with them after all. They were traveling faster than any horse could carry them, in the peculiar gait of the sigbin. A shimmering appeared in the air before them followed by the sound of thunder, then many things happened all at once.

The shimmering surrounded all of them until Tagkan could hardly see. It looked like they were traveling on a vast plain, but the sky was too close to the earth. Then the light became too much to bear, and Tagkan shut his eyes. At the same time, he heard the terrible shout from the tikbalang again and the shrieks of the frightened sigbin. He opened his eyes, but the blinding light forced them shut again just as he saw Amtalaw drawing his blade, and the tikbalang, teeth bared, grabbing hold of the sigbins' makeshift harnesses. Then they were falling, all three of them, upwards to the sky. Then came the pain.

Just before Tagkan passes into sleep, he realizes that this isn't a dream at all. It is a memory. He realizes he has failed. Saragnayan has waylaid them, and Tagkan will never reach Sun Girna Ginar in time. The giant of Gawi-Gawen will reach the Bone Gate unopposed, and it will crush the city underneath its feet. Tagkan struggles to wake up, but sleep will not let him go.

Part III: Gods and Heroes

'You have heard this story before,' Humitau, daughter of Tau-mari-u, says, 'of how Aponi-tolau saved the earth from the flood. But you do not know the truth. It is there in the words, but only if you listen to their meaning.

'I shall tell you the story again, not just so that you may know the truth, but also so that others may know the truth. And with every re-telling of my story, the voice of the truth will become stronger until all the lies have been silenced.

'They call Aponi-tolau a hero. They say he is my husband. But he is neither of those things. He is my captor, the man who kidnapped me from my home. He is my rapist.

'Aponi-tolau is indeed the son of a goddess, but that union spawned a mountain demon. That is how I came to know him, when he came down from the mountain and into the sea, the kingdom of my father.

'The demon came without warning. He crossed the gate of our home without asking for permission and broke through the circle of stones that protected the palace of Tau-mari-u. He found us—my sisters and I—in front of the palace gates. In one hand, he held a spear, and in the other, a length of rope with a cruel hook tied to one end.

'He declared, "I am Aponi-tolau, son of Lang-An of Kadalayapan, god of the mountains. Kneel before me."

'We refused the demon, and my oldest sister told him, "There is only one lord in the kingdom of the sea, and that is Tau-mari-u. Beware of your demands, and be gentle with your words. We are Tau-mari-u's daughters. Our father will reward your temperance with kindness."

'But Aponi-tolau would not listen. He grew angry and launched his spear at us. My sisters swam away, but I picked up his spear where it fell and turned to face the demon.

'I rushed at him, seeking to impale him with his own spear, but I only cut his arm. That was when he threw his hook at me. I tried to swim away, but I was not fast enough.

'The hook was poisoned, and my strength abandoned me as soon as it pierced my side. I couldn't swim, couldn't shout, and soon I was unconscious.

'When I awoke, we were on land, in a filthy fisherman's hut. Aponi-tolau and three men were trying to force-feed me some rice because they knew that if I ate their food, I would belong to their world, instead of the sea. One man held my arms.

One man sat on my legs. Another pried my jaws apart. Then, Aponi-tolau shoved the rice down my throat. I tried to fight them as much as I could, but it was no use.

When I had eaten their food, they left me with Aponi-tolau. He raped me. He kept saying that I belonged to him now, that I was his wife.

When he was finished with me, my father's flood found us. But the demon only laughed. He picked me up by my hair and swam out to sea where he began to drown me.

'Of all the things he did to me, this was the cruelest. I had lived all my life in the sea, and yet I was drowning in it now. At that moment, I knew I could never go back. I had lost everything.

"'Send back your flood, Tau-mari-u!" the demon said. And seeing his daughter dying, my father did what was asked of him. I do not blame him. What father would have done otherwise? But sometimes I wish he killed us both instead.

'Now you know the truth of my story, I beseech you, not to forget. Tell the others what you know now. I may live on in captivity, but at least the truth will be free. Lies have no power over us.'

1

Bagilat

Bagilat returns to Sun Girna Ginar to visit the old woman and gloat. He spots her selling bottles in a different alley this time and stalks her. In his cat form, he crouches low and travels swiftly between the market stalls, making sure to stay in the shadows. He crawls closer and closer and stops when the old woman's head turns in his direction. When he is close enough to touch her stall, he jumps and lands in front of her. She lets out a shriek. Bottles fall to the ground and break. A bottle full of red sand bleeds onto the dirty wet ground of the market as a bird escapes its glass cage and flies away.

'I have won!' the cat proclaims. 'Your datu's rebellion will soon be crushed.'

Recovering from her shock, the old woman clutches her breast with one hand and tries to catch a falling bottle with her other hand. She fails, and the bottle breaks with a loud crack. The smell of vinegar fills the air. To Bagilat's eyes, the old woman looks tired and defeated. He spots a flash of anger underneath.

'My Lord,' the old woman greets the god, but she forgoes the formalities of bowing. It does not matter to Bagilat.

'Do you concede that I have won?' he asks her. 'Adlao's rebellion will be crushed. His servant Magat is in hiding. Your champions have failed.'

The old woman raises her eyebrows. 'Have they now? Vizier Humadapnon is dead.'

Bagilat sneers. 'The vizier was never important,' he says. 'He was always a petty man who mistook wealth for power.'

'He was the Sultan's right hand,' the old woman argues.

'The Sultan will find another,' Bagilat dismisses the issue.

The old woman lets him have his victory.

'Kalaon is free,' the old woman says.

Bagilat pauses.

'That is interesting,' he says, weighing his words. 'Where is he?'

'I do not know, my Lord.'

'Well,' Bagilat says, 'if he is not with the Sultan and not with his enemies, it is of no consequence.'

'I do not think so, my Lord. The Sultan has no power now.'

'Is that what you believe?' Bagilat asks. 'He is the Sultan. He was great even before he enslaved Kalaon.'

When the old woman doesn't answer, Bagilat goes on, saying, 'I will have to prove it to you then. It is time for my heroes now. Have you heard their stories? No? I shall tell them to you. If you already know them, I shall tell the stories to you again because they are worth repeating. Centuries from now they will tell and retell the stories of these great men. They are etched in our memories and have become one with our being. How much poorer we would be if we forgot! And as long as we remember, we will have some of their greatness too. That lives on and never dies.'

The old woman says nothing and listens.

2

Lam-Ang

Lam-Ang traveled in the footsteps of his father, along the road that crosses the mountains and leads to the coast. After three days, he reached the Giant's Spine, and the road became a winding path that made its way up the mountains to the head-hunter's country.

After a day's climb, Lam-Ang reached a clearing and saw the tallest tree he had ever seen, one that dwarfed all others. That tree marked the border to the Igorot nation, and it was the largest balete tree in the sultanate. Like all of its kind, it had a hollow heart.

Lam-Ang rested for the night, and in his sleep, he was visited again by the ghost of his father. In the dream, they both sat inside the hollow of the great balete. The floor was littered with the bones of dead animals. The very top of the tree was open to the sky and through this opening, Lam-Ang could see the moon.

'Lam-Ang,' his father said, in a voice that Lam-Ang clearly remembered—strong, sonorous, made for song. 'Right now they feast around your father's skull.'

In an instant, Lam-Ang was transported to the Igorot village through a vision. He saw his father's killers celebrating beside a large bonfire. Beside the fire, lit by torches all around, were the heads of a hundred men impaled upon sticks. Lam-Ang saw the head of his father right away. It spoke to him.

'Lam-Ang!' it said. 'Make your revenge terrible. Your father demands it.' Now all the heads were speaking in unison. 'Your ancestors demand it. The price of blood is blood. Hurry. You are close now.'

Lam-Ang woke with a start. He reached for his machete and found it by his side. It was still dark. The moon had begun its descent on the other side of the sky. He stood up, got his campilan, his spear, and his kalasag, and headed towards the Igorot village. At daybreak, he reached his destination.

* * *

Lam-Ang stood in front of the village with twenty dead Igorot at his feet. They had been the first ones to hail him and question what he was doing there. Lam-Ang killed them without saying a word, working silently as if he were butchering pigs. Next came some men who were prepared for battle, enforcers of the local warlord. Lam-Ang killed them all as well, cracking their shields with his machete, and cutting off their heads. Now, all of the men in the village stood in front of him with their spears and long shields. They stood in a formation—ten groups of fifty men each, encircling Lam-Ang and advancing slowly.

'Is that all of you?' Lam-Ang taunted them. 'It will be a short day then. I have come here to find the Igorot armies who raid the villages along the Giant's Spine. Instead, I find this rabble.' Lam-Ang threw his machete to the ground and picked up his spear.

'How can I be satisfied with your number?' he continued to taunt them. 'Send your messengers to the other Igorot villages. I will fight you all. My quarrel is with all of you.'

As he said these words, he hurled his spear at the closest group. It impaled three Igorot warriors and knocked down all the others.

By the time the Igorot got to their feet, Lam-Ang pounced upon them, hacking and hewing with his campilan. Soon, all fifty warriors in that group lay dead before Lam-Ang.

The other Igorot launched their spears, which rained upon Lam-Ang. But he merely brushed them aside with his sword and caught the rest with his kalasag. Seeing this, the remaining Igorot stopped their advance and retreated to a safe distance. Lam-Ang saw a messenger run into the forest.

'Run!' He called out to him. 'Bring your allies. I am not satisfied by your number.'

* * *

It took half a day for the other tribes to arrive. They came from Dardaret and Padang, from their houses in Dagodong and Topaan, and from as far as Tabtab and Caocaoayan. They came and filled the plain to surround Lam-Ang. They assembled before Lam-Ang just out of spear range and their number was great beyond count.

A man, arms raised, his axe at his belt, approached Lam-Ang. He was the largest man Lam-Ang had ever seen, the half-breed son of an Igorot woman and a giant. He was twice the size of Lam-Ang, his axe was as long as Lam-Ang's height, and its head as broad as Lam-Ang's chest.

The man was heavily tattooed, like all the Igorot. His chest and arms were covered in black ink. Upon it were countless lines that ran from the bottom of his ribcage to his shoulders. Each line represented the life of an enemy taken to defend his tribe. The giant's chest was as wide as a hog is long and on its breadth were hundreds of these lines.

Lam-Ang stood up when the man was near. He drew his campilan, but did not hold it for battle. Instead, he placed the double-pronged tip into the ground and leaned on the sword with one arm, like an old man leaning on a staff.

'The time for words is over,' Lam-Ang said.

'If blood is what you want,' the man said, 'you shall have it. But the Igorot honour their enemies. Tell us your name and why you seek war with our great nation.'

In reply, Lam-Ang said, 'I am Lam-Ang of Nalbuan. Did you ask my father his name before you beheaded him? If so, I would ask your name before I take your head.'

The giant bristled at these words. 'Bumacas!' he said, his voice deep and proud. 'I am the chieftain of this tribe. If your father's head belongs to our tribe, then he should be grateful. It is a great honour.'

'Honour?' Lam-Ang spat. 'What foul thing did he do to deserve this honour?'

'I do not know who your father was. I only know that you should go home to Nalbuan, or your head will join his. You have spilled blood already. Be satisfied with that. If you are not satisfied, more Igorot will die, for yes, you are a skilled warrior, but our number is great and we will kill you. Then we will kill everyone in your village, Lam-Ang of Nalbuan.'

'No,' Lam-Ang said. 'It ends here. You will all die. There are not enough of you to satisfy my revenge.'

As Lam-Ang spoke these words, Bumacas reached for his great axe, but Lam-Ang was faster. Just as Bumacas swung his axe, Lam-Ang raised his campilan and leapt high into the air to avoid Bumacas' blow. In the same motion, Lam-Ang brought his sword down across the giant's neck.

Bumacas' head tumbled to the ground and landed at his feet. It rolled a short distance as the rest of Bumacas' body fell forward.

The Igorot charged and let loose their spears when they saw their leader fall. The spears fell upon Lam-Ang like rain. He embraced them all but none struck him.

Seeing how they had failed to hit him even once, the tattooed Igorots rushed forward like a black river. Soon, Lam-Ang was surrounded from all sides.

'Now comes my turn,' Lam-Ang said.

Lam-Ang beckoned to the south wind, and with it, lunged upon his enemies. He raised his campilan and struck. Left and right, he cut his foes in half. Nothing stood in the way of Lam-Ang's sword. Again, Lam-Ang rushed at the Igorot. Wave after wave, he cut them down. Each time he charged, there was the sound of thunder. Death lay in his wake.

They battled for days, but Lam-Ang did not tire. His sword arm never wearied. Night and day, he killed until there was only one Igorot left standing.

The last Igorot warrior rushed toward Lam-Ang, thinking death was coming, but Lam-Ang let him live.

Lam-Ang cut off the warrior's legs so that he could not run away, then he cut off his arms. The warrior cursed Lam-Ang as his killer got to his knees beside him.

'The gods will punish you for what you have done. Our allies will hunt you down and destroy you. They will skin you alive. They will eat your liver, and make you watch. They will rape your sisters and your mother before they kill them. They will burn down your village. They will make you pay, demon. The gods do not forget.'

Lam-Ang cut off the man's ears and tore out his eyes, saying, 'That your blood and your tribe may see you.'

After the battle, Lam-Ang walked back to the balete tree, and found the path back to Nalbuan. Meanwhile, the blood of the Igorot ran down the mountain. It seeped into the streams so that all the rivers in the land ran red for days.

Exhausted, Lam-Ang kept walking until he reached his home. On his return journey, he did not eat, nor did he sleep. He just walked— his campilan heavy in his hand, his shield unbroken. It was done.

* * *

Years passed and peace came to Nalbuan, but a restlessness came to Lam-Ang's spirit. His dreams were full of the Igorot that he killed. Their spirits haunted him, demanding payment for their slaughter. An oracle augured that he would pay for these deaths, along with countless more, at the end of his days, when the giant fish Berkakang the Old will swallow him whole and consume the hero's body for a thousand years.

It is said in other songs, that Lam-Ang journeyed to Sun Girna Ginar and became the champion of the sultanate, winning war after war with his mighty campilan and single-handedly bringing nations to their knees. In the great city, he married Cannoyan, a maiden of unrivalled beauty.

The singers tell of how Lam-Ang became the friend and ally of General Marandang until he gave up his campilan to pursue peace and trade with the king of Puan-Puan of China, like his father had before him. Other songs tell these tales. This one has come to an end, and will endure for as long as those who have heard it remember and retell it in their own words.

3

Tagkan

When Tagkan wakes up again, the moon is low in the sky and the horizon is brightening. It is almost daybreak. Once again, Tagkan is disoriented, this time because the moon is larger than he has ever seen it. Then, he remembers the betrayal of the tikbalang, and he sits up, his hand going to his side where he keeps his machete. Its hilt is reassuring in his hand.

Saragnayan is gone. Tagkan finds himself on a wide, dry plain, and he can see for miles in every direction. There is no sign of the tikbalang. The sigbin are gone too. A few feet from Tagkan is a sleeping form, Amtalaw, snoring gently. By the light of the moon, Tagkan can tell that he is scratched and bruised from his struggle with the tikbalang, but otherwise, he is well. Tagkan soon learns that the same can't be said about him. His knee is swollen. His arm is bleeding. When he looks closer, he sees that his arm bears the bite marks of a large beast, but the bleeding has stopped. He puts weight on his leg, and a sharp pain shoots up its length. After a moment, the pain subsides. Tagkan discovers that he can still walk.

Tagkan limps to Amtalaw's side and wakes him. At first, Amtalaw doesn't move, then he gets up with a start, kicking and screaming.

He pushes himself away from Tagkan but calms down when he sees Tagkan's face.

'Where is the tikbalang?' Amtalaw asks, a part of him still in that dream-like place between Skyworld and the earth.

'Gone,' Tagkan reassures him.

'He tricked us,' Amtalaw goes on. 'He attacked us. Where are we?'

'Skyworld. He brought us to Skyworld.'

'What? Why?'

'I don't know. But this is where he wants us to be. He took the sigbin, so we can't go to Sun Girna Ginar now. But he doesn't want us dead. He tended to our wounds.'

Amtalaw is confused for a few moments. He pieces Tagkan's words together and looks at him with admiration on his face.

'You are a very intelligent man to figure that all out so quickly. I am impressed.'

'There's one more thing.'

Amtalaw waits for Tagkan to speak.

'If Saragnayan went through all this trouble to bring us here, the question we have to ask ourselves is, what does he want us to do here?'

Amtalaw nods his head vigorously.

'You are right,' he says. 'And why couldn't he just ask us nicely? He could have killed us!'

'What do you think we should do now?' Tagkan asks Amtalaw.

'You are fortunate that I decided to come with you,' Amtalaw says. 'I know where we are. My lady's business has brought me to Skyworld a few times, and I recognize this place.'

'Then you know how we can get to Sun Girna Ginar.'

A mischievous look takes over Amtalaw's face as a thought occurs to him.

'Actually, I do know a way. But you won't like it.'

'Tell me anyway.'

'Do you see that mountain to the east?'

Tagkan nods.

'There, you will find many gods as well as my Lady's residence on this plane. You can take counsel with her again if you wish.'

Tagkan frowns as he looks at the mountains.

'The mountains must be many days away.'

Amtalaw squints. 'I'd place it at six days,' he says.

'Even if the sigbin brought us three days into the past as we had hoped, the giant will be at Sun Girna Ginar's gates long before we get to the gods' mountain.'

'There is another way.' Now Amtalaw smiles fully, showing more than a few gaps in his teeth. 'To the south is a marshland. Luckily, it is the direction we are going anyway. It is not far, half a day's travel at most. You can see the start of the bog along that line of trees over there. The land dips downwards from there, so you can't see anything more.

'Somewhere in that marsh is a dragon, the stone-skinned crocodile called Isarog. You are an intelligent man, so you must know that dragons fly and Isarog would have you at Sun Girna Ginar's gates faster than any stupid sigbin.'

'Now you are mocking me.'

Amtalaw raises his hands.

'I am only telling you what your options are. You said you want to go to Sun Girna Ginar. Well, these are the ways that you can get there.'

'Indeed. If we go to the mountains, we will fail to save Sun Girna Ginar. If we go to the marsh in search of the dragon, we will probably die.'

'Your intellect is like the sun, too bright to stare at . . . '

Tagkan grows annoyed but doesn't show it.

'Of course,' Amtalaw goes on, the sly look returning, 'all dragons have a weakness, and this one is no exception.'

'What is it?'

Amtalaw laughs, showing off his black, rotting teeth. 'Now you are being stupid, my friend,' he says. 'If I knew the great dragon's weakness, I wouldn't be an alipin, would I?' Then Amtalaw becomes serious. 'I do wish I knew. I do. It is a hard life being an alipin, no matter how kind your master is. Look where it has brought me today. And I don't want the city to be destroyed any more than you do. I have never been there, but I have heard it is beautiful.'

'Then the dragon is our only choice.'

'I knew you would say that,' Amtalaw replies. 'My master was right about you.' Amtalaw puts on a falsetto as he mimics the Witch Princess' voice. '"Amtalaw," she told me, "this timawa is just an ordinary freeman, but he has a noble spirit. He will always choose the right path. Be careful. Watch out for him. The right path is full of danger."'

'You can go to the mountain. You don't have to go with me. You are not my slave.'

'You can go to the mountain as well,' Amtalaw says. 'What makes you think the general needs your help? I'm sure he's capable of defending the city without you. Even I have heard of his deeds, and I am not from the city. I have heard of how he defended Sun Girna Ginar from the giants two hundred years ago, with an army of magical beasts and the gods of Skyworld. He rode into battle upon the back of a two-headed dragon covered in golden scales, wielding a spear that was forged from the metal of a star that had fallen to earth.

'What use has a man like that have of a man like you? I think you are a fine man, but the general can take care of himself. He killed dozens of giants in his day. He can handle this one, I am sure. I say, let's live to see another sunrise.'

Now it is Tagkan's turn to smile.

'You are right, Amtalaw,' he says. 'The general doesn't need me. Nothing I do matters.'

'Good, then let's go.'

'But Lady Gaygayuma is wrong. I am not a man of noble spirit. I lied to her.' Tagkan grows ashamed and looks at the ground. 'I told her that I did not seek revenge for the murder of my family. That was a lie. Of course, I want revenge.

'I am just a man with insignificant ancestors. If I were a slave, Amtalaw, you and I would have a lot in common. How can a man such as myself hope to kill giants? That is for other men.'

Tagkan smiles with regret, eyes still fixed on the ground.

'What you say about the general is true. He could probably kill the giant on his own. But even a great man like the general is not alone. He has lieutenants, foot soldiers, and slaves. I want to be a part of that, even if just as the man who will tell the general's army that the giant of

Gawi-Gawen is coming. And in that way, even a man with insignificant ancestors will have a role to play in killing the giant. I will be part of the songs.'

He looks at Amtalaw, and the alipin sees a kind of madness in Tagkan's eyes and a hunger for greatness.

'Saragnayan told me that one of my roads leads back to Sun Girna Ginar. I don't know what his reasons for betraying us were, but I believe he wanted me to find that road.

'I have nothing else but this, friend Amtalaw. That is why I am going to the dragon.'

Amtalaw stands up then and returns Tagkan's gaze. He is a full head shorter than Tagkan. He bows at Tagkan's feet like a slave. Then he stands up and grasps Tagkan's arm like a freeman.

Amtalaw says, 'Leave it to Bathala. He will guide your feet, your hands, your voice.'

Tagkan realizes that Amtalaw is praying.

'Here, take my amulet. My master made it. It will protect you. Maybe not against dragons but other things; you will be just fine. Take my machete too. It is better than yours.

'From here, you must travel south. The dragon's bog spreads wide so you cannot miss it. You should be at the bog's edge in a few hours.

'As for the dragon, I have little advice to give. Be polite. Dragons are as old as the earth, so they are worse than cranky old men. I was with my master when she spoke to one before. It was not pleasant.

'It will take more than asking nicely for the dragon to agree to take you to Sun Girna Ginar, so please, if you want to live, make Isarog a good offer. Beyond these useless vagaries, I am afraid I cannot help you more . . . '

Amtalaw's voice trails off and he shrugs.

Tagkan bows deeply to Amtalaw. 'Thank you,' he says. There is nothing more to say.

4

Lam-Ang and Adlao

'Remember, they are beasts,' the Sultan told Lam-Ang. 'They do not recognize the laws of man. They do not want peace. If you let them, they will break into your house and destroy everything, rape your wife, devour your children. They are animals, nothing more.'

Lam-Ang stands at the crossroad that leads to the Maharlika Quarter and remembers the Sultan's words. He watches the tide of people gather from all directions. They are beyond count—men, women, and children from the Slaves' Quarter mostly, but freemen too.

Lam-Ang's soldiers block the road. A battalion of shieldmen stands ready, waiting for his order to march forward. They are wearing armour made of hardened leather and steel helmets. Behind them are archers and cannons.

Seeing the soldiers, the crowd prepares to fight. They lock arms and walk forward in unison, taunting the soldiers to attack. Others create shields from pieces of wood. They arm themselves with their machetes and rocks and sticks.

Lam-Ang has fought many battles, but none like this. He has slaughtered a nation of head-hunters and clashed swords with berserkers of foreign armies. He has butchered countless giants, and demons from the underworld, winged, fanged, four-legged, or crawling on their bellies. He knows these people are not beasts.

Near the front of the crowd, he sees a man apart, leading the crowd, fist raised to the sky.

This is Datu Adlao, the Sultan's enemy, Lam-Ang thinks to himself. But he sees only a mirror of himself: a tired, middle-aged man who has fought too many battles, caught in one more, bound by duty and honour, and full of regret.

* * *

Adlao has always known how this would unfold, but seeing the soldiers lined against them, he begins to lose hope.

The golem with the face of Adlao has stopped. With the soldiers a hundred paces away, it has nowhere else to go. The people have stopped as well, forming a line opposite the shieldmen. Some hurl rocks into the soldiers' ranks.

The glint of sun on metal flashes. Adlao sees it in the crowd near the golem. *Not now,* he thinks. *Not now when I am so close.*

Adlao pushes closer to stop the man with the knife and is five feet away from the golem when he sees another flash of steel. It is a man carrying a diamond-shaped blade called a balarao.

Adlao shouts a warning, but it is too late. The golem is already surrounded by four of the Tyrant's assassins. More balarao flash in the sunlight and the golem is butchered on the streets before his own eyes. Some try to stop the assassins, but they are struck down too.

In an instant, the assassins are gone, lost in the crowd. The golem staggers for a few moments, blood flowing from its wounds, and then falls to the ground.

Someone shouts, 'Adlao is dead!' Fear ripples through the crowd.

Adlao hears commands being shouted to the soldiers on the front lines. He looks up and sees a volley of arrows raining down on the crowd. After the arrows fall, those who can still run abandon Datu

Adlao's rebellion as fast as their feet can carry them. The Sultan's shieldmen advance. The cannons fire.

* * *

Adlao runs until he reaches the market. There, the narrow winding alleyways stop the advance of the Tyrant's soldiers and give a chance for the surviving freemen and slaves to escape.

Adlao stops to catch his breath. He looks behind him and sees only other people running away. The soldiers are not chasing them anymore. He is safe.

Adlao is shaken. He doesn't know what to do or where to go. To his surprise, he finds that he is on a familiar street. By some coincidence, he is exactly where the old woman sold him the dream bottle with the golem. She is in the same spot he left her as if nothing has happened.

Adlao approaches the old woman's stall.

'Datu,' she says. 'I am glad to see you again.'

'Your magic saved my life,' Adlao says, struggling to breathe.

'And now you cannot die,' she says.

Adlao thinks the old woman's choice of words is strange.

'No, no,' Adlao shakes his head, still disbelieving the march of the golem and the sight of his own murder. 'The Tyrant thinks he has ended me, but I am still very much a mortal man.'

'No,' the old woman replies, sure of herself. 'Now you are more than a man. You are a martyr for your rebellion. You are an ideal for your followers.'

Adlao shakes his head again and desperately looks behind him for any sign of assassins. 'The Tyrant will find out. He will hunt me down.'

The old woman is filled with calm. 'No,' she says, 'you are beyond the reach of the Sultan. You cannot be killed again. You have won.'

'You do not understand,' he says, growing short. 'The rebellion is over!'

The old woman looks at him gently as if he were a child. 'No, my Datu. It is you who does not understand. You are beyond death. The Sultan cannot kill an idea. Your rebellion has just begun.'

5

Tagkan

Tagkan reaches the dragon's marsh a few hours after midday. His leg is giving him more trouble than he anticipated, and he is forced to stop a number of times to rest. The pain often becomes too much to bear.

The marsh is exactly where Amtalaw said it would be. First, the plain begins to slope downward ever so slightly. It becomes easier to walk, and Tagkan picks up the pace. Then the land becomes wetter. The earth darkens. Low plants appear, then trees. Green things grow everywhere. That is around the time when Tagkan begins to smell the marsh. The smell of rot fills the air. The earth turns to mud. The mud turns into a pond of scummy green water. The pond joins other ponds just like it. Insects swarm.

Tagkan continues forward. He stops when he comes to a lake.

Amtalaw said nothing about a lake, so Tagkan is unsure what to do. He can barely see the other side; it will take him a long time to go around.

In the middle of the lake, closer to the bank he is on right now, is an island. Nothing grows on the island, and the rocks steam gently, as hot springs do.

Tagkan sits down to rest and contemplates his next move. Three spotted deer walk out from behind a clump of burned-out trees, and

Tagkan watches a young doe approach the lake nervously, step back, return, then finally take a drink.

That is when the island moves. It moves forward so fast that it catches the doe before it can turn around to run. As it does, more of the island rises out of the water to reveal a giant reptilian head and the double-lidded eye of a crocodile.

It is the dragon Isarog. To Tagkan's terror, the dragon opens its long and terrible mouth. It is filled with teeth that are each longer than Tagkan's arms. In one bite, it swallows the doe, lifting its head to help the doe go down its gullet. Then, it exhales fire to incinerate the other two deer. They continue to run for about ten feet, engulfed in flames; then, they fall dead.

Tagkan watches all of this happen in the space of a few breaths. He is frozen in place, unable to move. Then, the dragon turns its massive head in his direction and sees him.

The dragon rises out of the water in a long, slow motion. Its head is massive. Its mouth alone is the size of two war boats turned in on each other. Twin ridges travel from above the dragon's eyes down its body to its tail, like a crocodile. It has little of a neck. From its head, sprouts a long, serpentine body, covered in scales that look like stone.

The dragon pulls itself out of the lake with two short arms. Half of its body is still submerged. Its tail rises out of the water and hangs in mid-air.

Isarog stares at Tagkan with yellow eyes. When the dragon opens its mouth, a laboured voice fills the air.

'You are a long way from your world, Human,' Isarog wheezes, as the ground trembles around it.

Tagkan tries but he cannot speak. He knows he must but fear has claimed him. His mouth is dry. His throat is constricted. He opens his mouth and finally, after too long a pause, some words come out.

'Oh, mighty Isarog,' Tagkan says, for he doesn't know what else to say. 'I am humbled by your majesty. Truly, you are the greatest of your kind.'

Steam begins to rise from Isarog's nostrils. 'Tell me, Human, what is your business with Isarog? I am curious why one as insignificant as you would be so brave. And foolish.' The ends of Isarog's mouth turn upwards, an expression Tagkan assumes is meant to be a smile.

Tagkan's mind races to find an answer. He has nothing to say. He has nothing to offer the dragon, nothing to trade, nothing to even amuse it, and nothing to coerce it. An idea sparks within Tagkan's mind, and he blurts it out before he can think it through.

'What makes you think I am a human?' Tagkan does his best to sound haughty. He is afraid that his voice is trembling. 'Do you not recognize a god when one stands before you?'

Isarog moves its head backwards ever so slightly, but it doesn't back down. More black smoke escapes from its mouth.

'You are trying to trick me. You reek of human.'

'But what if I am not? What if you are wrong?' Tagkan asks, and now he is just thinking aloud, trying to delay his death. 'What if, in your arrogance, you strike me down? What then? What would the gods on the mountain say? What would they do to you? What if I am just testing you?'

The dragon pauses before it replies, and Tagkan knows he has succeeded. He is not going to die just now. Maybe he will die a little later.

'Foolish human,' the dragon says. 'Isarog can tell truth from lies. A lie is easy to sense. I hear its pitch in my ears. I know its taste in my mouth. Sweet at first, always, then bitter.'

Tagkan's mind races. If this is true, he thinks to himself, then at least death at the hands of a dragon is swift. And yet, Tagkan thinks, he does not want to die. Maybe there is another way. Maybe creating doubt will be enough.

'I assure you, mighty Isarog. I speak the truth. But test me if you wish.'

Now the dragon rises out of the water completely, moving onto land with its short crocodile legs. It is immense, but it is fast, serpentine. Isarog turns to face Tagkan and lies on its belly. Again, there is an upturn of the corners of its mouth.

'Good. I like games,' Isarog says. 'It will make devouring you all the more delicious. If you lie even once, I will eat you where you stand.'

'Very well. You start. Ask me a question.'

The dragon's yellow eyes narrow.

'Do you come from the mountain?'

'No,' Tagkan says. 'I come from Sun Girna Ginar.' He shrugs inwardly and says more. 'Just the other day, I was there in the form of a human, but I travelled to the Giant's Spine on a whim, by magic. Now I am here in Skyworld. Must we go on with this game?'

'The gods live in Skyworld.'

'Some live in Sun Girna Ginar.'

'If you are a god, where are your alipin? Even the slaves of gods are powerful.'

'I have no more need for them,' Tagkan says. Then he takes a deep breath, and once again speaks a truth of sorts. 'The Witch Princess, Gaygayuma, and the tikbalang nation have conspired to bring me here. But now that they have served their purpose, I have sent them away. I do not care for their company.'

A rumbling sound comes from somewhere within the dragon, but Isarog says nothing more. Tagkan looks around at the mounds of rotting vegetation just under the lake's surface, at the wasteland that surrounds him, and he wonders what a creature as powerful as Isarog is doing here. It is at that moment that Tagkan realizes something.

The dragon is afraid of the gods of the mountain, Tagkan thinks to himself. *They have imprisoned him here.* All becomes clear. *It must have been here for aeons. Once, the dragon must have been mighty and beautiful, but over thousands of years, it has changed, taking the shape of the marsh, crawling on its belly, eating whatever it chances upon, fish, frogs in countless thousands, the occasional deer or traveller.* Suddenly, Tagkan pities Isarog. *This is no place for a creature of the sky. Isarog must be hungry.*

'What do you seek from Isarog?' the dragon asks.

Tagkan grows confident now. Still careful to speak the truth, he says, 'I have come here to purchase your freedom from the gods of the mountain.'

Isarog laughs, or at least the sound it makes is laughter. The dragon opens its mouth wide as it makes that sound, and for a moment, Tagkan thinks he is about to be eaten. He fights the urge to get on his knees and cower. With its mouth open, Isarog involuntarily releases spouts of flame that narrowly escape burning the man standing at his feet, pretending to be a god.

The dragon's laughter subsides. 'I will humour you. What would you want me to do for you, human, in exchange for ridding me of those cursed gods?'

'I would give the mighty Isarog a feast. A feast of giants. They march towards Sun Girna Ginar as we speak.'

Now the dragon becomes serious.

'Yesssss,' Isarog says, 'such a feast would sate my hunger. I have not gorged on the flesh of giants for centuries. You tell pretty lies.'

The dragon pauses.

'Very well, I have but one more question to ask you,' Isarog says. 'If you lie, I will take your life. If you are what I think you are—a human—and you tell the truth, I will take your life.

'Now tell me: are you a god?'

Tagkan almost doesn't hear Isarog's question. Just moments before, Tagkan realizes that everything he has said to the dragon is true. Everything about his incredible journey and the aid of others is all true. And that is when he discovers why the Witch Princess helped him. That is when it becomes clear what Saragnayan wanted from him from the start.

At that moment, Tagkan realizes who he is, and who he is destined to be. And knowing that, he is no longer afraid. The dragon has no power over him.

'Am I a god?' Tagkan says, repeating the dragon's question. 'No. I am just a man. But I am greater than your gods.'

* * *

When Tagkan arrives at Sun Girna Ginar on the dragon's back, the giants can be seen on the horizon marching towards the city. Tagkan looks at the giants with interest. There are more than twenty of them, each the size of a hill. None of them are the six-headed giant of Gawi-Gawen.

'There is your feast, Isarog,' he says and the dragon roars in reply.

Tagkan remembers walking under Sun Girna Ginar's Bone Gate. It was swarming with people and caravans heavy with goods stretched from the gate for miles. Now the gate is closed, and the bones that herald entry into Sun Girna Ginar are nowhere to be found. Only one thing stands before the gate, the tikbalang, Saragnayan. Everyone else has fled behind the walls upon seeing the shape of Isarog flying in the sky like a snake swimming through water.

The dragon lands in front of the gate and Tagkan calls out to the tikbalang.

'Saragnayan,' Tagkan commands. 'Come to me.'

The tikbalang walks to the dragon, its face impassive but its manner questioning.

'Do you know me?' Tagkan asks the tikbalang.

The creature shakes its head, and Tagkan smiles to himself. After the absence of the giant of Gawi-Gawen, this is the second proof that he is right.

'All the roads of my life lead to this place, this time,' Saragnayan says. 'So I am here. Who are you?'

Tagkan stands on the back of the dragon and says, 'I am General Marandang, commander of Sun Girna Ginar's armies, destroyer of cities, conqueror of this world and Skyworld, godslayer.'

Tagkan laughs to himself.

'Or, that is what they will call me one day, many years hence, if this road leads where I think it does. On that road, Saragnayan, many, many years from now, you will meet a man burying his family after his village is destroyed by a giant. He will try to go to Sun Girna Ginar to warn the city of the giants' return. You will tell him that you will help him, but you will not bring him to Sun Girna Ginar.

'Instead, you will lead him with all your cunning to Skyworld, to the plains between the mountain of the gods and the swamp of Isarog. You will do this when you ride with the man on the back of sigbin, between our two worlds, on lightning. You will lead him two hundred years into the past, to the day before this one.

'The man's name is Tagkan, an ordinary man without powerful ancestors. But one day, he will become great, when he understands who he is.

'You cannot tell him who he will become, for he will not believe you. He must realize it himself. Do you understand my words, Saragnayan?'

The tikbalang nods its horse-like head.

'Yes,' it says after some thought. 'That road is the best for all. But there is a price.'

'Ask your price, and I will give you an answer.'

'Years hence, Sun Girna Ginar's armies will climb to Skyworld and challenge the gods themselves. On your way, you will pass through the tikbalang nation. Spare us, and I will be your servant.'

Tagkan understands now. He comprehends the role Saragnayan played—or will play—in his journey. He understands his own destiny, and he welcomes it.

'It is done, Saragnayan. You have already upheld your side of the bargain.'

The general turns the dragon towards the Bone Gate.

'Guards!' he calls out. 'Put your weapons down. I am here to aid you. I have come to destroy the giants. I have come to save the city.' Then he commands them, 'Let me pass. I wish to speak with the Sultan.'

No reply is made, but commands are shouted from the walls and the guards move aside to let Isarog pass. General Marandang enters his city like a returning god.

Part IV: The Last Sultan

My name is Imugan. *She repeats this to herself every night. She says it aloud, careful not to speak above a whisper. They might hear her. Imugan. The name already feels strange on her lips.*

They call her by another name now. Menalam. It is not as strange as Imugan. She hears it often. She says it is her name when she meets someone new.

'They' are her new family, the ones who take care of her now, her new mother, and her new father. Having a father too is strange to Imugan. She has never had one before. He is kind to her. He gives her things and carries her on his shoulders, but she is uncomfortable when he touches her. Then there are her new brothers. Others call them Vizier Humadapnon, Sultan, and Datu Adlao. They insist that she call them 'big brother'. And she does. They tell her stories about who they are, who she is, and their dreams for the city. But every night, when she is alone, she repeats her story to herself—the real one, not the made-up one her big brothers tell her.

My name is Imugan. *Her mother—her real mother—told her that the name means 'charm'. She often joked that charm was the one virtue Imugan lacked. She is headstrong and defiant, like her father, mother said. Imugan never knew her father. He came from Skyworld and returned to the gods after she was born. Imugan grew up alone with her mother in a fishing village just outside the walls of Sun Girna Ginar.*

Like her mother, Imugan is a witch. Her mother taught her the craft. She taught Imugan how to see into the spirit world. She taught her to speak the language of the gods and the demons. She taught her how to make potions, cast curses, and give blessings. Imugan learnt a great deal. She was happy then.

Imugan would rather forget the rest of her story. She fights the feeling and forces herself to remember how the Sultan's soldiers came to her village in the middle of the night, looking for her. 'Where is the daughter of the witch?' the soldiers demanded. Imugan clung to her mother as they broke the door down.

'Don't be afraid,' mother said, but her voice was shaking.

The soldiers burst into the house and pulled the mother and daughter apart. Imugan had never seen soldiers before. They were dressed in steel armour that caught the golden torchlight. In their hands, they carried terrible weapons she never knew existed.

One soldier dragged Imugan away while another soldier slid a kris sword through her mother. It was Imugan's first time seeing such a sword, and she remembers thinking that its cruel, sinuous blade looked like a metal snake.

She wanted to jump into her mother's arms, cover her wounds with her hands and say the healing words, but the soldiers carried Imugan away as quickly as they had taken everything from her. She never saw her mother again.

The soldiers burnt down the village after they took Imugan away. She could see the fire lighting the night as they rode on horseback into the city.

The next morning, 'they' were all there. Her new mother said she had just dreamt the whole thing. She had always been here in the Sultan's palace. This was her home. None of that had happened. It was just a bad dream, they said. And bad dreams are best forgotten, isn't that what they always told her? They called her Menalam.

She knew they were lying. She could see the hunger in their eyes. They wanted something from her, she didn't know what. Until she found out, she knew she had no choice but to play along. There were times she fought, hid, and tried to escape from all the strange, new, kind people. But as the months passed, she accepted the fact that there was nothing more for her than this. She forced herself to smile at her new mother and father. She spent time with her big brothers and did what they asked. She let them call her Menalam. She learnt to answer to that name. Over the years, her memories became hazy and she began to doubt herself. But she never forgot.

'My name is Imugan,' she said to the darkness, to the air. 'My name is Imugan.'

1

Yumina

The Sultan's daughter looks at the city from her tower in the palace. It is night, but the city is full of lights. From her place on the balcony, the city lights below look like a sea of stars. She thinks to herself, *I am surrounded by stars from above and below, suspended by a single wish.*

Her nanny calls out, 'Yumina, come to bed now.'

'In a moment,' she replies. She does not move.

Yumina is not fooled by the city's tranquillity. Each light, she knows, belongs to a life. The yellow light by the gate, she muses, belongs to a poor guard who misses his family. She imagines that the soft glow she can barely see on a street in the Maharlika Quarter is the lamp of a man waiting to meet his lover in secret. The many-coloured lights in the Artists' Quarter are a drug-induced hallucination. The bright red bonfire in the market is a demon of greed. The silent blue flames lining the city walls are the spirits of her ancestors.

Again, the princess' nanny calls out, 'Yumina, come inside.'

With one last look over her shoulder, Yumina steps inside, leaving the city lights to their mysterious lives. She fears she will never know them.

'Look at you!' the nanny cries out, 'All goosebumps! And so pale!' She wraps the young girl in her fleshy arms and rubs the princess' arms with her hands. 'And so scrawny!'

'I'm all right,' the princess says, disentangling herself from her nanny's arms. 'I am going to bed now,' the princess proclaims. She sits down on her bed and waits for her nanny to leave.

'Of course dear, of course,' the nanny replies, and prepares to leave the room, putting everything in order on her way out. Before she closes the door behind her, she says, 'Oh, I almost forgot, there is a gift for you by your bedside, I don't know from whom.'

'Thank you. Good night.'

With her nanny gone from the room, the princess sighs and rises to extinguish the lamps by her bedside. She has handmaidens for this, but she prefers to be alone before she sleeps. She blows the lamps out almost in a ritual, lifting the glass covers of each lamp, inhaling with her eyes closed, and then letting out a gentle breath from parted lips.

She is tired, tired of living in the palace, of court intrigues, of audiences with foreign kings, of endless ceremonies. She is tired of the trappings of royalty, the dresses, the jewellery, the escort of soldiers, and the burden of tradition.

Before she turns out the last lamp, Yumina sees the gift her nanny was talking about, sitting beside a lamp on a low table. The gift is wrapped in golden paper, which she tears away. Inside is a plain wooden box. She opens the box and a fragile glass thing catches the lamp's light. In turn, Yumina catches her breath, for it is exquisite. It is some sort of crystal dome inset with diamonds and filled with delicate engravings of stars.

She searches for some clue as to where the gift could have come from, but she finds nothing. The princess sits on her bed, wondering which of her suitors could have sent the gift. She concludes that it is none of them, for none of them know the language of silence.

Yumina turns the thing over in her hands and discovers there is space underneath the dome for a lamp—possibly it was even made for one—so she places the dome on top of the last burning lamp. As she does so, the light in the room becomes muted, like the cold blue light of the night sky. She looks up to discover that her canopy is suddenly covered with stars.

She lays down on the bed, caught in the spell of the stars. Somehow, they are brighter than the stars outside, truer. Then she discovers that if she stares at a single star, its light grows and grows as if she is rushing towards it at incredible speed until the star becomes the image of a person. And she sees this image as if she is looking through a powerful spyglass.

When she looks at another star, it too becomes a person, and the previous star recedes. *They are the people of Sun Girna Ginar,* Yumina tells herself. *I want to know them. I want to escape from the palace and become one of them.*

That night, Yumina sees thousands of people this way. She watches a young couple making love by lamplight, a kulintang player practicing his art, and an old woman praying. She sees a courtesan preparing to escape from the palace, an assassin trying to break in. She sees a soldier who stands on the wall. She knows him.

Slowly, she drifts off to sleep and dreams. In one dream, she is running through the palace, through a series of doors marked with eight-pointed stars, lost within a labyrinth deep below the palace that leads outside into a new and beautiful, uncertain world.

2

Lumawig

The soldier watches the princess from the battlements of the Sultan's palace. Lumawig sees her, as he does almost every night, standing at the very edge of her balcony as if she is about to jump. Sometimes, she sits without fear on the balcony's railing, but not tonight. Tonight, she is deep in thought. He watches her in reverence as the wind toys with her long hair. He longs to be the wind, but he knows the Sultan would have the wind beheaded for this simple act. After all, touching the princess is a crime punishable by death.

Lumawig longs to speak to her, to call out to her from the battlements. That too would cost him his life, he knows, but he is not afraid. Even then, he keeps his silence, simply because he doesn't know what he would say to her. He reminds himself that he is only a soldier, no better than an alipin, and something of a fool.

The princess steps inside, and after a while, the lights in her quarters go out one by one. Then the soft yellow lamplight is replaced by a faint blue glow.

The soldier's heart quickens. *The slave gave the gift after all.* He had bribed a slave in the palace to deliver his gift to the princess, but he was never sure she would do it.

A smile makes its way upon his hardened face. There is no mistaking it now. He can see the stars released by the lamplight, just as the old woman described it. The princess received his gift.

In the afternoon he bought the gift, the old woman who sold it to him told him, 'I will give you two dreams for the price of one, young man: one dream for your lady friend and one for you.'

The soldier laughed. He had a powerful voice, well-suited for giving commands though he only took them. 'How did you know?'

'It's in your eyes,' she replied. 'I see hope and love and fear.'

'And what would you suggest for her?' Lumawig asked, looking at the bottles and trinkets, doubting any of the baubles would do.

'Ah, for such a princess, none of these things will suffice.' She dismissed the bottles in front of her with a wave of a withered hand. Lumawig was surprised by the old woman's choice of words, but he told himself that she was only teasing him. 'Princess' was a common enough endearment.

'Such a woman should have a dream without compare, a powerful dream.' The old woman searched among the things heaped carelessly about her stall and brought out a box. She opened the box, muttered to herself, 'Yes, this is the one,' and presented it to the soldier with a small bow.

Inside was a wonder of crystal, a fragile dome engraved by master craftsmen with stars. In the late afternoon light, it seemed to be on fire. 'When you place a lamp in it,' the old woman said, 'the crystal refracts the light. And it will fill the ceiling with stars. You will be the first man to actually give his woman the stars, eh?' The old woman chuckled.

She told him more. 'If your princess lights it by her bedside at night, allowing it to burn as she sleeps, it will turn her dreams into reality.'

Lumawig watched the fire in the crystal and he knew that the woman wasn't making fun of him. He was holding a priceless treasure in his hands. Somehow she knew he meant to give the gift to the Sultan's daughter.

'I cannot afford it,' he told the old woman.

The old woman shrugged.

'I think you can,' she said. 'The price is only everything you have now.'

The soldier looked at the old woman and saw that she meant what she said. She also knew he would not refuse.

The old woman nodded and took another package from inside her stall. 'This is for you,' she said. With both hands, Lumawig took the package, which was covered in coarse paper. His hands were rough and calloused, but he knew instantly what was inside. It was a knife.

'Take the glass knife,' the old woman said, miming what she wanted him to do, 'and cut your arm. The hilt is made of glass too, and inside is a potion. Break it and let the potion inside mix with your blood.'

'Like a blood compact.'

'Yes, exactly.'

'Then your dream shall be yours. And who knows? Maybe you and your princess will dream of the same thing.'

Beneath the window filled with stars, the soldier takes out the glass knife and cuts his arm in one swift motion. Being familiar with pain, he makes no sound as the dark blood pours from the wound.

Lumawig breaks the hilt of the glass knife, and from it flows a fluid the colour of blood. He mixes it with his own blood as the old woman told him to.

The potion spreads through his body quickly, burning like fire. When it reaches his heart, Lumawig doubles over in pain. He falls to his knees, holding a scream inside. His brain fills with pain, but his only thought is of Princess Yumina. It is his last thought before his heart stops.

3

The Sultan

'You are the greatest Sultan the world will ever know,' the old woman greets him, kneeling on the floor of the Great Hall. One hundred and forty-four steps above her, the Sultan sits on the Sky Throne.

The singers say that the Sultan's Great Hall is so large that a mountain can fit inside it, and the lantern that hangs from its vast ceiling contains the fire of the sun. This is not true of course, but still, the hall is large enough to fit the hundreds of Maharlika who hold court there, an equal number of ministers required to keep the sultanate running, along with thousands of soldiers to guard them all. Great doors open on one side of the hall, and these face the Sky Throne where the Sultan rules above all.

The old woman's palms are on the ground, her eyes are pointed at the ground, and her face is averted. This is the custom.

Seeing the old woman, the Sultan wants to hold the old woman's face between his hands and look into her eyes. She looks familiar to him somehow, but the memory is an old one. He does not trust old memories.

The Sultan has summoned the old woman because it is clear to him and his witches that the old woman who sold dreams in the market was working a powerful kind of magic. He wants to know if she is an enemy.

'You say that as if I will be the last Sultan,' he says in jest. The Maharlika and the ministers in the assembly laugh in unison. It is known that the sultanate will last until the end of time.

'No, my Lord,' the old woman says, 'you will not be the last.' She does not say more. The Maharlika look uncomfortable in the silence that follows.

The Sultan looks at the old woman's bent form for clues about her. She is dressed in a brown tunic, like a beggar. On her feet are old, worn sandals. She has no jewellery or anting-anting around her neck or wrists. From what he can see, there are no tattoos, runes, or wards on her skin.

'Where are you from?'

'I have the pleasure of being born in your great city, my Lord.'

'And where did you learn your craft?'

'My mother was a witch, my Lord. She taught me the craft when I was a child.'

'And your father?'

'My mother said he was a stranger who descended from Skyworld,' she says. For the briefest of moments, she raises her eyes and looks straight at the Sultan. Then she lowers her eyes again before anyone takes notice. Without pausing, she goes on, 'But I don't believe her. Countless women have told that lie to their bastards.'

The Sultan smiles. Few see it.

'My people tell me that there is an old woman in the bazaar who can make their dreams come true. Now I have heard this lie many times before. There is always some magician claiming to be able to cure their ills or some conjurer with love potions made of honeyed sewer water. Are you one of those liars?'

'I am just an old witch, my Lord,' she replies.

'Ah, then you have true power,' the Sultan says. 'You see, I know a little about these things. From what I know, and from what my learned magicians tell me, you would have to be a powerful witch indeed to grant the wishes of thousands.'

'I am happy my Lord is so knowledgeable,' the old woman says. 'I will not have to explain to him that that is not how it works.

The magic is not mine. It resides in each of us. I merely unlock the cage, and let the magic out.'

'That is still a difficult kind of magic nonetheless. You are no ordinary witch.'

'I'm afraid my Lord misunderstood me. I said I am not powerful, but I did not say I am unskilled. I have been a witch for a very long time.'

A silence passes between the Sultan and the old woman as he weighs her words.

'What do you seek to gain?' the Sultan asks.

'Nothing,' she replies. 'I am old. I am close to death. There is no longer anything to gain. There are only things to be lost, things to be left behind.'

'Why are you doing this then? What do you seek to achieve? What are you trying to leave behind?'

The old woman shrugs.

'It makes me happy to see people get what they want,' she begins, then frowns, and then says. 'It amuses me to watch them waste their lives on what they think matters. I do not know. I am not sure why I do what I do. If I dared, I might ask my Lord a similar question. Why did you create this city? This nation? What would you answer? I do not know. I would not dare to ask. How does anyone answer such questions? I do not know. I am just an old woman and a witch. This is what I do. You are a man, older than I, ruler of the world. You must have found more answers than I. I have few, and they are not worth much.'

The Sultan remains silent. The soldiers beside the old woman prepare for the order to strike her down for her insolence, but no order comes.

'Sell me one of your dream bottles, woman,' the Sultan says.

At an unseen command, a dozen soldiers carry the old woman's stall into the Great Hall. It takes them minutes to walk from the entrance to where the old woman stands. Four of them carry the wooden stall itself. One of them brings the old woman's stool. The others carry the old woman's stock of glass bottles in seven chests that sing like wind chimes as they cross the distance from the hall's great doors to where the old woman is kneeling.

The old woman stands up. She is bent at the waist and looks like she needs a walking stick, but she has none. She hobbles to her stall and rummages among the boxes until she finds what she is looking for, then she returns to her place at the foot of the stairs, and kneels. She places a small bottle with a black liquid inside in front of her, like an offering. Once again, she bows and averts her face.

'A gift for my Lord,' she says.

'What is it?' the Sultan asks. He cannot see it from where he is sitting on the throne.

'A trinket, my Lord. I am afraid it is quite insignificant. It is just a crystal inkwell, a memento of our meeting. What else is one supposed to give to the ruler of the world?'

As she speaks, a minister picks up the inkwell and walks up the steps to where a dozen or so other ministers are gathered. They inspect the item and debate about it in hushed tones for a minute. Upon reaching a consensus, they hand it over to one of the Sultan's magicians, who climbs more steps and delivers it to a group of bearded men who examine the inkwell under magnifying glasses and coloured lights while muttering incantations under their breath. When they are satisfied, they hand the inkwell to a member of the Maharlika, who climbs the final steps that lead to the Sky Throne. He climbs the last twelve steps on his knees. He bows down at the Sultan's feet while raising his arms to offer the inkwell to the Sultan, who takes it between two manicured fingers.

'My Lord,' the old woman says, 'may it grant you the power to turn your will into reality.'

At this, one of the magicians gets on his knees to address the Sultan. 'The inkwell is enchanted, my Lord,' he says. 'What the old woman says is true. With it, you could choose to do any number of miraculous things. You could redraw the map of the world. Or sentence your enemies to death. And these things would happen, become truth. It is a very powerful enchantment.'

The Sultan looks at the inkwell, holding it at arm's length.

'What would I do with such a thing?' he asks to no one in particular. 'I already possess this power.'

No one answers. After a few moments, the old woman speaks.

'If used that way, my Lord, then yes, it is true. You have no use for it. But there are other ways to use it.'

'Tell me.'

'To tell stories.'

'Stories? And of what use would these stories be?'

'Why, my Lord, a great many things. Stories begin as truths, though they resemble lies, and they grow to become much greater. They birth new ideas into the world. They teach us who we are, and what we desire. They give power to the powerless. They free the imprisoned mind. They break the boundaries of what is possible. They turn mortal men into gods. And stories live forever.'

* * *

Alone in his sanctum, the Sultan thinks of his audience with the old woman. She was talking about him, he realizes now. And in his arrogance, he refused to see. How did she know? When did she realize that he was trapped and powerless?

From below his tower, somewhere in the city, a muezzin calls out the hour in a single line of song. The Sultan hears him and knows it is time to attend to his duties. He does not move. For a few moments, he sits still, not breathing, as if he were a statue of himself carved in stone, or a monument to stand watch over his own grave.

He opens his eyes. Without haste, he reaches for a quill with one hand. With the other hand he opens the crystal inkwell the old woman gave him, then dips the quill into the black liquid. He half expects something to happen—a flash of light filling the room or fire erupting from the quill—but nothing does. It is only ink. Its stink is familiar to him.

With his free hand, he grabs a clean piece of parchment paper. He exhales.

The Sultan writes:

There was once a Sultan who ruled over the earth below and the Skyworld above. He was the greatest Sultan the world had ever known, and the people believed that he was a god.

The Sultan was old and tired. He possessed the world, only to find that it could not be owned. He achieved immortality, only to discover that he longed for death. One night, in his despair, he promised to give the sultanate to any man who could give him this death. His killer would be the new Sultan. This is the will of the Sultan, the living god, long may he reign.

4

Adlao, Magat, Asuang

Adlao and Magat sit in a dark corner of the longhouse waiting for Asuang. They are safe from the Sultan here. The longhouse belongs to opium traders and slavers, and the vizier turns a blind eye to their business. Like all longhouses, this too has a large hall that stretches from one end of the building to the other. From the hall, there are rooms where families live. In the common area, open to the night outside, lanterns are lit low as other men come and go, chewing betel nut, drinking tuba, and talking in low voices.

The two of them have been there for almost an hour now. Adlao drinks nothing, only sits there in his stiff way. Occasionally he looks around the room, scanning every face. As the minutes pass, he begins to scowl. A nervous tick along the corner of his eye begins to twitch. Magat scratches his arm where it is amputated above the wrist. Unlike Adlao, he looks disinterested. He drinks tuba alone.

With a shake of his head, Adlao gets up to leave. Magat follows him. As they step outside, a small man walks from the darkness to where Adlao is waiting for Magat. His face is hidden.

'Come with me,' the man says.

'Who are you?'

The man doesn't answer his question. He replies with a question of his own, 'Did you ask to see me or not?'

Adlao laughs. 'You can't be Asuang,' he says.

'Then maybe I am not.' He walks away. Adlao loses sight of him in the darkness.

Adlao searches for the man and calls out, 'Wait!'

The man steps out of the darkness and motions to Adlao and Magat to follow him.

'We will speak only to Asuang,' Adlao says to the man's back.

The man continues to walk at a brisk pace, not once looking behind him. 'That is one of my names,' he says.

'Forgive me,' Adlao says warily, 'but we need assurances. I must ask you for some proof that you are Asuang.'

'And how do you suggest I prove that?'

Adlao hesitates then says, 'They say that Asuang killed Vizier Humadapnon. If you are Asuang—and only Asuang could have killed the vizier—then tell me, how many locks are there on the door to his quarters?'

Asuang replies, 'Only one. To open it I needed the golden key that hung from the vizier's neck. I also needed to whisper a secret into the keyhole, the vizier's secret.'

'You are Asuang,' Adlao says.

Asuang continues, 'The vizier wept like a woman when I killed him. He begged me not to take his life. I slit his throat and still, he continued to beg. Some men do not know when it is over.

'Now, no more tests. You know who I am. I know who you are. Your name is Datu Adlao. Once, you were the right hand of the Sultan himself. You returned from exile, and the Sultan had you killed. Yet, somehow, you are still alive.

'Your name is Magat,' he said to the one-armed man. 'You left Adlao's hideout this afternoon, and you went to the market to purchase items for a bomb you are building, disguised as the lantern in the Sultan's Great Hall. One of the Sultan's men followed you there, and you did not see him. I killed him with a kitchen knife from the knife sharpener's stall.'

Magat betrays no emotion, but his hand goes to the hilt of his knife.

Asuang says, 'I could kill the two of you as easily as I killed that man, but I won't. Instead, I will tell you why I will help you.' He pauses. 'I want the Sultan to die at my hands. Now give me what you promised. Tell me how to get inside the Sultan's tower and defeat Kalaon.'

Asuang stops walking. Without moving, he begins to disappear into the darkness. All that's left are his eyes, black on white.

'Kalaon is already free,' Adlao says to the night. 'You don't have to worry about the enslaved god.'

'And the Sultan's tower?'

'Promise me you will succeed,' Adlao says.

'The Sultan will die, old man,' the night replies.

Adlao nods, and Magat tells Asuang the secret he learned from Aya, 'On the wall of the palace that faces Bathala's temple is a mark the size of your hand: an eight-pointed star. Breathe onto the star and a door will open. The door leads into a labyrinth beneath the palace.'

5

Magat

Magat spends the next few days waiting for the signal. After Aya left for the last time, he decided it would be safer to live somewhere else and moved to a borrowed room on top of a smithy.

Most days he sits by the room's only window, looking out at a piece of sky. It is a small window placed high on the wall. From his chair, he can't see the street below, but he can see many other things: processions of clouds, the towers of the palace, and the mid-afternoon sun. There, on his chair, he looks, and he listens for the signal as the bellows in the back of the smithy breathe fire and the blacksmiths hammer on metal with the sound of warring armies.

In the Great Hall of the Sultan, the lantern awaits. Inside it is a bomb made of gunpowder and oil, but also a demon of fire. When released, the demon will grow with everything it consumes until the entire palace is destroyed.

It took many months of work to create the bomb, infiltrate the palace, and place it, in secret, in the lantern in the Great Hall. And soon its time will come. The bomb must be triggered through witchcraft by lighting a small replica of the lantern itself, which now hangs from the ceiling in Magat's room.

The replica of the lantern is always ready. The golden yellow ball hangs from a long chain at eye level so Magat can reach it easily. He always keeps a candle lit on a nearby table. His few belongings are scattered on the same table: a knife, some clothes, the ampoule he bought from the old woman.

'It will give you what your heart desires,' the old woman said to him.

'But I don't know what my heart desires,' he argued, thinking the woman was just making promises to make a sale.

'It doesn't matter what you know,' she replied. 'This will give you what your heart desires.'

Magat awakes from his reverie and looks outside the window again. He doesn't know what he is waiting for. Perhaps there will be a sign in the sky or a signal fire by night. Or, maybe he will hear a code tapped out on the wall by an enchanted bird. Magat has no way of knowing what it will be, so he is constantly on the lookout for signs.

The only thing Adlao told him is: 'You will know that we have won.'

Magat sees signs everywhere. He listens to the musical agong bringing news from all over the sultanate and deciphers hidden secrets where there are none.

On his walks, Magat thinks he sees Aya sometimes. Once, he called out to her and ran after her, but he was mistaken. She didn't even look like Aya.

When he sleeps, he dreams of her. But there are other dreams as well. In one, he is in Sun Girna Ginar from a distant time, many generations from now. In this version of Sun Girna Ginar, the city gleams like silver, with metal and glass towers and chariots in the sky. Up close, nothing has changed. A different tyrant rules over the land. The Maharlika are there as well, feasting on the suffering of the freemen and the slaves. The alipin have multiplied in number. They cover the city like a plague.

Adlao is in this dream as well.

'It's our fault, Magat,' he says.

'Why?' Magat asks. 'We didn't do this to these people. They made their own tyrants.'

'You could have ended it,' Adlao says. 'But you didn't.'

Magat wakes up and sees the moon framed in his little window. For a moment, he wonders if this—his dream, and the moon in the window—is the signal. He doesn't fall asleep again until sunrise.

* * *

When the signal finally arrives, Magat hesitates.

There is no mistaking it. The first shot is so loud that Magat thinks the house is collapsing. He falls out of his chair and scurries under the table. Then, he realizes that it is a cannon, but louder than any cannon he has heard before, save for one. It is the God Cannon.

Since the general turned away the giants two hundred years ago, the God Cannon has been fired only for ceremonial reasons: once when the Sultan takes a wife, twice when a new Sultan is crowned, and thrice when the Sultan dies.

Another shot shakes the earth, and Magat waits. He knows it is coming. He holds his breath. The third shot follows soon after. There are cries of 'The Sultan is dead!' on the streets.

Magat knows he has received the sign.

He gets to his feet and steadies himself. With one hand, he grabs the candle on the table. With one simple move, he can light the lantern and trigger the magic that will make the lantern in the Sultan's Great Hall explode. With one motion, he can kill all of the Sultan's allies. With one gesture, he can set the people free.

But Magat cannot do it. He places the candle back on the table.

He doesn't know why he can't light the lantern. He only knows that he can't let everyone in the Great Hall die. He agreed with Adlao that the Maharlika, the ministers, and everyone in the palace must die. But now, faced with their deaths, he cannot do it. He keeps seeing Aya in his mind's eye.

He imagines the people in the hall burning in the firestorm unleashed by the cursed lantern. He sees the Sultan's children burning beside corrupt ministers and the palace guard, all howling as their hair burns away, their skin blisters, and their blood begins to boil.

In his head, Magat hears Adlao chastising him. 'We have failed.' He imagines Adlao saying, 'We were supposed to do this for the people and their children, that they may live in a world where there are no tyrants and no slaves.'

The children will create their own world, Magat says to himself as if replying to Adlao. *They are the hope for the future, not this instrument of death.*

Magat's eye catches the ampoule he bought from the old woman sitting on the table, and he decides to use it.

'Now,' he says to himself, 'now I know what my heart desires.'

Magat grabs the ampoule and throws it against the hardwood floor. It breaks immediately and releases its dark liquid. The liquid evaporates and fills the small room with a sharp smell. It is some kind of gas, Magat realizes. It is his last thought as the gas catches the fire from the candle and explodes. The whole room is engulfed in flame. The lantern is lit.

6

The Sultan and Asuang

'The witch's magic works fast,' the Sultan greets Asuang.

The Sultan looks at the man who has just entered his sanctum. The man is small and lean, but there is a deadly look in his eyes. His clothes belong to one of the palace servants, and a dark red stain emblazons his shirt. It is not his own blood. In his hands, he holds a small knife. He says nothing.

The assassin contemplates the Sultan's words but says nothing. He considers the old man still sitting in his chair. He doesn't recognize the Sultan, but he knows it is him.

Stripped of his lies, the Sultan is grotesque. His obese body is full of rot, bulging with cancers. His skin is a sick grey colour, covered in pustules. And even the tip of his bloated, pockmarked nose is rotting.

'You know I could stop you,' the Sultan says with the confidence of kings and puts down the quill in his hands. His fingers are blackened, and the tips of some have fallen off.

The assassin says nothing.

'These walls have ears, you see,' the Sultan goes on. 'It is an enchantment that came at no small cost. All I have to do is speak one word and fire will engulf everything in this room except me.'

Asuang smiles at the threat and decides to speak. His voice is low and menacing, not suited to his stature.

'Perhaps my knife is faster than your words.'

The Sultan shrugs. 'Perhaps,' he says in return. 'And yet that word escaped. As have these.'

Something crosses the assassin's face. Amusement? There is almost the hint of a smile. *He is not afraid,* the Sultan thinks. *He is confident he can kill me.*

When the assassin doesn't reply, the Sultan goes on, saying, 'If you think that is the only enchantment that protects me, then you are gravely mistaken.'

'Kalaon is no longer under your control,' Asuang says.

The Sultan raises an eyebrow.

'If you summon him, he will not come to your aid.'

'The witch's magic is quick indeed,' the Sultan says. He grows curious about the assassin. 'Was she the one who sent you? Tell me before you kill me.'

Asuang doesn't want to talk anymore. He tenses his body to strike.

'I have other enchantments,' the Sultan says when Asuang doesn't answer. 'Let's talk. Please.'

Asuang relaxes when he hears the last word, for it is a word that Sultans never learn to speak.

'There are other enchantments,' Asuang says, 'yet you do not use them.'

The Sultan shrugs.

'Perhaps I have been waiting for you. Sit with me. Have a drink. I promise it is not poisoned. The food is meant for me, and my taster would be dead if it were so.' The Sultan stops as if he thought of something. 'He would be dead, or well-rewarded,' he adds.

A smile? A joke? Asuang cannot tell. He has faced many men at the moment of their death, but few have welcomed their killer.

'You wish for death,' Asuang says. There is no other explanation.

The Sultan sees the assassin's surprise and realizes he is the one who is mistaken. The assassin knows nothing about his wish for death.

'The witch didn't send you,' the Sultan says after he recovers from his own surprise. 'Who was it then? The merchant kings? Separatists? Tell me.'

'If I speak the name of my client, I would be a poor assassin indeed,' Asuang replies.

The Sultan dismisses Asuang's words with a wave of his rotting hand.

'Obviously, that is not true. No other assassin has made it this far. You have scaled the highest tower of my palace undetected, eluding the guards and the spells that protect this place—an impossible feat, I was assured. That means you are uniquely gifted at what you do. Yet, I do not know you. I employ many assassins, and I have never heard of one with abilities like yours. Unless . . . '

Asuang remains unmoving.

'Unless,' the Sultan continues, 'you are the legendary Asuang. They say Asuang is not a man at all, but a spirit of retribution and judgment.'

Asuang says nothing, only tips his head in the direction of the Sultan.

The Sultan sits back in his chair. He looks amused.

'I have searched for you for a long time,' he says. 'We could have achieved great things together. I never expected to find you like this.'

'They never do,' Asuang says.

The Sultan laughs, a rich sound that fills the room.

'I'm sorry,' the Sultan says, still smiling, 'Forgive me if I find our situation amusing. You think you have the upper hand, but I'm afraid it is I who has you at a disadvantage. You were sent to kill me, but I welcome you. You will deliver me from this prison. You will set me free. This time, you are not justice. Not retribution. I am truly sorry.'

Asuang sits down on a chair in front of the Sultan's table. He stares at him from across the table with eyes that are chips of cold stone. If he wanted to, he could cut the Sultan's throat from where he sat.

'Do you know why you never found me?' Asuang asks the Sultan.

'Because you didn't want to be found, no doubt,' the Sultan answers, sure of himself, absently picking at a pustule on his arm.

'That's right.' Asuang allows himself a small smile, but there is no joy in it.

'When I was a young man,' Asuang says, 'your soldiers killed my wife and my three children. They burnt down my village in your name, and I lost everything.'

'Ah,' the Sultan says, 'you are the client.'

'I devoted my life to killing everyone responsible. And one by one, I found the men who took everything from me, and I took everything from them. Now you are the only one left.'

Asuang stares at the Sultan, and the Sultan stares back at Asuang with eyes full of cataracts.

'Then I fear we are at an impasse,' the Sultan says finally. 'I am weary of this life, and I want you to release me. You are the only one who has that power. But you cannot get what you came here for without giving me exactly what I want. This must be very difficult for you.'

Asuang doesn't want to talk anymore.

'You know,' the Sultan says, 'I have had a great number of people killed. And many more have died in my name without my knowledge. Like your family.

'I am not absolving myself. You are correct in believing I am responsible. But there are reasons why we do the things we do. It is never easy—though it does get easier—but it is always *necessary*.' The Sultan emphasizes the last word. 'You slaves should be grateful. You will understand one day.'

Asuang moves. Quick as a snake, the hand holding the knife strikes the Sultan's hand, nailing him to the table. In the same motion, Asuang stands up and draws another knife from his belt. The Sultan screams, and as he does so, Asuang reaches into the Sultan's mouth, grabs his tongue and cuts it off. The Sultan writhes on the table, making horrifying animal sounds with his throat.

Asuang steps away from the Sultan's thrashing body and throws his tongue into a corner of the room.

'I never said your death would be painless,' Asuang says.

Asuang wipes the blood from the knife on his sleeve and approaches the Sultan again.

7

Yumina

In the Great Hall, Yumina sits ten feet away and twelve steps down from the Sky Throne. There are no other seats between her and the empty throne. Twelve steps below her is the new vizier—a nervous and unsure man who has replaced Vizier Humadapnon upon his sudden death. Twelve steps below him to the left are the seats of the ministers, three hundred in all, dressed in identical robes that are the colour of blood, signifying what they would sacrifice to the Sultan. Twelve steps further below the vizier to the right are an assortment of datus, kings, and princes who rule the nations of the sultanate.

The Sultan is not there, but his absence is nothing out of the ordinary. He is often too busy to attend to all of the sultanate's affairs. After waiting for two hours, the vizier signals that the ceremonies should begin.

A gong sounds and the doors of the Great Hall open wide. The merchant kings enter, each attended by eighty-eight eunuchs. Each of the kings is borne on gold palanquins, but they get down before they step into the hall, as custom demands. Each merchant king gets on his knees and bows to the Sky Throne three times, then they bow to Yumina. The last hundred steps are taken by the merchant kings alone, without their entourage of eunuchs, and on their knees.

The sight of the old men hobbling about on their knees is so pathetic that Yumina has to hold back her laughter by biting her lip. After an eternity, the merchant kings make it to their seats—single cushions at the foot of the stairs where the sultanate's ministers and royalty sit. Once they are seated, the speeches begin.

Yumina soon loses interest in the proceedings. For a moment, she almost falls asleep, but she is able to catch herself before her head falls forward and sends her metal headpiece crashing to the floor. She bites her lip again, forcing the pain to wake her up. Her handmaidens, kneeling three steps below her with no seats of their own, look at her with concern.

Suddenly, without warning, a sound erupts and fills the entire hall. It expands to fill the palace and beyond. It jolts Yumina awake, and she feels like her head might explode from the intensity of the sound. It brings some of the guards to their knees.

Slowly, the people in the Great Hall realize the sound they just heard is that of the God Cannon. They know what it means.

In the moments that follow the first shot, there is silence. The old men cease talking. Everyone stops to listen. They wait. It seems as if everyone is holding their breath.

Another shot breaks across the night, and it fills them with terror for what they know must come next. The God Cannon sounds one more time then goes silent. The Sultan is dead.

The silence remains after the cannon fires for the third time. One of the merchant kings whispers something to a servant, and the boy bolts out of the hall as fast as his feet can take him. A low murmur begins to rise as the others begin to realize what this means for them. In the distance, the agong begin beating out a message for the whole sultanate to hear: THE SULTAN IS DEAD. THE SULTAN IS DEAD. THE SULTAN IS DEAD.

Yumina stands up and surveys the room. The vizier is shouting orders at a group of Maharlika. The low murmur in the hall rises gradually at first, but it gets louder and louder, and soon everyone is shouting. Servants are running to and fro. Ministers argue over what their course of action should be. The Maharlika have broken into groups, betraying their alliances. No one pays any attention to Yumina, who stands alone twelve steps below the Sultan's throne.

The hall's great doors burst open, and chaos erupts. Outside the door are the merchant kings' eunuchs armed with spears and shields. Behind them is the merchant kings' royal guard: fifty heavy cavalry and three hundred armoured spearmen. Within seconds, the merchant kings are safely behind the spearmen's lines. Then the cavalry charges, running down the palace guards before they can organize themselves, then wheeling around to cut through the Maharlika and the Sultan's ministers, dealing death with each pass.

None of this is possible, Yumina thinks to herself. *Only the palace guards are allowed to carry weapons within the walls!* She knows there are enchantments that prevent entry to anyone with a blade. *Someone must have helped them. It could be anyone. The Sultan has many enemies.*

'Father' has many enemies, she corrects herself. *Now Father is dead.* Yumina has no time to grieve as she gathers her handmaidens to get as far as possible from the carnage in the hall.

At that moment, the lantern that hangs in the centre of the Great Hall burns brighter than ever. All eyes travel upwards, and it is as if they are all standing outside in the light of the noontime sun. The light becomes blinding, and Yumina covers her face with an arm as she turns her head away from the fire and the pain.

The giant lantern explodes. Everyone in the hall is knocked off their feet. Molten fire falls from the lantern to the ground below, killing hundreds of the Maharlika and ministers who stood underneath. Once on the ground, the fire rears and rises, growing larger with each passing moment. It is a living thing, and it consumes everything it touches. It reaches out with long arms to set a group of fleeing servants on fire. It swallows soldiers, exhaling black smoke. It grows and looks around the hall to consume more.

Yumina has nowhere to go. There is only one entrance and exit to the hall, and that is blocked by the tall, dark eunuchs who are moving steadily forwards and killing all in their way. So, she runs up the twelve steps and hides behind the Sky Throne. The throne is massive, twice as tall as a man. At the throne's back is a carving of the sun's corona erupting in golden rays where the Sultan's head would be if he were sitting on the throne. This is enough to cover Yumina and her three handmaidens.

Hidden behind the throne, with her handmaidens praying to their gods, Yumina knows that eventually, they will find her, but she is not afraid. For the first time in all her years in the Great Hall, she notices the sun carving on the Sky Throne. And seeing it, she is filled with calm and determination. The sun carving is an eight-pointed star, like the one in her dream.

8

Lumawig

Time is short.

A light erupts in Lumawig's head. At the same time, pain explodes in his chest. His heart begins to beat again.

Get up. Time is short.

The light in his head begins to fade as quickly as it came. His vision returns, only to disappear moments later. He looks around as his eyesight goes from dark to light and back to darkness. He is lost, and he doesn't know where he is. There is a voice in his head that is not his own, telling him to get up. The pain in his chest is almost more than he can bear. His heart feels like it is trying to escape his ribcage. His blood is on fire.

There is no time. You need to start running.

He tries to stand up but he falls instead. He was on a table and now he is on the floor. He raises his head and looks around. The room snaps into focus, then his eyesight dims as his head crashes to the floor again. He can hardly control his body, and the pain in his chest is unbearable.

The princess is in danger. You must save her.

The princess! She was his last thought before his heart stopped. He takes a deep breath and lifts his head again. He knows this room.

He has been here before. It looks like some sort of barracks. He gets up on one knee and shakes his head to silence the pain. Yes, he remembers now. This room is inside the palace. He was brought here to meet the captain once, many months ago.

'You will guard the wall,' the captain said, 'and you will never step inside the palace again. You will follow orders. You will live, and then you will die. When you die, if you die while guarding the wall, they will bring you here. You will be wrapped in a shroud before your body is given to your family. You will never see the palace again otherwise.'

Lumawig is not dead. Yet here he is. They must have brought him here when his heart stopped. They must have thought that he was dead. *Where is everyone?*

Time is short. You must save her.

The princess. He gets up on his feet and walks a few steps, his legs buckling underneath him.

'Who are you?' he asks aloud. His voice is dry and catches in his throat. No one answers.

Lumawig looks around. The pain in his chest is subsiding now, but his vision remains dim. He sees the table he was lying on and uses it to support his weight. Behind him stretches a row of spartan beds for the palace guards, all empty. To his right is a closed door that he remembers leads to the quarters of the Captain of the Guard. In front of him is a spiral staircase hewn in stone.

Run. You must save her.

This time, he does not question the voice. He propels himself forward, at first in a few stumbling steps. Gradually, he finds his legs and heads towards the stairs. Something inside him knows that the voice is right: he has to hurry.

Without thinking, he grabs a helm and a sword, the captain's, he guesses, by their quality. Then he runs. His heart races as he climbs. This time it is from exertion and fear. Death awaits him if he is found inside the palace. If the voice is right, death awaits the princess if he cannot reach her in time. He flies up the steps as fast as his body can take him. He finds that he is strong. He feels his burning blood bringing strength to his limbs.

The star. Search for the star.

Now the voice is speaking in riddles, Lumawig thinks. He continues to climb until he runs out of stairs; then, he races down a long hallway with recessed alcoves. He is running so fast he almost misses it. There is a palace guard at the end of the hallway, but the guard has his back to him. Lumawig rushes into an alcove to hide, and as he crouches down, he sees it staring him right in the face: an eight-pointed star carved into the stone.

He reaches out to touch it. His face is so close to the star that he can see how dirt has collected in the engraved lines that form the figure. He exhales just before his fingers touch the star, and as he does so, he hears the sound of turning gears, and the wall opens with a click, revealing a hidden passageway and another stairwell.

Hurry. Climb. Time is short.

The voice urges him on. This time, he doesn't hesitate. He enters the passageway, closing the wall behind him; then, he climbs the stairs. He takes the steps two at a time until he reaches a narrow corridor just wide enough for two men to walk abreast. Every twenty feet or so, there is a narrow slit in the wall at eye level, some kind of spyhole hidden in the wall.

Lumawig looks through the slit and sees the palace's Great Hall. It is so large he has difficulty seeing the other side of it. Though muffled through the wall, sounds of combat reach his ears. He can hear the clash of steel, horses running on stone, and the shrieks of the dying. Through the slit, he can see little more than smoke, but he also sees people running and soldiers giving chase. He doesn't know who the soldiers are.

Lumawig moves from one slit to the next trying to get a better look at the hall and find a way in. He looks for the princess, but he cannot find her.

At the fifth slit, he sees it: another eight-pointed star. This one is at waist-level, and Lumawig gets on his knees, touching the star to activate it and eventually breathing on it as he did with the first star. Again, there is the sound of metal gears turning. The wall opens with a click.

Lumawig tumbles out into the hall and stumbles over the bodies of several slain ministers.

The hall has become a battlefield, but it is unlike any Lumawig has seen before. There are no clear battle lines. A large group of soldiers is advancing from the door, a phalanx of men carrying small round shields and short spears. At their feet lie the bodies of palace guards. Caught by surprise and not even in formation, they were easily killed.

Some palace guards are making a stand close to the throne where they are protecting a group of Maharlika by surrounding them in a shallow phalanx. Many other guards are scattered about the room, but they are being harried by the enemy's cavalry. Their numbers are not large, but they are able to break the palace guards' ranks time and time again. Lumawig knows that the Great Hall is said to be protected by a thousand guards at any time of the day. Today, it seems there are less than two hundred of them standing.

In the middle of the hall is an inferno. Hundreds of corpses lie burning, engulfed by flames. Above the burning bodies towers a creature of fire. It has the body of a lion and a dozen heads in the shape of snakes. The merchant kings' guard is advancing on the beast, but soon they are surrounded by fire. Lumawig looks away as the flames engulf them.

Next, he sees a group of guards and ministers cowering behind the bodies of their slain comrades and approaches them. Seeing his captain's helm and officer's sword, one of the guards salutes him and reports, 'C-Captain, we're trapped. What should we do? They're . . . butchering everyone . . . '

'What happened here?' Lumawig asks.

Voice shaking, the soldier replies incoherently, 'The merchant king's eunuchs . . . they attacked us . . . no time to form ranks. Then, the lantern exploded . . . fire everywhere . . .' The soldier runs out of words to describe the horror of the fire demon.

'Grab a hold of yourself,' Lumawig says in a tone that makes the soldier stand straight. 'We'll survive together. Take that banner,' Lumawig says, pointing to a pole with a banner with the Sultan's colours, red and gold, lying on the ground. 'To me!' he cries. 'To me!'

He knows that the men will remember their training. He is sure of it because it is the same training that he went through. They will follow commands. They must follow.

Soon, a dozen guards have formed ranks beside him, shield to shoulder to shield.

'Give me a spear,' Lumawig commands, and a spear is given to him. He surveys the hall for any signs of the princess.

He sees her on top of the steps, looking at the battle from behind the Sky Throne. But he is not the only one who sees her. Six riders spot her and head towards the throne.

Lumawig throws his spear without thinking and lands a blow on the last rider's helm. He has rushed his throw, and it should have landed a glancing blow, but somehow the rider's head is torn clear of his body.

What did the witch do to me? What is this demon's blood flowing through my veins?

The lead rider wheels around on his horse and sees his fallen comrade. He barks an order to the other riders and they all gallop in Lumawig's direction.

'Forward!' Lumawig commands his men, breaking into a run to close the gap between himself and the riders. 'Form a wedge at my command!' The frightened soldiers grunt acknowledgement in unison as the riders bear down upon them.

'Another spear!' Lumawig commands and as his hands wrap around the shaft of the spear, he signals to his men: 'Now!'

The men line up and crouch low, forming the shape of a spearhead with Lumawig as the tip of the spear. Their timing is perfect as the lead rider's horse is so surprised it stops and rears on its hind legs. Lumawig and the men to either side of him rush forward to spear the horse's underside, and it falls to its side, crushing its rider.

Two other riders plow straight into the right side of the wedge in a clash of breaking steel. Horse and riders tumble to the ground, trampling Lumawig's men and killing three of them. Once on the ground, the riders are killed by the palace guards.

The remaining riders swerve along either side of the wedge, facing a series of spears aimed at their horse's flanks. Two of them manage to escape, but Lumawig throws his spear at one rider's back and strikes him between the shoulder blades, throwing the rider off the horse.

Lumawig's men look at him in fear, but they have no time to stop. He urges them forward. They have to keep moving if they hope to save the princess. They make their way up the one hundred forty-four steps that lead to the Sky Throne.

The princess rushes out of her hiding place behind the throne as soon as Lumawig and his men are nearby, and Lumawig runs forward to meet her. She implores him with her eyes to save her. Yumina's headdress has come undone and there is terror behind her eyes, but she bears her situation with a strength of spirit that moves Lumawig. He takes the princess by the arm. It is a crime punishable by death.

'I will take you to safety,' he tells her.

'Where?' she asks him. 'How?'

'There is a passageway,' he assures her. Then to his soldiers, he gives the command, 'Form around me!' and they form a tight phalanx that surrounds him, the princess, and her handmaidens.

Lumawig leads them to the part of the wall with the secret passageway. As they approach the foot of the hall's one hundred forty-four steps, he begins to fear that the passageway may be gone, closed forever, or only accessible from the other side. But as they come close, the princess exclaims, 'The star!' and Lumawig knows that great forces have moved them to this place—this moment. He knows he has nothing to fear. They will make it out of the palace alive with the worst behind them and everything to hope for.

The creature of fire grows with every moment and almost fills the entire hall as Lumawig kneels to breathe upon the eight-pointed star. The passageway opens and he steps in first, making sure it is safe. From inside, he offers a hand to Yumina, their eyes meet, and she takes his outstretched hand.

9

Asuang

When the Sultan finally stopped breathing, six hours after his tongue was cut out, Asuang started to think, for the first time, of his escape. He had thought he would die in the Sultan's tower. He takes a deep breath and savours the fact that he is still alive.

Through some magic unknown to Asuang, the Sultan's death has triggered a series of events. Somehow, an alarm was sounded. He doesn't hear it, but in the courtyard below, he sees the palace guards pouring out of the barracks. Patrols are sent out. An entire legion prepares itself for battle at the foot of the Sultan's tower. On the walls, a company of soldiers prepares to fire the God Cannon. The cannon fires once, twice, thrice: THE SULTAN IS DEAD. THE SULTAN IS DEAD. THE SULTAN IS DEAD.

Asuang hides in a corner of the room on his knees and covers his ears until the cannon fire is over.

His next thought is of self-preservation: *It is time to go.*

He could end it here, Asuang thinks to himself. He could jump out a window and disappear into the night forever, his body broken on the stones of the courtyard. Yet he does not.

They are all dead now, those who took everything from him—the foot soldiers who killed his family, the captains who gave the order, the commanders who planned the invasion, the vizier who executed the Sultan's will, and the Sultan himself. It is over now, but Asuang wants more.

Asuang guesses that now it is a matter of moments before the Sultan's soldiers break down the door in search of the assassin. They will want his blood for killing the Sultan. They will not be ordinary soldiers. The most dangerous men in the sultanate will take his head.

The Sultan wanted to die. His eyes welcomed his death even though he knew in the end that the way to the death he so desired was through pain. Asuang did not make it easy for the Sultan. He savoured every wordless cry that escaped from the Sultan's throat. He prolonged the Sultan's pain for as long as his art made possible. But Asuang could see that there was gladness in the Sultan's heart no matter how slowly the end came. This infuriated Asuang at first, but after the first few hours, his anger cooled, and he was left only with a bitter taste in his mouth, and curiosity. Why did the Sultan long for death?

The Sultan had tried to tell Asuang something before he died. Asuang didn't think much of it at the time, but now that he reflects on what transpired, he realizes that the Sultan's words were strange. 'You will understand one day,' the Sultan said. He said it with certainty.

Asuang's eyes are drawn to the Sultan's table. Much of it is covered in the Sultan's blood, but he sees a piece of parchment at the edge of the table that bears the Sultan's signature, his seal, and his dried blood.

Asuang reads the words on the parchment, and he remembers his own wish, made in the presence of the old woman in the market. He also remembers the old woman's words, 'When your revenge is complete, open the bottle and let the wind have the ash inside.'

All is suddenly clear. Asuang opens the vial of ash he bought from the old woman and empties it on the wind. He drops the vial onto the floor where it breaks, then without pausing, he walks to the door that leads outside the Sultan's sanctum. He senses people on the other side of the door, but he is not afraid. He opens the door and steps outside.

There are dozens of people in the room, and they all fall to their knees when Asuang enters. They bow until their foreheads touch the floor. They bow a total of twelve times and then raise themselves to a sitting position, all the time never making eye contact with Asuang. Half of them are soldiers bearing arms, palace guards, and an assortment of generals. The other half are ministers, withered old men carrying scrolls, priests, and Maharlika.

One of the ministers enters the Sultan's sanctum and retrieves the parchment with the Sultan's last command. Others also enter the sanctum and tend to the Sultan's body, muttering prayers over the corpse. A priest who has the most elaborate headdress begins chanting in an ancient tongue and the others soon take up the chant. When the chant is over, the priest bows seven times and says:

'All hail Sultan Sakandal, ruler of the earth and Skyworld, beloved of the gods, who was once known as Asuang. Long may he reign.'

I am Sakandal again, the Sultan muses.

Sakandal hears the God Cannon sound again, once, twice: LONG LIVE THE SULTAN. LONG LIVE THE SULTAN.

Part V: The Flood

The people in the market make way for the god and kneel as he passes. He is twice as tall as a man, and a golden light streams from his being. He heads straight for the old woman's stall.

The old woman is surprised to see the god approaching her stall in the market. Blinded by the light that surrounds him, she struggles to identify which god he is. But when she looks at his eyes and sees the rain inside them, she recognizes Bagilat. She gets down on her knees, places her palms on the ground, and bows her head.

'Lord Bagilat,' the old woman says.

'Get up,' he commands. 'I told you we will have none of that.'

The old woman gets to her feet slowly. Impatient, Bagilat speaks before she has fully risen.

'I am here to give Sun Girna Ginar what its people have been praying for. Rain will fall upon this land again.'

'My Lord,' the old woman says, bowing her head in a gesture of gratitude.

'It is,' Bagilat says with a tilt of his head, 'because of you, I realized. I can no longer deny the people. Their voices have grown strong. And loud.

'I asked myself, "What happened? Where have the people found this power?" And the answer was clear. It was the demon's doing.'

The old woman looks at Bagilat with her palms open in a gesture of false humility.

'I did not tell them what to dream,' she says.

'Ah,' Bagilat replies, 'but you gave them hope when they had no right to hope.'

The old woman doesn't reply. She folds her hands in front of her.

'I underestimated you,' Bagilat says. 'You are a powerful witch. You honour your ancestors.

'Years ago, I sought to deny the Sultan for what he did to Skyworld. I withheld the rain, and the drought began. But the Sultan is dead now. Was that your doing as well?'

The old woman looks down and shakes her head in a gesture of humility.

'No,' she says. 'I had little to do with the Sultan's death. Our hunter found his quarry, that is all.'

'You were right about your champions,' Bagilat says. 'But you have not won yet. The city still stands. For how long? I don't know. It doesn't matter. I have

called the north-easterly wind that your people call Habagat. The rain will be here soon. It would be best for you to move to higher ground.'

'What about the storm, my Lord?'

'Do not be too eager. That too shall come in its time. You will not have to wait long. Be patient. All of your prayers will be answered, Imugan.'

1

Pinantaw

Weeks before the old Sultan died, Pinantaw, the fortune teller, knew something terrible was going to happen.

It began with dreams, as these things always do. It was always the same dream, a simple one but full of meaning: she couldn't breathe.

At first, Pinantaw thought nothing of it, but when she kept having the same dream every night, she began to wonder. She thought that perhaps some spirits were playing tricks on her—like the demon Bangungot that sat on your chest while you slept—but she didn't know which spirit it was. She told her mother, a manghihilot who possessed the healing hands, about her dreams but her mother ruled out the spirits from the start. 'There is nothing wrong with you. It is only a dream; it must be some kind of vision.' She was right, of course.

The readings should have told Pinantaw everything, but she ignored all the signs. She would slaughter a pig and inspect its liver for omens. She would then take a little of the liver between her teeth, and this would trigger visions. Lately, all the visions had become the same: it was always water. She saw water filling the streets of Sun Girna Ginar, the rain falling in torrents for days, the sea crashing over the city walls.

Pinantaw apologized to those who came to her for a reading. 'Something is wrong with my sight,' she told them.

* * *

The day the old Sultan died, Pinantaw wakes up from the same dream she's had for weeks now, and finally realizes what it means. In her dream, she could not breathe because she was drowning. Pinantaw realizes that there are no hidden meanings at all. It is a simple vision of what will come to pass. She is going to drown.

Once she realizes this, all the other visions begin to make sense as well. The rain will return. There will be a flood. The sea will claim Sun Girna Ginar. *We will all drown,* she realizes with terror.

Pinantaw sits up in bed. Her heart races. She can't breathe. *It is not yet time,* she tells herself. *The rain isn't here yet. The flood hasn't risen.* The anxiety passes. Her lungs are able to find air again.

She puts on clothes and sandals, and heads out of her house. She needs to tell someone about her visions. There must be something that can be done. She doesn't want to die, not yet, and not like that.

'We are all going to drown,' she says. The people on the street give her a wide berth. To them, she is just another crazy woman.

'We have to leave the city!' she shouts at the top of her voice.

The people ignore her. Some of her neighbours see her and begin to approach her with concern on their faces.

Mother, Pinantaw realizes. *I must tell mother.* She runs away from her neighbours and heads towards the market. Her mother does her healing there.

Once Pinantaw is in the market, she has to slow down. It is impossible to run because of all the people. She pushes her way through the crowd as fast as she can, but she makes little progress.

The steady crush of the crowd calms her down. She tells herself that she doesn't know when the city will be destroyed. First, there will be rain, and it hasn't rained in years. *The end is still far away,* she tells herself. Pinantaw relaxes. The movement of the crowd hypnotizes her. Above the noise of the street, she hears a voice.

'Dreams!' a barker says, 'Dreams in bottles!'

Pinantaw finds herself drawn to the barker. He ushers her inside a tent without saying a word.

It is dark inside the tent. As Pinantaw's eyes adjust, she sees that the tent is full of wooden shelves crammed with bottles. These shelves are behind a makeshift wooden counter where a crone sits, like a Chinese herbalist.

Once inside the tent, Pinantaw is gripped by the rarest kind of vision: a waking dream. She sees the world through the eyes of her vision, without the aid of sleep.

In her vision, Pinantaw sees the world as if she is underwater. Sun Girna Ginar has become a sandcastle swallowed by the tide, and she is in a tent at the bottom of this sandcastle city. The sun is far away, through miles of ocean, touching all around her in a faint light. Everyone has become blue, with bubbles of air escaping from their noses and mouths. All sound has disappeared.

Pinantaw swims to the crone, who asks her, 'What is your dream?'

'There is no more point to dreaming,' she wants to tell the old woman, 'when all will end in a watery death.'

Instead, Pinantaw says, 'I want to live.'

The old woman looks surprised. Her eyes come to life.

'I don't want to drown,' Pinantaw goes on. 'I don't want to die like that.' Pinantaw thinks her voice sounds like it is coming from far away.

A smile breaks the old woman's cracked face.

'You know,' the old woman says. She says it again, almost to herself, 'You know.'

The old woman turns around and swims to the end of the tent where she looks around and picks a bottle that has floated almost to the top of the tent. She returns to Pinantaw by kicking off a shelf. She swims like a frog. Pinantaw can't help but laugh. More bubbles escape from her mouth.

In the crone's hands is a plain jar. At first, Pinantaw thinks it is empty, full of nothing but water and some air trapped inside. Upon closer inspection, she sees that there is a glass amulet on a piece of string floating inside.

'Put the amulet on if you want to live,' the old woman says.

Pinantaw takes the jar with the amulet and pays the old woman.

When she steps out of the tent, her waking dream comes to an end, and again she finds herself on the dusty, crowded street in the market of Sun Girna Ginar.

She continues to walk towards her mother's house. She has so much to tell her. They need to make plans to leave the city.

Pinantaw's thoughts are broken by a loud sound that crashes overhead. At first, Pinantaw thinks it is thunder, but a second shot follows, then a third. It is cannon fire, but there are no cannons as loud as that. There is only one cannon that loud.

'The Sultan is dead!' someone shouts. Others take up the cry. 'The Sultan is dead!'

There is growing panic in the crowd. Some people try to run away, turn around, or go home to their loved ones. Some rush to find a safe place. There is pushing. Fights break out. Then the pushing turns to a steady pressure behind her; it is no longer individuals trying to escape but a sea of people behind her with nowhere to go but forward. A stampede has erupted.

Pinantaw moves forward because she has no choice. She either pushes forward like everyone else, or she gets crushed under the sea of people behind her. A man pushes her hard in the back and her head jerks up.

The sky is dark. She feels something moist land on her face.

Pinantaw is filled with fear. It is a raindrop.

2

Liddum

Liddum looks out at the desert from his place on the city's wall. His helmet is heavy from the heat of the sun. It would burn his brow were it to touch his skin. So, Liddum has wrapped his head in cloth first. Still, it is stifling under his helmet, and the sweat trickles down his face. He is accustomed to standing under the sun at this hour, but today the heat is brutal. His spear is heavy. His strength has been sapped away.

Liddum knows that the heat has been known to play tricks with the mind. Nevertheless, he entertains a fantasy of his. He dreams of a day like this. On that day, he will be staring into the desert when he will see a god traveling over the dry earth. He will watch the god travel across the desert, like lightning from Skyworld. He won't even be able to tell the other guards because, by the time he opens his mouth to speak, the god will be gone.

In Liddum's fantasy, he will see the god again the next day. It will happen at the same hour. There will be a fire in the corner of Liddum's eye as Skyworld opens and the god descends to the desert. But this time, Liddum will be at the spot where the god descends to earth. He will be waiting for him.

The hours pass slowly, the sun hides behind the horizon, and Liddum's watch comes to an end. Another hour later, he finds himself in a stall in the market, eating a meal of salted fish and rice with a small overripe tomato. Still, he thinks of the god falling from Skyworld.

Everything will be different with the power of a god, he tells himself. He knows it is possible. *Didn't the Sultan enslave a god?* He would just have to find a way. He will catch the god as it comes down from Skyworld, vulnerable and unsuspecting.

With the power of the god as his own, nothing will be the same. He will leave the wall guard and live with the Maharlika in their mansions upon the hill. And every day, the Sultan will seek Liddum out to ask his counsel on things great and small.

Liddum will not use the god's power only for selfish things. He will become the defender of Sun Girna Ginar, replacing General Marandang who has grown old and senile. When the city comes under attack from giants or demons of the underworld, as it has come under attack before, it will be Liddum who defeats the monsters, not the general. The people will sing songs about *his* deeds. They will throw flowers at *his* feet.

After Liddum's meal, he hands the vendor a small bead, and then stands up to return to the barracks.

'Two streets down, turn right, look for the stall with the bottles,' the vendor says.

Liddum looks up and questions the vendor with a look. She does not see him. Her head is down. She is busy with cooking.

'Sorry? Did you say something?'

'Two streets down, turn right, look for the stall with the bottles,' she says again.

Liddum blinks, not understanding.

'You look the type,' she says as if that explains everything. 'There's an old woman over there who can make dreams come true. I have a cousin who swears it worked for him. He became a rich man overnight. You look like you have a dream or something with your faraway looks.'

Liddum shakes his head.

'I'm just a soldier who guards the wall,' he says. 'I don't have time for dreams.'

She shrugs. 'Funny. I thought you'd have all day for that sort of thing . . . I mean, you never know . . . '

Liddum turns around and walks away without saying anything more, but two streets down, he turns right.

He almost misses the old woman's stall. In the darkness, it is difficult to make out the wares on sale. The vendors have lit lanterns that release an oily black smoke. They cast shadows everywhere and illuminate little. Liddum scans the stalls for any signs of glass bottles and almost stumbles over the old woman.

The old woman is a sad, spent thing, and she looks as if she is as old as time itself. She barely has the strength to lift her gaze towards the soldier. At first, she says nothing and closes her eyes to focus on the task before her. For a second, Liddum thinks the old woman has fallen asleep. Then, the old woman opens her rheumy, half-blind eyes, and speaks.

'A soldier of the wall,' she says and raises her hand above her head. 'Bless you. How can I help you?' Her voice is the rustle of dry leaves.

'Forgive me,' Liddum begins, then realizes he has nothing to say. 'I was told . . . I am only looking . . . I am afraid I do not know what I am looking for . . . '

Liddum pretends to inspect the bottles in the stall. There are not many left. There are plenty of gaps in the shelves, and in the empty spaces are circles of dust where the bottles once stood. Even in the dim light, he can see that. He is not sure what he is looking at though. Each bottle is a different shape, and inside each are strange things. Here, there is a glass flask full of dark blood. There, a golden wine inside a wide carafe with an unborn child curled up and sucking its thumb.

Again, there is that rustling of leaves as the woman speaks. 'Ah,' she says, 'but you do know . . . ' For a moment, Liddum loses himself in his vision again.

The people will call me a hero. I will defeat the enemies of the sultanate, and end their wars. Then when the time is right, I will replace the Sultan and his

Maharlika. With the power of the god, they cannot stand in my way. I will rule Sun Girna Ginar as a benevolent god. I will be just and merciful. I will heal the sick, punish the wicked, protect the little children, and give my people dignity and prosperity.

Liddum snaps out of his reverie with a shake of his head. The old woman looks at him with a blank expression, then she reaches from underneath the stall. There is the tinkling of glass as she rummages among the bottles. She stands up and hands the soldier a bottle without saying anything more. The bottle is broad and square and cool to the touch.

Inside the bottle, Liddum can see the sky. The smoke from the food stalls in the alley has risen and blocked the sky; the stars are barely visible above them. But in the bottle, Liddum can see the stars in vivid detail. To the soldier, it seems like entire constellations are trapped inside and shrunken. He can see their colours, intensity, their subtle pulsing, and the clouds of nebulae that surround them.

'It is Skyworld,' the old woman whispers like a dry wind. 'That is what you wish for, yes? To have a piece of that place, to command the gods like our Sultan?'

The soldier doesn't answer, doesn't dare to answer.

'Take it,' the old woman goes on, even softer than before, and it sounds like her voice is receding, retreating to the place where it will find rest. 'Go to the place where Skyworld meets the earth. You saw it in your vision. A god will be travelling from Skyworld to the earth. When he comes, open the bottle and the god's spirit will be drawn inside. Close it, and the god will be your slave.

'I waited a long time for you. You will be a great hero.'

The old woman sits down, blows out her lantern, and begins putting the remaining bottles on the shelves into a wooden box by the light from the other stalls.

'Go,' she says. 'It's time to rest. You will need it. A storm is coming.'

3

Cayapon

Cayapon's feet are swollen, and walking has made her tired. The midwife told her that she needs to walk now that her time is near. The baby is still too high, she said, and walking will help it find its way out.

At first, it felt good to walk after too many weeks of hiding from the heat. Cayapon liked setting out in a different direction every morning. But today, she took her walk in the afternoon instead. Now, she finds herself unable to bear the heat, and she sits down on the first seat she sees, somewhere in the middle of the market.

Cayapon stretches her legs and winces. She thinks her left leg is about to cramp and braces herself for the pain. In front of her is a tiny stall with a few oddly-shaped bottles on a pair of shelves. Behind the stall is an old lady who looks half-asleep, or half-dead. Cayapon is not sure which she is.

'Are you hoping for a boy or a girl?' she hears a withered voice say. It is the old woman behind the stall.

Cayapon looks up and forces herself to smile.

'Anything,' she says, 'as long as it's healthy.'

'Of course,' the old woman says right away. 'Of course. But if you could choose, would you rather have a boy or a girl? Most say "a boy" because boys will make your house strong. But you would be surprised, girls are good too.'

Cayapon is tired of this game. She has heard it all by now.

She has heard of how her baby will be a boy because her nose is bloated. She has been told that if she eats conjoined bananas, she will give birth to twins. She has been warned against sleeping alone. If there is no one to guard you at night, a tiktik will eat the foetus. It will insert its snake-like tongue into your belly button, they said, and consume the child from the inside.

Few have ever asked her what she wants, so Cayapon answers the old woman's question.

'A girl.'

The old woman's eyes go wide, waiting for more.

Cayapon shrugs and says, 'I just think it is a girl.'

The old woman stands up. To Cayapon's surprise, she sees that the old woman is extremely bent. She must have been small, to begin with, but her twisted back makes her about half of Cayapon's height. Seated, Cayapon is almost at eye level with the old woman.

The old woman gives Cayapon something, her old hands placing something smooth into Cayapon's palm.

'Rub this on your belly,' the old woman says, 'and no harm shall come to your baby girl. She will be as strong as a carabao, and as beautiful as the dawn. And should she need help, heroes shall rush to her rescue. When they hear her cry, the defenders of the city will come to her aid with all the powers of the gods.'

'What is in it?'

The old woman smiles. 'It is just water,' she reassures Cayapon, 'taken from a spring on a holy mountain. The water comes out only once a year and healers from all over the sultanate congregate there to harvest the water. It carries the blessings of the gods.'

'I can't . . .' Cayapon begins. 'I'm afraid I have nothing to—'

'Nonsense!' the old woman cuts her off. 'I won't take your money. Let me be a grandmother. I have no children of my own, you know. You are all my children.' She waves vaguely around her, gesturing towards the people in the streets.

Cayapon is moved by the old woman. 'Then I would be honoured,' she says, 'If you would be the one to give the blessing, Nanay.'

'Here?' the old woman asks.

Cayapon shrugs. 'This place has seen stranger things,' she says.

The old woman doesn't need to bend over or kneel to reach Cayapon's belly. She only has to step closer. Then she lifts Cayapon's shirt, opens the bottle, pours some of the liquid on her hands, then lays her hands on Cayapon's belly. As the old woman does this, Cayapon feels the child kick.

She hears the old woman say some words under her breath and realizes that she is praying. Cayapon waits for the old woman to finish. After a second of silence, the woman removes her hands. They are both silent for a moment, then the God Cannon changes everything.

Cayapon turns to where the sound comes from, clutching her stomach as if to protect her baby. All around the street, people hide behind market stalls or huddle on the ground. Cayapon turns back towards the old woman and finds that she has disappeared. There is no trace of her. It is impossible that she could have gone anywhere so quickly.

The God Cannon goes off again. Cayapon hears shouting coming from down the street. She gets to her feet and decides to return home. Then the cannon sounds for a third and final time, but Cayapon hardly hears it. She is rooted in the place where she is standing. She knows she has to find a midwife soon. Her water has broken.

From out of nowhere, a man runs headlong into her, pushing her aside. She turns around to see what he is running from and sees a stampede heading towards her faster than she can move, a flood of people, desperate, afraid, trying to escape the city. As the rain begins to fall, Cayapon braces for the flood to hit her.

4

Liddum

Liddum is ready. He has been at this spot in the desert for an hour now. The god will be here, Liddum believes. In his vision, this is where lightning struck the ground.

Today, Liddum isn't wearing armour. On his head, he has wrapped a white cloth to protect himself from the sun and keep the sand out of his eyes and mouth. At his side is a flask of water. In front of him is the bottle from the old woman. Inside it, the sky.

The sky inside the bottle has taken on the colour of the sky above, blue with clouds coming in swiftly on the Habagat. The north-easterly wind used to bring rain, but not anymore.

Maybe, finally, it will rain today, Liddum muses. *Maybe I should return.*

Liddum laughs at the notion. There is no turning back now. The captain may be fat and lazy, but he will still have Liddum's head for abandoning his post. It is the law. It is the will of the Sultan.

Another hour passes. Liddum stands, ready with the bottle in his hands. Nothing happens except for the slow advance of the clouds from the sea. He sits down and places the bottle in front of him once again. He waits. He watches the sun's slow march across the sky. It is time.

No, the time has passed. Was the vision false? Did the old woman lie?

Liddum begins to fear that the god is not coming. Skyworld will not open today. The Sultan's soldiers will capture Liddum for abandoning his post, and the captain will have him executed.

Liddum decides to stay until nightfall just to be sure. He has nothing to return to anyway.

Just before sunset, a sound erupts from across the desert, and Liddum's heart gives a leap. He thinks the moment has arrived.

I must have missed the flash of lightning. I must have fallen asleep. The god is here!

Liddum springs into action. He kneels in front of the bottle and opens it. The liquid inside the bottle evaporates in an instant, but nothing else happens. Liddum examines the bottle and touches what remains of the liquid inside. It is only water.

He looks around and realizes that there was no thunder, no lightning. No god has fallen from the sky.

It is cannon fire. But there is no cannon as loud as that.

As the cannon sounds a third time, Liddum realizes it is the God Cannon. And he knows that the Sultan is dead.

After a few moments, Liddum hears the sound of the agong sending the news to the other cities of the sultanate. Liddum also hears another sound coming from the city: the sound of thousands of voices screaming. Then, he sees smoke rising from the Sultan's Palace.

Liddum pushes aside his disappointment about capturing the god. He gathers his things and rushes back to the city. If they discover that he has abandoned his post, they may sentence him to death. But it doesn't matter. They need him there.

Liddum runs towards the burning city. In his haste, he doesn't notice at first. But soon it becomes impossible not to notice. There is water on his face, on his chest. The cloth that wraps his head is wet. It is raining!

The rain falls like a light mist at first. The parched earth drinks the rain, and Liddum finds himself running through a watery mud made of sand and dust and water. He looks above him and sees that the clouds now cover the sky from horizon to horizon. The sun has almost set, but there is still a faint orange glow from behind the clouds, just above the mountains.

Liddum stops and squints at the horizon. Was he disoriented? Was the rain playing tricks with his eyes? He knows there are no mountains there. To the north, there is only a vast plain. He squints through the rain in the failing light. He definitely sees something. Liddum's mind confirms what his eyes know to be true. Those aren't mountains on the horizon.

He counts eighteen of them in all. They are so large it would be easy to mistake them for mountains. They are giants. He has heard of them in tales, of how General Marandang defeated them two hundred years ago, of how a prophet said that Sun Girna Ginar's doom would come when they returned. And now they are here—here to destroy the city at last.

5

Cayapon

Cayapon knows it is impossible, but she can't deny what she hears: a newborn's cry. Just minutes ago, there was a heartbreaking silence. She had lost all energy to push, and somewhere, somewhere below, Kagayha-an, the manghihilot, was doing what she could to get the child, pushing aside flesh and bone, pulling at the baby inside her.

Cayapon had tried to push all day. She pushed when Kagayha-an commanded her to push, screaming when the pain became too much. It was late in the afternoon when the labour began, and Sun Girna Ginar had just begun to flood, with water trickling in from the manghihilot's doorway. By noon, the water was just below her knee. Now it was completely dark outside, and the water was higher. It went past her ankles from where she sat in the high birthing chair. A flood of relief spread through her when the baby came out, followed by fear when the manghihilot attended to the baby without smiling. She cleared the newborn's airways, reaching into the mouth with her old fingers, then she slapped the baby's back and buttocks with a cupped hand, once, then paused, then slapped the baby again. Cayapon held her breath and closed her eyes. There was no sound. Her baby wasn't breathing. In the dim lamplight, she could see that it was a girl.

She doesn't remember what Kagayha-an said then. She said something, but Cayapon wasn't paying attention. She didn't look at Kagayha-an either, couldn't look at the old woman and her sympathy. She kept her eyes closed and wept. Later, still, with her eyes closed, she felt the afterbirth slip between her legs. Then that impossible sound filled the air, and she opened her eyes.

She finds Kagayha-an cradling a baby in her arms. Cayapon knows immediately that it is another child. This one is darker and smaller, hairier. It almost looks like it was born before its time. Kagayha-an cleans the child of blood and then places it on Cayapon's breast. It finds her nipple and suckles hungrily, like a beast.

'I can't explain it,' Kagayha-an says, searching for words. 'The afterbirth. It came to life. It is a boy.'

Cayapon has no time to ask questions. She has no words for questions—she cannot speak the unspeakable about what happened to her child or form the questions about who or what she is holding in her hands. The manghihilot has no further explanations. Her face was full of grief when the baby was stillborn. She turned pale when the afterbirth came to life, but she moved swiftly to ensure that all was well with the child.

Now, Cayapon can feel the water rising from where she lies in the birthing chair. Kagayha-an breaks her silence.

'We have to go,' she says. 'The water is rising fast. Do you think you can get up?'

Cayapon thinks that she can't. She is so tired but she says, 'Yes. Give me a moment. Where are we going?'

'Not far,' Kagayha-an replies. 'Just across the street to the next house. They have a second floor. My daughter is already there.'

Later—too soon it seems to Cayapon—she finds herself on her feet, thigh-deep in water. She feels weak, afraid that she will topple over into the water at any moment, but Kagayha-an is there with one arm across her back and under her arm. With her other arm, the old woman is cradling Cayapon's child, the stranger.

The little one begins to cry halfway to the neighbour's house. Both of them pay the child no heed. The street outside has become inundated with garbage. Massive drifts of trash float by. Some get stuck on doorways or against walls as the rising water pushes forward relentlessly. The current is not strong, but Cayapon quickly grows tired of pushing her body through the water. If the water were deeper, it would be easier. She would be almost weightless. But now, with the water level creeping slowly up her thighs, everything is full of weight. The rain pushes down and soaks her clothes. Cayapon wants to stop when they reach the middle of the street—she just can't go on anymore—but Kagayha-an won't let her.

'We are almost there,' she says. 'We cannot stop here.'

They press on, taking one step and then another until they reach the front door of the house. With each step, Cayapon feels weaker. There is a pain in her womb, which has now expanded to fill her. Now, there is also the pain in her weak, tortured legs and a lightness in her head.

The door to the house opens and inside is a middle-aged woman with her skirts tied around her waist.

'Come in,' Pinantaw, the manghihilot's daughter, says. 'Hurry. The baby is getting wet.'

* * *

The rain beats down without any respite, and before midnight, the water has reached the roof of the house. It was just an hour earlier when they moved from the second floor to the roof of the small house by climbing out the window. Kagayha-an went first, and they passed the baby to her. Cayapon followed, supported by Pinantaw. Finally, the others in the house followed onto the roof. Soon, everything they had would be underwater, but they didn't look back.

Other survivors have joined them now because this house, along with another further down the street, are the only ones with a second floor. There is a family of three with them—mother, father, son. They were a family of five when the day began, but the two youngest were carried away by the flood. There is a ten-year-old boy who won't speak. In all, there are now fourteen of them on the roof of the house.

They managed to salvage a banig and a parasol. The two older women take shelter under the woven mat as Cayapon and the baby hide under the parasol. The rain is so strong that soon they are all soaked. The baby begins to cry.

'Give him your breast,' Kagayha-an says.

Cayapon doesn't move. To her surprise, she feels nothing. She feels nothing for the child in her arms. She feels nothing for the loss of her child, the real one, her daughter. She feels nothing for the flood, the destruction of the city, the giants on the horizon, her own death. Even the pain has gone away. Now, she feels only a dull ache all over. A part of her is relieved that she doesn't have to deal with emotion, here, at the end.

As the baby continues to cry, Cayapon looks at the stranger in her arms. He is a hairy little thing with soft, fine black hair on his forehead. He even has the same fine hair on his arms. It is almost fur-like. She half-expects to see a row of monstrous, sharp teeth in his mouth, but there are none. His pupils are very black and very large. She imagines they are asking her a question.

Cayapon looks away and returns to staring at the floodwater. It has risen again. The roof of the house is sloped at a slight angle and the water is now slowly climbing to where they are sitting. Soon it will be time to go and search for shelter elsewhere. Beyond the edge of the roof, now submerged, the water is a lake. A few hours ago, it was merely a river traveling through the streets. But the floodwaters flow sluggishly now. The drifts of garbage on the street have been carried elsewhere, to the sea perhaps.

The rain doesn't allow her to see far, so Cayapon doesn't know if there are still any other roofs above the flood. In the Maharlika Quarter, surely, but that is far away. Maybe up the hill towards the temples in the Holy Quarter. That is still some distance away, she thinks, but it is closer. She doubts she can make it. She doesn't have the strength to swim, and she was never much of a swimmer anyway. If the water reaches where she is sitting, she tells herself, then it will be the end.

The prayers of the old woman who blessed her with the holy water will go unanswered. There will be no one to protect her child from the world, no gods or heroes to save her from her fate.

She will go quietly. First, she will submerge the baby in the floodwater, silence his crying, then let go, let the current take him where it will, to safety or to the bottom of the sea, whichever the gods choose. Then, she will follow. She will step off the roof without a word, and before anyone else will be able to reach her, she will be sinking, down into the cold, letting the breath out of her lungs, taking in the flood. It will be painful, but she will be beyond pain, soon. Just this one last trial, and it will be over. She will be free.

6

Dunungan

It's just bad luck, Dunungan tells himself. **You make your own fortune.** Still, Dunungan cannot deny that it all began when he started sweeping the floor just before he went to bed.

'You'll sweep the luck away,' his wife, Perena, told him.

He replied, 'I like it this way. It's cleaner.'

She shrugged and didn't argue with him, but two weeks later, an accident happened on his boat, and he had to pay for repairs. Money was tight ever since, not that there was ever much to begin with.

Things became worse when Dunungan jumped over a termite hill without asking permission from the little people. Dunungan's bosun was lost overboard in a storm.

'Maybe an enemy cursed you,' Perena said.

'I have no enemies,' Dunungan replied. 'I have a boat that takes people to Sabah and back. I'm not the vizier.'

'You should have yourself cleansed.'

'That costs money. We don't have money.'

'You should ask forgiveness from the gods.'

'I've tried that. What can I do? I'm unforgivable.'

'You should look for that old woman in the market.'

'What for? I'm already married to you.'

Perena did not look amused.

'Maybe she will give you a good price,' she said.

'Or, maybe, she will take my arm along with my money!' Dunungan thought that would put an end to the discussion, but Perena was persistent.

'All my friends say her magic works,' she said.

Dunungan gave up. 'Why not? You are right,' he said and left the house. He needed to get out anyway.

Dunungan's ill-luck found him almost as soon as he left the house. He travelled through an awful commotion at the mouth of the market. There was some kind of riot because the general fired his big cannon three times, and people thought the Sultan was dead or something. Dunungan thought that would probably be bad for business, but he saw no point in returning home. He had been fortunate to escape the riot by climbing onto the roof of a house. Maybe his luck was turning.

An hour after he left his house, Dunungan finds himself standing in front of the old woman who sells dreams in bottles. She is in front of an empty market stall. There is nothing in it except for a wooden box containing a few of her things. He is holding a bottle in his hands, a thin glass flask with briny seawater inside. It is the last bottle the woman is selling.

'This will bring me luck?' Dunungan asks. He looks sceptical. 'What am I supposed to do with it?'

'Pour it onto the deck of your ship.'

'How did you know I have a ship?'

The old woman fixes Dunungan with a look and says, 'You believe I sell magic in bottles, and yet you have to ask how I know such things.'

Dunungan lets the question go.

'That's all there is to it, then?' he asks.

'That's all there is to it.'

Dunungan shrugs. If it works, then he will be grateful. He needs a change in luck. If it doesn't, he loses a little money, which makes little difference to him. He is already poor.

'How much?' Dunungan asks. He prepares for an answer that will shock him. He doesn't want to give away his reaction. He will offer her half of whatever price she says.

'Free passage on your ship,' the old woman replies. She picks up her box of belongings.

Dunungan's mouth hangs open. He doesn't know what to say. Instead, he blinks rapidly. He scratches his head.

'It's yours,' the old woman says as if she needs to explain something to a child. 'Just take me on your ship.'

Dunungan is still confused. He opens his mouth to ask a question, but no words come out.

'What time do you depart?' the old woman asks, ignoring the bewildered look on Dunungan's face.

Dunungan is uncertain about the arrangement, but he answers anyway with a well-rehearsed statement that comes out involuntarily. 'We leave for Sabah tomorrow morning. But be there early. Sometimes we leave before sunrise to avoid bad weather.'

'That is perfect,' the old woman says, pleased at something. Dunungan almost asks her what she is so happy about, but something tells him he will not get an answer.

'May the blessings of Magbabaya be upon you,' she says and walks away, leaving the market for the last time.

7

Liddum

Liddum returns to the wall. At the Bone Gate, people are streaming out. They are fleeing from chaos behind—the Sultan's palace is burning. They are running towards danger—giants are on the horizon. There is no way out. The giants have surrounded the city.

When the giants start throwing boulders at the city walls, many run back inside Sun Girna Ginar. Liddum enters the city with them. The Bone Gate begins to close, pushed by a battalion of the wall guard. The stone boulders break against the walls and fall on the people outside trying to escape. Many are crushed. The survivors cry for help, and Liddum almost runs outside to save them, but the gates are closing. There is no time. The gate is slammed shut. Stone boulders continue to strike the outside of the gate.

Liddum heads towards his brothers in the wall guard, but now that the Bone Gate is closed, they break ranks and join the crowd now trying to get as far from the wall as possible.

Liddum stops one of the guards, grasping him by the arm.

'Brother,' he asks, 'where are you going?'

'Liddum,' he says, recognizing the soldier. 'It is over. How can we hope to defend the wall against *those*?' The guard points in the direction of the giants.

'It is our duty,' Liddum says.

'We have done our duty. We have closed the gates. There is no one left,' the guard says. 'The others have abandoned their posts. The captain was the first to go. The Sultan's armies are not coming to our aid. They say the general has locked himself in the palace.'

The guard shakes himself free of Liddum's grasp.

'The Sultan is dead,' the guard says. 'If you don't want to end up like him, you'd best find a way out of this cursed place.'

Liddum watches the guard go. He looks up at the sky and sees a column of smoke rising from the Sultan's palace. He runs towards it.

* * *

The moon is high in the sky. Liddum has still not reached the palace. Throughout the night, the rain fell in torrents and flooded the streets. The entire city was submerged quickly. Everywhere, people abandoned their homes to swim to buildings whose roofs were still above water. Liddum helped them get to safety, then went on, always swimming in the direction of the palace.

I was a fool to believe the old woman, Liddum tells himself. *She told me what she needed to earn a few gold beads, and like a fool, I gave up everything when she said that I would be a great hero.*

Liddum's regret is interrupted by voices in the distance. He hears them shouting for help in the darkness, and swims towards them. There are a dozen, or so, of them, mostly women and children, standing on the roof of a house. He treads water when he is near them, and they call out to him.

'She fell into the water,' they tell him. 'She had a baby with her. A newborn.'

'One of us went after her, but she hasn't surfaced either.'

Liddum dives to look under the water, but he can't see anything in the darkness. He surfaces to hear more screams. As he catches his breath, he sees the people on the roof pointing in the direction of the sea. In the darkness, Liddum has difficulty seeing.

'What is it?' Liddum calls out.

'There is a wave coming,' someone says, then he sees it.

From horizon to horizon, the wave towers over everything in Sun Girna Ginar. There is no escaping it. Liddum knows he won't survive the coming of that wave. No one will.

Part VI: Giants

After Imugan helped her brothers enslave the god Kalaon, they planned to kill her. They thought she did not know, but she noticed a great many things. She was twelve years old already, no longer a child. And she was a witch. She always had been.

Before their plans were set in motion, Imugan had a vision. She saw the Sultan giving Adlao a long knife.

'You do not have to do this, brother,' the Sultan said. 'We can poison her, or we can have the assassins kill her for us.'

Adlao shook his head.

'What difference does it make who kills her?' the Sultan asked Adlao. 'The child has to die. We knew that from the start.'

'It should be one of us,' Adlao said. 'She calls us her big brothers. We betrayed those words. She thinks we will protect her. But we never meant to. We used her and tricked her. It is only right that one of her brothers takes her life in the end. I want to be the one to do it.'

The Sultan showed no emotion.

'Then take the knife. It is enchanted with spells to ensure the death of her spirit. And remember, she is dangerous. She is a child, yes, but remember, you kill baby snakes the moment you see one.'

Adlao took the knife.

Since Imugan had the vision, she has been on her guard. She fashioned her own knife out of a broken mirror and cast what spells she could to protect her. She kept the knife with her at all times. After she bound her father Kalaon to the Sultan's amulet, she knew she wouldn't have long to wait. She was correct—Adlao made his move that same night.

Imugan woke up to see Adlao in her room, at her bedside. She reached for her knife but found no knife at her throat.

'Menalam,' Adlao whispered, 'come with me.'

'Why?' she asked, afraid of the answer.

'We are leaving the palace. You are not safe here. You never were.'

'How do I know it is not a trick?'

'Trust me. Am I not your big brother?'

Imugan looked at Adlao's face in the darkness. She could see that he was afraid too.

'How will we get out?' she asked Adlao. 'There are guards in every corridor. There are spells in the doorways, and the gates are watched by the Sultan's witches.'

Adlao raised a finger to his lips. He walked to a wall, knelt down, then placed his face close to it as if he were looking for something. There was an almost inaudible click, then a door that wasn't there before opened.

'Come,' Adlao said. 'Bring nothing.'

They walked for what seemed like hours through the passages behind the walls. Adlao walked ahead with an oil lantern lit low. Imugan followed in silence. They did not speak. They travelled through narrow stone passageways and climbed down winding staircases. Always, they headed downward and southward until they reached a door.

'When you walk through this door,' Adlao said, 'you will be outside the palace walls, in the Maharlika Quarter. Take the first road you see and keep going until you reach the market. Go to the other end of the market and look for the road with the dragon's bones.'

'I know, Isarog's bones.'

'They are not Isarog's,' Adlao said. 'The Sultan lied. They belong to the dragon of Laon. We caught him in a volcano in the north and slaughtered him here in Isarog's place. The Sultan lied about a great many things. He lied about enslaving your father. He lied about your mother as well. He killed her long ago. He even lied about your name. It is not Menalam. Your name is Imugan.'

She stared at Adlao and thought it was strange to hear someone speaking the truth. She was weaned on lies. They were familiar to her. These truths were painful and uncomfortable, but Imugan preferred them.

'I know,' she said simply.

Adlao nodded. He always suspected that she had never forgotten.

'The dragon's road is many miles long. At the end of it is the Bone Gate. When you step past the gate, you will be safe from the Sultan's eyes. But his reach is long. Travel as far as you can from this place.'

'You are not coming?' For a moment, she was filled with panic.

'No,' Adlao said. 'I can't leave. I have to help the Sultan see the error of his ways. That is how I can best serve him. He will not harm me.'

Adlao blew out the lamp and opened the door. Outside, the night was bright, and the air smelled like flowers from the gardens of the Maharlika.

'You need to live,' Adlao told Imugan before he closed the concealed door in the palace walls. 'Live a prosperous life. Forget about us. Forget about this place.'

1

Marandang

General Marandang looks at the giants on the horizon and struggles to find the hatred he has nurtured for more than a hundred years. It is raining—the first rain since the drought—and it hasn't stopped yet. He has difficulty seeing the giants through the rain. His cataracts have dimmed his sight, but there is no mistaking what he sees before him. It is the six-headed giant of Gawi-Gawen. Marandang has been waiting for its arrival for a long time.

'It's just you and I now,' Marandang says to the giant's shape on the horizon. 'Everyone is dead now.' The Sultan is dead. Adlao was murdered by the Sultan's assassins. Gaygayuma has travelled to Skyworld before her time. Even the tikbalang has passed on. And then there was the dragon Isarog but Marandang doesn't want to think of the dragon right now.

'What does it matter now, old friend?' he says. 'I will kill you, or you will kill me. That's all there is. Whoever survives will be killed by someone or something else. If I kill you, maybe some enemy will send an assassin to end me. Or, maybe, my own heart will betray me and stop beating. If you kill me, well, you may live longer than I ever will. But even giants die. You may be too arrogant to believe it, but I've seen it happen. They simply let go, stop moving, and allow the earth to reclaim them. So you and I, we'll both end up in the same place. The only difference is who put us there. But I think it will be worth it.

'You killed my family. You destroyed what was my world. Come. Finish the job.'

With these words, Marandang feels the fringes of his hatred. It is a fire that has gone out, leaving only its embers behind. But, it is still there. Marandang knows he can feed the embers and turn them into a fire if he wishes. Or, he can let it all turn to ashes. Either way, Marandang knows he is at the end.

* * *

The six-headed giant of Gawi-Gawen stops when it reaches Sun Girna Ginar's Bone Gate. The features of its six heads are carved from different minerals. Granite covers its faces. Sandstone forms its ears. Jagged black limestone pillars are its teeth, and obsidian is in its eyes. The six faces themselves are almost a parody of mankind. One is the face of a retarded child, while another is the lined face of an old man. One face belongs to an obese glutton, and the one beside it is a gaunt and half-starved beggar. One face has the vacuous eyes of a fool, and the last has the noble visage of a king.

The giant surveys the city silently, then it speaks.

'Is this the greatest city of man?' it says, all six heads speaking at the same time. Together, its voices sound like thunder. 'Sun Girna Ginar! Your doom has come.'

The giant of Gawi-Gawen walks through the walls of Sun Girna Ginar and they crumble at its feet. The giant hardly breaks stride. Great pieces of the wall tumble to the ground, landing on the shanties below. Close to the walls, the flood has risen above the roofs of most of the buildings, but from that point, the land rises gradually, leaving half the city above the flood. At the centre of the city, the Sultan's palace crowns the city, waiting for the giant. It walks forward, destroying everything in its path. The earth shakes with each step.

'Is this the city created by the gods?' the giant taunts, six voices as one. 'Where are your mighty protectors? Where is your Sultan and his magic? Where is your general and his armies?'

There is no reply. The giant continues to walk forward, crushing the city underneath its feet. Then, a sound fills the air. It is the God Cannon.

The shot echoes over the floodwater, and something explodes on the giant's chest. Chunks of the giant's body fall into the water below. The giant lets out a low grunt. It staggers.

A voice is heard from the Sultan's palace. Amplified by witchcraft, the voice shouts directly into the minds of all in the city.

'I am here,' the voice says.

'Who are you?' the giant's six heads ask in unison.

'I am your death, giant.'

Now the giant's heads are laughing. They are a discordant crowd. The fool's head guffaws, the child's head giggles, the old man's head closes its eyes and laughs in a hoarse croak. The king's head is thrown back and laughs with pride.

'We have been here since the gods made these islands,' the king's head says as the other heads continue to laugh. 'We have seen your people arrive on their boats and build their cities. We have seen these puny cities burn like fireflies in our vision. Your people are nothing compared to the gods or the mighty giants of the earth. We have witnessed the eons pass. Death is not for us.

'And now you threaten us? Who are you? Who is so brazen in the face of their death?'

'I am here,' the voice says again, but now there is more. 'At the centre of the city, on the battlements of the walls of the Sultan's palace, you will find me. And you will find your own death. Come to me if you dare. I am not afraid of you. I have killed your kind before.'

The God Cannon fires again, filling the air, and this time the cannon strikes the giant higher up, at the base of its neck. Great sheets of stone fall from where the giant is shot, but it continues to walk forward as if it is unaffected.

From the top of the Palace walls, Marandang watches the giant make its slow progress towards the centre of the city. He calculates how long it will take for his men to reload the cannon, and where the giant will be when they are ready to fire. He orders his men to aim the cannon higher still.

The giant makes its way towards the Sultan's palace, each step bringing destruction to the city. It begins the long climb from the Holy Quarter to the Maharlika Quarter, stepping out of the rising floodwater, knocking down the towers of the temples in its way, and destroying the mansions of the Maharlika that lie at the foot of the Sultan's palace. This destruction is punctuated by the deafening shots of the God Cannon. Five more times the general hits the giant. Five more times the rocks that form the giant's flesh tumble to the ground below. The shots strike the giant's chest, abdomen, shoulder, and neck. Once they hit the giant's hand when it raised its arm to protect one of its heads.

Nothing stops the giant's advance. It stops in front of the Sultan's palace and scans the walls for the man who dared to threaten it.

'Where is my death?' the giant's king head mocks the general.

'I am here,' Marandang says. This time he uses his own voice, and it carries far past the walls.

The six-headed giant of Gawi-Gawen kneels in front of the Sultan's palace so it is now at eye-level with the top of the wall, the God Cannon, and General Marandang.

For the first time in over a hundred years, Marandang looks at the giant, and he finds a little of his old hatred. He is surprised at how much he has forgotten about the giant. He has forgotten the size of it. In his mind, it had grown to the height of the clouds. Now, he thinks the giant is smaller than he remembers, not much larger than the other giants he killed, and just as mortal. He stares at the kingly face in the middle and studies the cruelty carved on its stone visage. He looks into the indifference of its obsidian eyes. The hatred in Marandang flares then burns steadily at last.

Marandang swears to himself that this will be the end. He steels himself for action. He speaks.

'I am General Marandang of Sun Girna Ginar.'

The giant looks for the source of the voice, finds the old man standing on the wall, and laughs.

'You are nothing but an old man,' he says.

'That is true,' Marandang says. 'And once I was a foolish boy whose life you spared so that I could tell Sun Girna Ginar that you were coming to destroy the city.'

The giant pauses as if it is trying to remember.

'Yes,' the giant says, 'I remember now. You begged and cried and told me of the great general. And now you are old. And you say you are the general. How has this come to pass?'

'It is simple,' Marandang says. He pauses, and the giant waits. 'I have become a god. To kill you.'

The giant has had enough. All six heads turn towards Marandang.

'Little man,' the giant says. 'I care not for your tricks. You are the general. It is your turn to die. Then, I will destroy the rest of your city.'

Marandang gives the signal, gets down on one knee and covers his ears. The God Cannon fires.

The shot strikes the king-head of the giant just below its eye. Half of its face explodes. Stone fragments from the explosion strike the other heads. The remaining half of the king's face hangs limply from the giant's massive neck.

The giant stands up, shocked by the blow, then it reels backwards. It is falling.

When the giant falls, the earth shakes. The floodwaters surge. The giant's fall has crushed a large section of the Maharlika Quarter, flattening estates and mansions. Its remaining five heads land somewhere in the Holy Quarter. Clouds of dust rise from the destruction. The dust, together with the heavy rain, make it difficult for Marandang to see what has happened, or if the giant is still alive.

But it doesn't matter to Marandang. He is already in motion. He strides across the walls with his aides and captains behind him.

'Set him free,' Marandang says to one of his captains who disappears into a door that leads into the walls. From there, the captain gives the command to his lieutenant who orders a messenger to send the signal.

The messenger runs down the stairs that lead outside the palace. Once outside the wall, the messenger transforms into a bird, and in that form, he flies into a building behind a small temple in the Holy

Quarter. There, he transforms back into a man and gives his message to another soldier who rushes to the building's basement. There, a chasm travels deep into the earth.

The soldier steps into the chasm and floats down into the darkness. At the bottom of the chasm, he wakes a dozen giants, each as tall as five men. At their feet is a chain with links as wide as a tree. The chains are bolted to the walls of the cavern with massive iron spikes. The other end of the chain disappears into a black cavern.

The giants busy themselves in breaking the chain. Two giants hold a steel wedge over the chain. Another pair of giants hold a stone slab over the wedge, while four giants take turns driving sledgehammers into the stone, like women husking rice in a pestle. At first, it seems like nothing is happening. The soldier commands the giants to pick up the pace, then he starts to whip them. Inch by inexorable inch, the wedge moves downward through the iron chain. Then, the chain breaks.

From deep within the cavern, something stirs. It is large, ancient, and hungry.

Above the ground, Marandang watches what is left of his army spring into action. The rebels infiltrated his army, but there are still those who are faithful to him. It is these men who are now attacking the fallen giant. Thousands of men pour out of the palace gates. They are all armed with bows and a magical orange fire.

The giant is not yet dead. It gets up, raising itself with one arm from its position on the ground.

The closest battalion lets loose a barrage of flaming arrows. The volley buries itself into the stone legs of the giant and burns everything that the fire comes into contact with, even the giant's stone skin begins to melt.

To the giant of Gawi-Gawen, it is nothing but a nuisance. Now, half-sitting, it swats at the soldiers closest to him. Hundreds die under the giant's palm. Then, it stands up and shakes its remaining five heads. A thick black liquid pours out of wounds inflicted by the God Cannon. Meanwhile, volley after volley is fired by the general's soldiers, and now the giant's legs are engulfed in flame.

The giant lashes out at the troops with its burning feet. Blocks of the city are destroyed with a single kick. What is not destroyed is engulfed in flame. Again and again the giant kicks. The army is in disarray.

A low rumble begins deep in the earth. Some of the soldiers believe it is another giant, and they break ranks, running away from the sound, away from the giant of Gawi-Gawen.

The rumbling increases in volume, and then goes silent.

The earth erupts. Something large comes out of the ground in an explosion of rock. It isn't clear right away what it is with all the dust and dirt in the air, but it is large, almost as large as the giant of Gawi-Gawen itself.

It is the dragon Isarog, and it has grown. Marandang had kept it chained underground for all these decades. After feeding it on legions of the Sultan's enemies, unleashing it on rival cities, and having it devour hordes of magical beasts from Skyworld, Marandang imprisoned the sated dragon with chains and magic. Since then the dragon has not fed, and now that it has been set free, Isarog is hungry.

The dragon, in its hunger, consumes everything it sees. It charges at the giant and bites the giant's right leg. The force of the dragon's charge sends the giant tumbling to the ground again, destroying more of the Maharlika Quarter and part of the palace walls. Once the giant is on the ground, the dragon spins from its belly to its back, just like a crocodile, and as it spins, it breathes fire, engulfing the giant in flame. The spin breaks the giant's leg off and the dragon releases it, finding another hold on one of the giant's heads and most of its shoulder. Again, it spins like a crocodile and a terrible rending sound fills the air. It is rock breaking, stone burning. Isarog is feeding.

The giant stops moving, and Marandang knows that it is done.

All around the general, his men are celebrating the defeat of the giant, but Marandang knows it is only the beginning. He knows the dragon will consume the giant of Gawi-Gawen and then move on to the next giant. It will devour the giants one by one until none are left. If any of them turn to flee, it will give chase. They will not get far. When there are no more giants to consume, Isarog will return to the city and destroy its captor.

The general tells his captains to go and leave him.

'Sun Girna Ginar is ruined,' Marandang says. 'There is nothing more to do here. Go. Leave this place. You have fought with honour. There is nothing more your Sultan, your country, or I can ask from you. It is time to think of your wives and your children. Find your families. Make sure they are safe.'

His men do not move.

'Go!' the general commands. 'I release you from your vows. The fight is over. We have conquered two worlds together, but now we have come to the end. There is no honour in staying at my side. There is only death.'

A few of his captains bow low and leave, but most of them stay. Every soldier in his personal guard stays as well. Marandang knows he cannot convince the rest of them to leave, so he says nothing more, just watches Isarog feeding on the giant of Gawi-Gawen.

2

Sakandal

Sakandal—he is Sakandal again, no longer Asuang—thinks it is all over when he sees the dragon return to Sun Girna Ginar. He thinks it has returned to devour what's left—the bones of the palace and the few remaining Maharlika and petty ministers cowering in the water-filled halls below his room in the tower. Sakandal doesn't try to save himself. Where else is he supposed to go?

Then a miracle happens. The dragon stops at the part of the wall where the general is standing beside the God Cannon. The two speak, and before Sakandal can hope that the general will kill the dragon, like he did the six-headed giant, the dragon eats the general.

It is a simple motion. The dragon opens its mouth, moves forward, and closes its mouth. It is so large that it takes a chunk of the wall into its mouth as well. The God Cannon tumbles from the wall and falls into the floodwater. Between one moment and the next, the general is gone.

Sakandal watches the dragon rise towards the clouds, and fly towards Skyworld, swimming through the air like a snake through water. The massive beast grows smaller and smaller until it disappears somewhere over the horizon. Sakandal realizes that he still remains. He is alive.

The light is fading. From the dying light, he can see what remains of his city. By now the flood has risen to cover everything. The flood has submerged the mosques in the Holy Quarter. Only the minarets can be seen, and occasionally the top of a dome.

As for the Maharlika Quarter, little survives. Here and there, a roof peeks out of the water, but most of the great mansions are submerged—monuments to their masters' greatness, preserved in a watery grave where the grave robbers cannot reach them. Here, their riches will stay, buried under silt and sand. Or where the flood water meets the ocean, all will belong to the sea. Gilded thrones will grow barnacles, golden baths sprout coral, growing richer and more varicoloured than they ever were in the days when they were the playthings of royalty.

The floodwater stops halfway up the walls of the Sultan's palace. Currents carry the dead to the Sultan's gate like an offering. Hundreds of bodies converge there. He does not know why or how, but they are naked, bloated, and stiff. They hardly look like people, more like the carcasses of pale cows or hogs. The following days will bring more of the dead. Soon they will begin to rot, and the flies will come. Maybe carrion eaters will come too, but he is not sure. Maybe the rains have killed them too.

From the palace wall, the flood water goes around and through the barrier, down through secret passageways, in between cracks in the wall, through open doorways and cunning arrow slits in the wall. Nothing stops the water. Once inside the palace, it climbs the steps and seeps into the Sultan's receiving rooms. It enters the Great Hall unannounced, climbs the one hundred forty-four steps of the Sultan's dais, and swallows the Sky Throne.

The flood will do this all with no one to bear witness. Sakandal looks at the destruction from afar, safe in the certainty that the flood will not reach the top of the Sultan's tower. He will venture out one day when the floodwaters have receded. Or, if the waters never return to where they came from, he will set out on a makeshift raft crafted from a table, and survey his kingdom because, yes, all of this, everything as far as the eye can see and more, everything above the water, the sky, the clouds, and everything swallowed by the flood, it all belongs to him now.

Sakandal laughs. It is a bitter sound he does not recognize. He isn't sure why the laughter is escaping from his mouth in wave after hilarious wave. This was the previous Sultan's joke on Sun Girna Ginar, its millions of people, his allies, his enemies, his killer. This was the Sultan's power, that beyond the grave, he could take it all with him, the greatest civilization the world has ever seen, and in one day, make it all disappear. There would be no monuments, no songs, no epics, no statues of great men and their powerful ancestors. Not even a memory would be left.

Hundreds or thousands of years later, the children of the Sultan will continue to live on these islands and never know that once they ruled the earth and the sky. Other empires will rise and rule over them, and they will be like slaves, never knowing that once they had the power of gods—and he, Sultan Sakandal, long may he live, who was once the assassin known as Asuang, will be the first ruler of these people, a new nation born in water and blood.

He can't stop laughing. The joke is too damn funny.

3

Lam-Ang

The dream is always the same. He is falling through water. He knows that is impossible, but that is what it feels like in the dream. He is falling through the water as if he were falling through the air. In his dream, there is no bottom to the sea. It just goes on and on, into the deep, into the dark. Then, he stops falling and a great fish comes out of the darkness, a fish as large as the Sultan's palace. It is Berkakang the Old, who hatched at the same time as mankind was born.

Lam-Ang wakes halfway through the voyage. A hand is shaking him firmly. The hand belongs to his wife Cannoyan, still beautiful to his eyes after all these years.

'Beloved,' she says, 'you must see this.'

He stands up to find that the earth is moving underneath him. Cannoyan steadies him, and then Lam-Ang remembers that they are at sea.

He remembers everything that happened in the past day, the tolling of the God Cannon, the drums heralding the giants' return, the rain, the flood.

Like many of the Maharlika, Lam-Ang was prepared. They had heard of the plans against the Sultan long before they were put into motion. Some of them had a hand in it, while others paid for plotting against the Sultan with their lives. Others sided with the Sultan, reporting traitors in return for favours. But most, like Lam-Ang, simply watched events unfold, and prepared.

When the God Cannon sounded three times, Lam-Ang looked for Cannoyan and found her already gathering their children. Together, they headed for the harbour where a ship was waiting for them. By the time the ship left Sun Girna Ginar, along with a flotilla of ships from the other Maharlika, the palace was burning. Lam-Ang could see a thick column of black smoke rising into the sky.

Now Lam-Ang is standing at the same spot in the stern of the ship watching a different spectacle, one that terrified him more.

It is the middle of the night and the moon is hidden by clouds, so Lam-Ang can't see much. From what little light escapes the clouds, he can see ships dotting the dark sea. Many of the ships they left the city with are going to the same place, to Sabah. Some ships are small, but most are barges built to carry the glittering fortunes of kings and datus.

Once his eyes adjust to the darkness, Lam-Ang sees it, and he understands why they awoke him. Close to the horizon, he sees a swell rise from the ocean. It is so far away that he thinks it is only a small wave, but as it approaches one of the ships in the distance, he gains a sense of scale. The swell obliterates the ship, reducing it to driftwood, and then it moves on to the next ship, which it capsizes and then swallows. The wave is getting closer.

Lam-Ang turns around to tell the captain to make the ship go faster, but he sees that all the sails are fully furled despite the bad weather and he knows they are already going as fast as they can.

'Cannoyan,' Lam-Ang says to his wife. 'Tell the alipin to throw everything into the sea, all of the gold and our belongings and the food. All of it. Throw it overboard.'

Cannoyan hesitates.

'You must do this, my beloved,' Lam-Ang commands. 'It is our only chance.'

Cannoyan nods and passes the message on to the alipin.

Lam-Ang looks into the darkness again and what he sees confirms all his fears. He sees the swell heading straight for Lam-Ang's ship, and at its centre, a giant fin rising out of the water like an island being born.

'Berkakang is coming for me,' Lam-Ang says.

Lam-Ang looks around him, at the faces of the frightened crew and the face of his beloved Cannoyan. He holds her close, inhaling deeply as if he could take her with him if he did so.

'We always knew this day would come,' Lam-Ang tells her. 'The dreams told me this would be my fate.'

Cannoyan shakes her head, denying everything.

'You must live,' Lam-Ang continues. 'The children must live. Fly as fast as you can. If the beast has me, maybe it will return to the deep.'

'No,' Cannoyan says, still denying him, but Lam-Ang knows that she will obey him. She knows that he is right. This is their only hope. He kisses her farewell and then steps to the very stern of the ship. He looks around one last time, but it is dark and there is little to see.

He jumps into the water and begins to fall as he did in his dream.

He is calm. It feels good to be in the sea. The water is almost warm, and it locks out all sound, all memory. The roar of the wind, the unrelenting rain, the merciless waves breaking upon the bow of the ship, they are all gone now. It is all in the past, together with all the pain and the suffering he experienced. There are other things too such as his love for Cannoyan and the songs he left behind—things that cannot die. But Lam-Ang doesn't give them another thought. He looks forward as all light recedes, and he plummets into the deep.

Soon it becomes clear that he is not falling at all, but sinking as if he is weighed down by stones. Lam-Ang realizes it is Berkakang bringing its prey to itself. It has waited so long for its prize.

Just as all light is about to disappear, Lam-Ang sees it: an eye reflecting what little light there is left in the world. It is huge, a sphere as large as a house, and milky white. At first, Lam-Ang thinks it is blind, but it isn't. Lam-Ang feels it see him, sees Berkakang the Old turn towards him, and open its mouth. The darkness inside is the void.

'It is your fate,' the oracle told Lam-Ang a lifetime ago before he left Nalbuan for Sun Girna Ginar. 'You have escaped a thousand deaths. But you will not escape Berkakang. The gods demand that you atone for killing all those Igorot. I know, I know. You did it for your village and your father, but debts must be paid. And more blood is to come, which you must also pay for at the end of your days.

'In the end, your life belongs to Berkakang.'

'When will this happen?'

'Oh, not soon. Don't worry. That old fish doesn't count time like you do. It will happen in your twilight years. At the end of the world. That is all I know.'

Lam-Ang grew despondent.

'Take heart, Lam-Ang,' the oracle said. 'They sing songs about you! That will never die.'

Lam-Ang stares into the void that is Berkakang's mouth. He closes his eyes and lets out the remains of his final breath, knowing this was the beginning of immortality.

Part VII: The Immortal City

The young girl runs along the docks looking for the old woman. It is raining and the water has soaked her clothes and her hair. She is barefoot. She looks like she has been crying. But few stop to look at the beautiful child. They are busy trying to escape from the city and the giants. They seek passage on ferries, fishing vessels, or any boat that will take them to safety. There is an air of silent desperation, and the beautiful young girl weaves through it all, between the skirts of the women begging to be taken on board the ships, over boxes and bales of goods left to rot, like a flying fish bursting from the sea and sparkling in the sun.

The diwata Humitau, daughter of Tau-mari-u, lord of the seas, finds the old woman sitting on a bench in the harbour, waiting to board Dunungan's ship.

'My husband told me about you,' Humitau says, 'about how a mighty witch was giving away her power to the people of the city. It was you who made it all possible, he said.'

'Yes,' the old woman says. 'I remember Aponi-tolau. You must be Humitau.'

'You gave your power to a demon,' Humitau says with spite. 'Your hands are full of blood. These people don't deserve your gifts. They don't know what to do with dreams. They are butchers and murderers, every one of them, and you were wrong to help them.'

The old woman takes Humitau's harangue without saying a word.

The young diwata is not finished. 'Now my father's flood is coming. The cruel men of this land will all drown.'

The old woman lets Humitau's anger burn itself out. When the young girl has nothing left to say, the old woman speaks.

'Do you think you are the only one who suffers?'

Humitau doesn't reply, but the old woman waits for her to answer.

'No, of course not,' the girl says.

'Do you think there are no other people in this city? Do you think there is just you, surrounded by demons?'

'There is no one blameless in this place,' Humitau replies quickly. 'They worship the demon Aponi-tolau. They think murderers are heroes. They believe their Sultan is a god.'

'And there are some,' the old woman says with a sea of patience, 'who simply don't care about the gods. They do not come from noble birth. But they go about their lives quietly and do others no wrong. They worry about their next meal, about

their children, about an endless tyranny of small things. What do they care about the gods and their quarrels?'

The old woman speaks slowly, emphasizing each word.

'And then there are those who suffer more than you. What Aponi-tolau did to you was wrong, and you are right to seek justice. But you do not own all the suffering in the world. Others have more. Others have borne their pain longer than you. Do not be so quick to condemn them. Many of them have more right than you to ask for the flood that you seek. And yet, not all of them do.

'Do not worry, child,' the old woman says. 'Your justice shall come in the fullness of time. I grant dreams to all who ask, both to the men who inflicted pain upon us and to those who suffered at their hands. And if good outweighs evil, then we shall live in the light of their justice. But if the wicked outweigh the good, then retribution shall be ours. Not your way, no. We will have it without vengeance.'

Humitau breaks into tears after being admonished by the old woman. She cries like a child, covering her face and bawling into her hands.

The old woman takes pity on the child and takes her into her arms.

'Do not worry, Humitau. If you are right, and evil reigns over the city, then the storm will come. And the storm will bring the flood. The flood will cover all in the mercy of your father. You should return to the mountain.'

Still weeping, Humitau shakes her head.

'I am staying here,' she says in between sobs. 'I would rather drown in the flood.'

The old woman understands. 'I am sorry,' she says simply.

They remain huddled together for a moment, then the old woman takes a flask from her belongings and hands it to Humitau.

'Drink this,' she says, and the young girl takes a tentative sip.

'I just wish I could return to the sea,' Humitau says.

'Soon,' the old woman replies. 'Soon.'

1

Yumina and Lumawig

It is him, Yumina realizes. Now that they are outside the palace walls, under the fading light of the day, she is sure of it. It is the same soldier from last year, the man whose life she saved.

Could he know? Yumina wonders. She shakes her head. *No, it is impossible.* She made sure he would know nothing about it. *And yet,* she thinks with some doubt, *he is here.*

'We must get the princess to safety,' Lumawig says to the small group of soldiers he commands. 'If the Sultan is dead, his killers will come after his children next.' He looks almost apologetic when he says that.

They make swift progress through the Maharlika Quarter. The mansions are closed like fortresses. Archers are stationed on the walls. Some streets are blocked by phalanxes of soldiers. Lumawig, Yumina, her handmaidens, and the soldiers travel through these streets, and soon they are in one of the city's poorer quarters.

The streets are full of people, despite the rain, which has started to fall in heavy torrents. Many are trying to escape the city. There is rioting on some streets and looting on others, and Lumawig is forced to avoid these areas.

'We must leave the city,' Lumawig tells Yumina. 'The docks are closer than the walls. We will hire a boat. Once you are safe, we will figure out what to do.'

He doesn't know, Yumina tells herself. He treats her like a soldier is expected to treat a princess. He gives away no hint of their shared history. And yet, she feels safe with him. She doesn't know why, or what it is about him.

She remembers the first time she saw him. That day, she had travelled to the Bone Gate to receive the maharaja of a distant kingdom. It took three hours for her handmaidens to dress her. She waited two hours more. The maharaja was late.

Yumina had her royal guard with her, and they were lined up on either side of her in ceremonial armour. In front of her, the maharaja's caravan approached over the desert. They looked almost frozen in time. Yumina couldn't tell if they were moving forward or not.

The sun beat down upon them without mercy. She sat on a golden throne in an open tent without walls, but she could still feel the heat. It was making her sleepy, and she was tired from carrying her heavy dress and headpiece. She could already feel her back beginning to hurt.

'How much longer do we have to wait?' she asked Datu Sakabandar, her companion for the day, and one of her suitors. He was fat and old, but he was unmarried and the ruler of a hundred islands.

'I estimate they are an hour away, my gentle princess. It shouldn't be long now. For me, the time passes only too quickly. Each second I spend with you goes away too soon.'

The princess ignored the datu's words. They changed little about him, or how she felt for him. She looked away. At that moment she felt a pair of eyes on her, and they didn't belong to the overweight datu. She looked to either side of her, but she saw only her guards, looking into the distance with stoic gazes. She looked behind her, but there was only the usual assortment of handmaidens, aides, Maharlika, and ministers. They all looked wilted underneath the sun, hiding in their tents with their alipin fanning them with anahaw fronds. They were also looking into the distance at the caravan of the maharaja. None of them were watching her now.

Yumina returned her gaze forward as Datu Sakabandar continued to prattle on. She wasn't listening to him. She was scanning the faces of her guards. It was unlikely that any of them were looking at her. Looking directly at her was a crime, and the punishment for that was a whipping. The soldiers knew better. But still, Yumina looked into every face. She did it not only because she had nothing better to do but also because the feeling had begun to bother her. It felt like an intense gaze that was looking through her ceremonial garb, the headpiece, the jewellery and makeup. The intruder was looking at her, not as the princess, or the Sultan's firstborn daughter, but as herself, Yumina, the girl, exhausted and a little hungry, uncomfortable in her clothes, sick of the tiresome company, trapped by duty, and lonely.

Finally, Yumina found the man whose gaze bore into her, and to her surprise, it was indeed a soldier, one of her guards. It was nothing like she had expected at all. He looked, upon first inspection, just like any of the other soldiers, tall and hardened from the constant training. Maybe he was a little taller, a little younger, a little more handsome than most, but he was not that different from any of them. What unarmed her was that in his gaze there was supreme confidence. He was completely unafraid. He looked her in the eye with bare-faced honesty but not lust or malice. He had the look of someone who had found what he had been looking for, and seeing it for the first time, discovered that it was beautiful. There was a kind of wonder in his expression, and maybe— she was not sure because she had never felt that emotion, but she had been told stories about it, and if all that were true, she guessed that was what it would look like—a trace of love.

Her first reaction was one of shock. No one had ever done what he was doing. No one looked the Sultan's daughter in the eye, especially not a low-ranking soldier. No one dared. Then, having caught her eye, he smiled. There was just enough of his face showing from behind his helmet that she could see a mischievous upturn of his lips. Yumina was completely disarmed by that smile.

Meanwhile, Sakabandar continued to drone on, eyes fixed on Yumina's face, but she didn't hear what he was saying. She didn't see him either; her eyes were locked on the soldier.

The soldier's expression changed. He closed his eyes—no, they were still half-open, whites showing, irises raised to the sky. His mouth was half-open, then he was blowing air through his lips, yes, he was pantomiming boredom, sleep, long snores. He was making fun of the datu.

Yumina laughed. She didn't mean to laugh. It just escaped from her. Datu Sakabandar looked at her with a confused expression, and a handmaiden came closer to see if she needed anything. 'I am happy that my story amuses you,' Sakabandar said.

Yumina composed herself and stifled a laugh. 'You are more beautiful when you smile,' Sakabandar went on, flattering her. Yumina was only relieved that her laughter hadn't seemed inappropriate.

With that small burst of activity, Yumina's soldier returned to staring ahead of him. Too soon, that was what she thought of him: 'my soldier'. Encouraged by her outburst of good humour, the datu launched into the telling of another story, but no sooner had he begun, Yumina stopped paying attention to him. She was instead memorizing the features of her soldier so she would be able to find him again among the hundreds of identical soldiers in her personal guard.

He had a proud face with kind eyes and a nose with a strong, high bridge—so different from the broad flat noses that were typical of the Sultan's people. She liked his face.

When the princess thought he wouldn't look at her anymore, her soldier blinked rapidly and then turned his eyes in her direction without moving his head. To the princess' shock, he winked at her.

This time Yumina was able to act angry. She hardened her face and looked away from her soldier, but deep down her heart was racing. She wondered to herself if she was blushing because she felt very warm. When she looked at the soldier again with the angriest face she could muster, he was once again staring at the desert, but though he was trying to look serious, he couldn't help but let a smile escape from the corner of his mouth.

Again, it was Datu Sakabandar who forced her back to where she was.

'Have I offended you?' he asked.

'No,' the princess replied, suddenly afraid that she would be found out, that they would discover her secret. 'No, I just remembered something. Please, go on.'

As she looked at her soldier one more time, her face softened. She couldn't help but smile as well.

* * *

Lumawig didn't know how long it took the maharaja to arrive at the Bone Gate. Underneath the sun, in full ceremonial armour, he lost all track of time. A minute seemed to stretch and grow elastic, circling back on itself and becoming infinity. After a thousand of those had passed, the maharaja's caravan was before them.

The doors to the maharaja's palace opened. The palace began to move, to shift, to turn and rotate, like the turning of a mechanical clock. A set of stairs were placed at the foot of the carriage door by a pair of slaves. Rich scarlet curtains were drawn aside, but still, there was no maharaja to be seen.

Anticipating the maharaja's arrival, the princess got to her feet, walked out of the cover of her tent, and made her way close to the maharaja's carriage, preceded by thirty handmaidens, and sixty of her guards. Together, they—Yumina, Datu Sakabandar, Maharlika, ministers, handmaidens, soldiers—advanced until they were halfway to the golden carriage. When Yumina was closest to Lumawig, ten feet to her right with no one between them, she said in a soft voice, 'This is far enough.' Because she was standing straight ahead of him, Lumawig saw her look briefly in his direction. There was something of a smile playing on her face.

Once everyone was in position, they returned to waiting. The wind blew, picking up dust and sand. The entourage squinted as the wind passed through their ranks. Somewhere in the distance, a dust devil danced over the burning sands. Where was the maharaja? Already, this bordered on insult. One did not make the Sultan's daughter wait.

Just as some of the ministers were beginning to mutter among themselves, there was some activity from inside the golden carriage.

The maharaja's entourage began to disembark, starting with the maharaja's guard then the maharaja's ministers, almost all of them obese, dressed in voluminous robes, and the royal members of the maharaja's house. Finally, the maharaja himself stepped out of the carriage. He was a large, middle-aged man with a thick black beard and hard, unsmiling eyes. Behind him followed his seven wives and all their children.

It took an hour for the whole entourage to be announced properly to Princess Yumina with all their titles and honorifics, and as the hour passed, without warning, Yumina fainted from the heat.

Lumawig was the first one to see it happen. He couldn't help but see because she was standing in front of him. He saw the subtle signs. She swayed backward then forward in place. Her eyelids dropped as if she were falling asleep. Then she was falling to her side, the crown on her head tumbling to the ground.

He moved without thinking. He took five steps forward to catch the falling girl. To touch the princess was a crime punishable by death, but he wasn't thinking of the law. He was aware of it; he had been told before, but it was the last thing on his mind. All he knew was that she was falling, so he caught her. That was all there was to it.

Many things happened in rapid succession. First, there was a collective intake of breath from the princess' entourage when they saw her fall. One lesser handmaiden let out a shrill high-pitched scream. This was followed by a second of shock where everyone stood frozen in their places. As Lumawig swooped in to catch the princess, there was more shock and inaction as they witnessed the forbidden: a low-ranking soldier, little more than an alipin really, holding the daughter of god in his arms.

The captain of the guard, who stood far away, at the end of the line of soldiers, saw what had happened, and sprang into action. He shouted a command. Lumawig turned his head towards his captain, but he didn't stand right away because that would mean dropping the princess. Then Datu Sakabandar stepped in and struck the soldier with the back of a mailed fist.

After that, everyone became unstuck and began to move. The princess' handmaidens took Yumina from the soldier and carried her to her tent. Meanwhile, a dozen of Lumawig's fellow soldiers surrounded him and held his arms upon the command of their captain. They took him to the side and made a big show of beating him until the captain of the guard said, 'Take him away.'

At first, Lumawig was confused. He didn't know why everyone had reacted that way or why the datu had struck him, but by the time his brothers were beating him, he remembered the warnings of his captain and the law. It was a stupid thing to die for, he admitted, but what else was he supposed to do?

* * *

When Yumina came to her senses, she was back in her room in the palace. She was in her bed, and she could see from across the room that all the windows were open. The curtains caught the wind like sails on a ship.

On a chair beside her bed, Yumina's nanny was dozing lightly. She woke up right away when Yumina stirred.

'Don't move,' the nanny told Yumina. 'You need to rest. You passed out. From the heat.'

'Yes,' Yumina said, 'I remember.' She remembered the golden carriage of the maharaja, the merciless eye of the sun, and the young soldier.

'How are you feeling? Are you still warm?' The nanny's hand was upon Yumina's brow.

Yumina remembered more. She remembered hearing a voice in the darkness—the soldier's voice she realized now—calling to her as she lay passed out in his arms. He had a kind voice. She remembered opening her eyes and seeing the soldier being taken away.

'What happened to him?' Yumina asked weakly.

There was concern on her nanny's face. 'Who?' she asked.

'My soldier,' Yumina answered without thinking.

The nanny furrowed her brow. 'What soldier? Maybe you should go back to sleep. You're talking nonsense, dear.'

'The soldier who caught me when I passed out. What happened to him?'

A horrified look appeared briefly on her nanny's face. It was only then that Yumina believed that her nanny knew nothing about what had happened.

'Surely he didn't dare?' the nanny asked.

'And what if he did? I fell. He caught me. What then?'

The nanny's hand flew to her mouth.

'He will be executed for that. It is forbidden for one of his station to touch—'

Yumina stood up.

'Yumina!' her nanny said in alarm. 'Where are you going? You need to rest.'

Yumina didn't answer the question.

'Call my handmaidens. I need to get dressed.'

* * *

Minutes later, Yumina sat with Datu Sakabandar and the Captain of the Guard on their knees in front of her. Their foreheads touched the ground as they bowed.

Yumina abhorred this room. It was the largest one in her suite of rooms in the tower, and it was the one where she received her guests. At one glance, you could tell that it was a smaller version of the Great Hall. On one end, there were double doors that led to a dais a few steps high. On the topmost level was a jade chair upon which Yumina sat now.

The datu and the Captain of the Guard stood up. Now that they were standing again, the arrogance of the datu returned. He did not know why the princess had summoned them. He thought it could only be good for him. The Captain of the Guard was less arrogant. He stood upright in a stiff fashion, duty-bound.

The princess didn't waste any time with greetings or formalities.

'Where is he?' she asked in an even tone.

Datu Sakabandar and the Captain of the Guard were both silent.

'Who, my Princess?' Sakabandar asked. He had no idea who she was talking about.

The princess continued in her cold, even tone. 'When we received the Maharaja, I passed out from the heat outside the Bone Gate. As I fell, a young soldier caught me. My senses were not entirely with me, but I recall that he was beaten and taken away. Where is he?'

'Ah!' Sakabandar said. 'That soldier. Do not worry, my Princess. It has been dealt with.'

The princess shook her head and her headdress tinkled prettily, but her face was dark.

'That is not what I asked,' she said. 'Answer the question: where is he?'

Somewhat taken aback, Sakabandar replied, 'I ordered the Captain of the Guard to beat him and execute him. That is the law. He dared to—'

The princess turned her head towards the Captain of the Guard and interrupted the datu by repeating her question, 'Where is he now?'

'They should be in the middle of whipping him.'

Yumina closed her eyes. He was still alive. She let out a breath to steady herself. She did not know if she could do what she needed to do next. Even then, she had learnt much in the past minutes. She confirmed that Datu Sakabandar and the Captain of the Guard were afraid of her, even though they treated her like a child. She suspected they had always been afraid of her, but if that were true, why? And what was she capable of? What was the power she commanded?

She knew that when she pushed them—when she was rude to them, interrupted them, or treated them poorly—they did not push back. Now she needed to learn if she had any power at all, or if the titles and honorifics were just meaningless words attached to her name.

When she opened her eyes, she was ready. She was determined not to let her soldier die. When he caught her, touched her, he was only being human. To save him, she needed to become more than that.

'Captain, go to the soldier and set him free. It is my will that he not be harmed for his offence.'

The captain was about to bow and leave, but the datu stopped him with a hand on his shoulder.

'My Princess!' Datu Sakabandar said. 'We cannot go against the law. As you know, the law is the will of the Sultan. It is the will of your father.'

Yumina stared at the datu and tried not to show her fear.

'It is true what you say,' Yumina said to Sakabandar. 'The law is the will of the Sultan.' She paused. 'What I want to know is this: do I have to remind you who I am?'

'My Princess, the law is clear. Anyone who touches your personage whose blood is not—'

Yumina cut him off. 'Who am I?' she asked.

Sakabandar hesitated to answer, so she asked the question again, this time to the captain.

'You are the princess,' the captain said.

'Go on,' she said.

'The daughter of our Sultan, long may he live, ruler of this world and Skyworld, our lord and god.'

'And what does that make me, Captain?'

'The daughter of our god.'

'No!' Yumina shouted the word with a force that surprised her. 'My father is a god. What does that make me?'

For a brief second, the captain paused to search for the answer she was looking for, then he said, 'A goddess.'

'Yes.'

She returned her gaze to Datu Sakabandar.

'Datu,' she said. 'Let me tell you what will happen if you choose to disobey me. You think I am a child, and a girl fit only to be married off by my father. But do not underestimate me. If you disobey me, I will find out, and I will make right the wrong you have committed against me with all the power at my disposal. You claim to be on the side of the law and the Sultan, but who can be closer to the Sultan than his own daughter? Do you think my father can say no to his daughter's wishes? I say the Sultan's will is the law, and his will and my will are one.'

Here, Yumina blinked rapidly. She knew this was not true. Her father cared little for her. She had not seen him in months. The truth was she had no power. But they did not need to know that.

Sakabandar bowed low, and seeing the datu on his knees, the Captain of the Guard bowed as well.

'As you wish, my Princess,' Sakabandar said.

'You will set the soldier free,' Yumina commanded the datu. 'It is your will as much as it is my will and my father's will. But the court will gossip. You must be prepared.

'You were mistaken. You realize this now. The soldier did not touch the princess. His fingertips merely grazed her dress as she fell. You begged the princess to spare the soldier's life. She relented. She commanded the captain to reduce his sentence to a whipping.

'Captain, you will transfer the soldier to another company, somewhere close. The palace guard, yes. Place him on the palace walls. You will not sentence him to die in one of my father's wars. You will not see him again. I will not see him again. But justice will be done. Kindness will be met with mercy.'

Yumina knew she had succeeded in saving her soldier's life, but a sadness overcame her. She did not know why.

* * *

After the whipping, Lumawig was roused from his sleep by his commander. He was expecting to be hanged, but instead, he was told to dress in his uniform, and was taken to see the Captain of the Guard. His wounds remained untreated, and the weight of the armour on his back made every movement a lesson in pain.

Lumawig entered the captain's room. The furnishings were better than in the rest of the barracks, but it was still a soldier's room. There was nothing there that didn't need to be there. There was a silver suit of ceremonial armour on one stand, and a simpler set on another made up of a steel breastplate and greaves. The captain sat behind a table writing on a piece of parchment by the light of the window behind him.

The captain didn't look up. Lumawig stood in silence trying not to think of the pain from his wounds. After a long minute, the captain spoke.

'I am transferring you to the palace guard,' he said. He made a movement to dismiss the young soldier then changed his mind. 'You are lucky to be alive,' he went on. 'You owe a great debt to Datu Sakabandar. He pleaded with the princess to save your life.'

Lumawig said nothing.

'If you had actually touched her, you would be dead now. It is fortunate that you only caught the hem of her dress.

'Report to the commander of the palace guard. He is expecting you. You are dismissed.'

Lumawig saluted the captain, and a sharp pain ran through his back. He tried his best not to show it, then he turned and left the room.

Back in the darkness of the barracks, Lumawig packed what few belongings he had. He stuffed his mat, the statues of his ancestors, and his few clothes into a rough canvas bag. He was alone, but he was not sure if his commander was watching him from his place across the common room. He turned his back to him to hide his face. He closed his eyes, then broke down into tears.

His life had been spared. As a soldier, he knew that the end could come at any time. His life didn't belong to him. When they took him away and whipped him, he thought he would be hanging from a tree before the end of the day. It did not bother him. But this—this he was not ready for. The captain said that Datu Sakabandar was responsible for saving his life. Lumawig didn't believe it. When it all happened it was the datu who had him arrested. It was the datu who ordered his beating. It made no sense for the same man to show him mercy. The datu knew that Lumawig had held the princess in his arms, touched her skin. It all happened before his eyes. He was an arrogant man who relished giving the order to the soldiers. He was accustomed to cruelty. No, the mercy was not his. And if the mercy was not his, then only one other thing was possible: it was Princess Yumina.

He knew she didn't need to show him mercy. The Sultan's family was responsible for the death of countless others. He was no fool.

He knew what was going on in the sultanate. But he also knew through their exchange of glances that the princess was kind. He knew it was her who had saved him, and he was grateful. He also knew one other thing, but his mind couldn't hold on to it, couldn't explain it. It had made too far a leap. He no longer had the words to explain it himself. But if he did have the words, he would have said one thing: that the princess did it out of love.

* * *

Once again, Yumina finds herself taking Lumawig's hand. This time he offered his hand to make sure she didn't fall as she crossed the wooden plank that led to the boat they would take to leave the city. 'It is slippery,' he cautions.

Earlier that night, the captain of the boat, Dunungan, decided to leave when he heard that the giants were almost at Sun Girna Ginar's walls. 'We are leaving now,' Dunungan told the passengers who slept on the docks awaiting their departure, 'while we still have our lives.'

'What about the storm?'

'The storm will only get worse,' Dunungan replied. 'Best to be on our way now while all we have is a little rain. Of course, you're welcome to stay if you want. I'll give you a refund. You'll be safe and sound with the giants.'

Yumina finds it difficult to think about the destruction of the city. Her father is dead. She does not know whether or not her brothers and sisters are safe. She only knows that the Sultan's enemies tried to kill her and a fire was still raging through the Sultan's palace. At least, she thought, if the Sultan's enemies find her, she will be with the rest of her family.

Yumina sits in the cramped passengers' area with Lumawig beside her. She holds on to him because the motion of the boat is unpredictable. Dunungan only had space for the two of them. Her handmaidens and the soldiers remained at the docks. They would have to find their own way out of the city.

Yumina has never been on a boat so small. The passengers' area is nothing more than a row of benches underneath a wooden roof on the deck of the ship. Below are crates filled with trading goods like mangoes and spices, as well as the passengers' things. Yumina, of course, has nothing.

To distract herself from the sickening motion of the boat, she scans the faces of the passengers and crew. The captain, Dunungan, looks calm, and that puts her at ease. The rest of the passengers are an assortment of free men and slaves, each one fascinating to Yumina. She has seen little of their kind before, aside from her own alipin, who were always passive and wordless. Here, they are unguarded. She sees that most of them are tired, full of worries for the loved ones they are leaving behind. In that way, she realizes, they are not that much different from her.

An old woman catches her eye. She looks gnarled and twisted, a spent thing with a shrunken head. The woman is asleep, so Yumina can stare at her all she wants. She sees that the woman is wealthier than the others. The old woman's mouth hangs open to reveal a mouth full of golden teeth as she snores. Yumina cannot hear the woman's snores above the sound of the rain, but she imagines it to be cacophonous, an ugly sound, the kind that makes children laugh. The woman's dress doesn't betray her wealth, but neither is it tattered and threadbare like the clothes of those around her. Yumina guesses that the old woman is some kind of merchant. Maybe, she muses, her business in the city is over. Maybe she is going home.

Whatever the old woman did in Sun Girna Ginar must have consumed all her strength. Yumina cannot comprehend how she can sleep in the boat. The wind carries the rain into the passengers' area, soaking all of them. The sea rolls and heaves and tosses the little boat on the waves. Yet, somehow, the old woman is sleeping. Somehow, this makes her look like a little girl.

After surveying the faces of the passengers and crew, Yumina looks up at Lumawig. He has a handsome face, she decides, strong but not without a hint of gentleness. He looks like he is always ready with a joke though Yumina has never heard him tell one. His appearance is not her concern though. What she is searching for on his face is an answer.

Why is he doing this? Why did he risk his life to save mine?

Yes, she saved his life, but he doesn't know that. He couldn't know that. She made sure of it.

While it is true that the palace guards swear to give their life to the Sultan and his family, when the God Cannon sounded three times, she witnessed the guards abandon their posts in droves. Why did he stay? Why did he go out of his way to protect her?

Or maybe he is more than he seems? He looks like a common soldier and talks the way you'd expect a common soldier to talk, but how did he know about the eight-pointed stars that led them to freedom? Why had she seen the stars in her dreams?

Why, she wonders, did all his actions say that he loved her? She had heard no proclamation, received no grand gifts, accepted no impossible vows. Instead, she received sacrifice after sacrifice from this gentle, silent man, who was capable of quick violence. He saved her from death, and now he is delivering her to safety without asking for anything in return.

He turns his head downwards to hers after he feels her gaze on him. She doesn't look away, looks straight into his eyes instead, still searching. When he sees her looking at him, like she did, like he did, at the start of everything, he smiles. All the weight of worry is lifted from his face, revealing hope for the future, together away from the world, and free as she had always wanted to be. Yumina receives her answer.

2

Cayapon, Pinantaw, and Liddum

It is deep in the night when Cayapon feels it. Cold wet fingers touch her legs, claiming her as their own. It is the floodwater. The survivors are now stranded on a fraction of the roof that remains above water. It is barely big enough for all of them.

Somehow, they survived the battle between the six-headed giant and the general. They saw the giant pass as it made its way to the Sultan's palace. It crushed a block of houses not far from where they are. Afterwards, there was cannon fire and the sounds of battle. The earth shook again and again, and there was fire in the direction of the palace, then all was still.

It is close to dawn now, but none of them have slept. The rain has hardly let up. The winds have died down, but the rain still pours from the sky.

The baby is still crying. He is tired, but it is impossible to keep him dry. He falls asleep sometimes, but he is soon awake and crying because of the rain. Suckling gives him little comfort, for Cayapon's milk has not yet come in. Even then, because he is tired, his savage cries have subdued into a steady kind of mewling.

The others have decided that they will leave the roof at daybreak. They have it all planned out. First, they will fashion a device for the baby out of a basket, some pieces of wood, and string. Then they will all enter the water and head towards higher ground. The stronger swimmers will scout ahead. The others will take turns pushing the baby along the water.

Of course, they don't know that it will never come to that. Cayapon knows what she has to do. She has decided, and the time has come. She stands up and rocks the child, swaying from one foot to the other, as the others try to rest. She gets ready to jump into the water.

Cayapon turns around to face the water, and as she does, she sees the wave. It climbs hundreds of feet into the air, and it is rushing towards them at an incredible speed. She knows they cannot survive it.

She calls to the others. 'A wave is coming,' she says. They get to their feet beside her. Some of them make sounds of terror. One of them begins to cry. Cayapon feels detached from everything. A thought occurs to her.

'We have to jump into the water before the wave hits us,' she says. 'We will end up in the water anyway, but if we jump from this side, the building might protect us.'

They start arguing among themselves. The wave is almost upon them. Cayapon jumps.

The cold is what surprises Cayapon the most. It makes her panic at first. Her free arm flails about and she kicks involuntarily, trying to get to the surface. Then, a calm fills her as she goes underwater. She exhales, and the air in her lungs rises to the surface in a long trail of bubbles. With the air gone from her body, she begins to sink. It is a long way to the bottom, twenty feet, maybe more. The surface is far away now. She feels the water pressing down on her chest, her eyes, her ears.

The sight that greets her at the bottom of the flood seems like a memory from far away: it is the street where Kagayha-an, the manghihilot lives. It was just this afternoon when she was here last. She doesn't know why, but she finds the thought funny. She laughs, but when she does, the last remnants of air in her lungs escape. She is breathing in water, and it is painful, so painful. Cayapon tells herself that this is the last pain she will ever feel.

The moment doesn't last long. Something drifts in front of her face, some kind of amulet hanging from a string. The string is attached to a neck and below that a face. It is Pinantaw, hanging upside down in the water, diving down to reach Cayapon. The fact that she is underwater doesn't seem to bother her at all. She is breathing like a fish.

Pinantaw rights herself, and in a swift motion removes the necklace and puts it around the neck of Cayapon and the baby. And to Cayapon's surprise, she finds that she too can breathe now. Then, Pinantaw wraps Cayapon in her arms as the wave hits them.

The impact pushes them down the street along with a thousand other objects caught in the wave. Cayapon is too weak to fight. Pinantaw just holds on to her with all her strength. She is determined to save them. They tumble through the water, and Cayapon feels Pinantaw's body go limp.

Cayapon thinks this is the end, but then she sees a man amidst the debris of the broken buildings, tumbling in the crush of the wave. She doesn't know it, but it is Liddum. He sees Cayapon and Pinantaw and swims towards them, fighting against the current. He wraps his arms around them and kicks towards the surface.

It feels like an eternity before they break the surface of the water, but they do. Both Pinantaw and Cayapon gasp for air. The current carries Liddum away. They never see him again.

Pinantaw is coughing up water. The baby is crying. He is alive.

3

Adlao

For a brief moment, the night clears, the moon appears behind the clouds, and Adlao sees the wave coming from the direction of the sea. He knows the end has come.

As the floods rose and the six-headed giant destroyed the city, all of Adlao's plans came to fruition. The Sultan was dead. His city lay in ruins. Adlao had won.

And yet the datu grieves for Sun Girna Ginar. It is true he wished for the destruction of the city, but not like this. The wave will destroy everything; he is sure of it. This is a sacrifice he was never willing to give.

Now, on a rooftop somewhere in the Holy Quarter he watches the ocean surge approach in the moonlight. He asks mercy for the role he played in the city's doom. He asks forgiveness from the dead, from the men he once called brothers—poor mad Marandang, Humadapnon, and the Sultan.

Overcome with grief, Adlao closes his eyes, and to his surprise, his sorrow takes shape in song. His voice rises over the flood water in a tune that was once Imugan's favourite, *Maiden of the Buhong Sky*.

The song tells the story of a diwata who came to earth from Skyworld seeking refuge. She had spurned the Young Man of Pangumanon, a cruel giant whose headdress grazed the clouds, and in return for her rejection, he burned her entire country and every country where the maiden hid thereafter.

On earth, the maiden chanced upon the hero Tuwaang who fell in love with her. And when the giant came, he fought the Young Man of Pangumanon for days in an epic battle. Tuwaang eventually triumphed and slew the giant, but his country lay in ruins.

Overcome with regret, Tuwaang took his people and the maiden on an airboat called a sinalimba to search for a new home. They settled at the foot of Skyworld, in a green and fertile land called Katuusan, a place that does not know death.

4

Dunungan

Dunungan finds Pinantaw, Cayapon, and her baby clinging to the roof of a temple in the Holy Quarter. They are the first survivors Dunungan has found all day.

To reach the temple roof, Dunungan's two men stand on the boat's outrigger to make sure the boat doesn't collide with the sunken buildings. They push off the walls with bamboo poles if they get too close. Though the boat isn't a large one, it wasn't made to manoeuvre along the city streets. The boat's prow is pointed as close as they dare to come to the temple roof. Lumawig and one of Dunungan's men jump into the water to help the two women cross the short distance from the roof to the boat. They escort them one at a time to where Dunungan stands on the prow of the boat. They bring the infant on board by putting him in a basket, which Lumawig brings to the boat. The baby cries and cries, but Dunungan, who raised two of his own, takes this as a good sign. That means the baby is strong, he tells himself.

Sun Girna Ginar has disappeared. Not a single roof remains above the water. It has all been lost in the flood. All that remains are some temples and the Sultan's palace, but even then, only the highest towers remain above the water.

Yesterday's downpour is now a drizzle that lands on the skin like a mist. While there is light, Dunungan and his crew navigate the boat from one corner of Sun Girna Ginar to the next in search of survivors. There are no more to be found. Pinantaw, Cayapon, and her baby are the first and last ones. In total, there are ten of them, no more. There is Dunungan, his wife Perena, and his crew—his two sons—the young soldier Lumawig and his bride, the fortune teller Pinantaw, the new mother Cayapon and her child, and the old woman.

They navigate by peering into the water. By looking at the rooftops below them, at the drowned fountains and monuments, they are able to tell where they are.

Before nightfall, they try to go to the Sultan's palace, but for some reason, the currents have carried the bodies of the dead there, thousands of them, and it is impossible to get closer to the towers.

They call out to any survivors, but no one answers. By sunset, they finish circumnavigating the city.

'Where are we going now?' Lumawig asks Dunungan.

'We will follow the river upstream until we find a town that hasn't been flooded,' Dunungan replies. 'I think that is best. Sabah is too far. And we cannot get there if another storm comes.'

'Do you think the rain will stop?'

'Maybe. I don't know. But it looks that way.'

The old woman interrupts them.

'It will be days before the rain stops,' she says. 'Too many people wished for rain.'

Lumawig recognizes the old woman for the first time. 'I knew you looked familiar,' he says. 'It is you! You sold me a dream.'

'Did it work for you?' Dunungan asks. 'I asked for good fortune, but since I met her, it has been nothing but bad luck.'

The old woman smiles. 'You are still alive, are you not?' she asks Dunungan. 'The rest of Sun Girna Ginar is dead. I would count that as good fortune.'

'She saved my life,' Pinantaw says, clutching the amulet she is wearing.

'So did it work for you?' Dunungan asks the soldier again.

'Yes,' Lumawig replies, glancing at the girl who sits beside him.

Across him, Cayapon looks down, avoiding the gaze of all. The baby in her arms begins to mewl. 'A hero saved us,' she says, 'just as the old woman said would happen.'

'Well then,' Dunungan says to the old woman. 'I don't suppose you have another bottle in there? Then you could wish us all to safety. I'm not sure we're getting far in this cursed boat.'

The old woman smiles at Dunungan. She reaches over to her side where her bag is hanging. She puts it in her lap, then she opens it and takes out a small vial about the size of her finger. Inside the bottle is a milky white liquid, the colour of yesterday.

'No need,' she says to Dunungan. 'Your good fortune will carry us all to safety. This last bottle is for me.'

'Ah!' Dunungan says, growing excited. 'May I suggest a sumptuous feast? We have far to travel and our provisions were washed overboard.'

The old woman shakes her head gently.

'What will you wish for?' Yumina asks the old woman. 'Please tell us.'

The old woman considers Yumina's request and then says, 'Very well, my child. It can't hurt.'

The old woman looks far and chooses her words with care.

'I gave Sun Girna Ginar everything I had, out of hate and out of love, payment for a crime and a kindness. It has led us here, to the end of all things. But also to beginnings.' The old woman looks at Yumina and Lumawig, and to the newborn in Cayapon's arms. 'There is only one wish that is fitting for both.'

The old woman pauses. She takes the bottle in two hands, then she opens it and lifts the bottle to her lips.

'I wish we would all forget Sun Girna Ginar.'

She drinks.

Glossary

agimat/anting-anting: a magical amulet or charm

agong: a wide-rimmed metal gong

alipin: literally a slave, but also, the slave class, those whom the Maharlika use for labour, and as domestic help in their households

anito: ancestral spirits, they are worshipped like gods

anting-anting: any magical charm, typically a necklace

babae: woman

babaylan: priests of certain sects, commonly homosexuals

balarao: a knife with a diamond-shaped blade

balete: banyan tree, believed to harbour evil spirits

baliana: priestess

banig: a common woven mat, essential in most households, used for many purposes; it is large enough for two adults to sleep on

betel nut chew: a mix of ingredients wrapped in a betel leaf, it is a mild stimulant

campilan: a long, two-handed sword with a double-pronged tip

carabao: indigenous water buffalo, often tamed to plow the fields

datu: a king

diwata: spirit or god

habagat: the north-easterly wind that brings the monsoon

Igorot: a mountain tribe of the North

kalasag: a tall shield used in the North

kamagong: a prized hardwood

karakoa: a large outrigger warship

kris knife/kris sword: a knife or sword with a distinctive wavy, serpentine blade

lalaki: man

longhouse: a relatively large building used for communal housing

Maharlika: the ruling class/royalty

manghihilot: a healer

nanay: mother, also a respectful way of addressing elderly women

prao: a small outrigger boat with a triangular sail

talampakan: a measure of distance, the length of a stride

timawa: free men who do not serve a lord, typically merchants

tuba: an alcoholic beverage made from the sap of palm trees

Epilogue

The survivors forgot. They forgot their beautiful city. They forgot the power they held in their hands, in little glass bottles, in each other. Over the centuries, they grew many. They built again. But nothing ever rivalled the city between two seas. Conquerors came to their land and they welcomed them. The conquerors took whatever they wanted. They took their names. They took their stories. They taught the people that dreams were dangerous things. The people laughed and smiled as they lost everything because that is what they always did. Or, so they believed. Some of them fought, revolted against their oppressors, overthrew their tyrants, and lost everything. They called them heroes, but few followed their example. No one remembers the old city or the time when they ruled the sky, except the old woman in the market. Her memory can't be trusted and she has grown senile, but sometimes she sees through the mist and tells the real story of these islands. Find her. Her words are everything we have lost.